TRUST IN ME

Linda should have been dazzled by Lester's smile. Maybe she would have been if she hadn't been thinking about that other face—the one without a smile. The one that closed against her every time.

"You didn't have to get out." She took the hand he offered.

"Of course I did. How else could I call it 'door-to-door' service?"

They reached the door and Linda tensed.

"Good night." His soft words let her relax. "See you tomorrow."

"Thanks for tonight. It's been a long time since I've been out like this."

"Hopefully it's the first of many."

Linda held out her hand. Lester took it and held it for a few seconds. When he let go, she unlocked the door and turned back to face him.

"Good night."

She stepped inside. He waved and went back to the car. She closed the door and leaned against it.

He's such a nice guy. Sense of humor, good-looking. There aren't many like him out there. Why don't I feel a pull for him instead of for someone who doesn't even like me?

BOOK YOUR PLACE ON OUR WEBSITE AND MAKE THE ARABESQUE ROMANCE CONNECTION!

We've created a customized website just for our very special Arabesque readers, where you can get the inside scoop on everything that's going on with Arabesque romance novels.

When you come online, you'll have the exciting opportunity to:

- View covers of upcoming books

- Learn about our future publishing schedule (listed by publication month and author)

- Find out when your favorite authors will be visiting a city near you

- Search for and order backlist books

- Check out author bios and background information

- Send e-mail to your favorite authors

- Join us in weekly chats with authors, readers and other guests

- Get writing guidelines

- AND MUCH MORE!

Visit our website at
http://www.arabesquebooks.com

TRUST IN ME

Alice Wootson

BET Publications, LLC
http://www.bet.com
http://www.arabesquebooks.com

ARABESQUE BOOKS are published by

BET Publications, LLC
c/o BET BOOKS
One BET Plaza
1900 W Place NE
Washington, D.C. 20018-1211

All Kensington Titles, Imprints, and Distributed Lines are available at special quantity discounts for bulk purchases for sales promotions, premiums, fund-raising, and educational or institutional use. Special book excerpts or customized printings can also be created to fit specific needs. For details, write or phone the office of the Kensington special sales manager: Kensington Publishing Corp., 850 Third Avenue, New York, NY 10022, attn: Special Sales Department, Phone: 1-800-221-2647.

First Printing: August 2002
10 9 8 7 6 5 4 3 2 1

Printed in the United States of America

ACKNOWLEDGMENTS

Thanks to Richard Bank, my Public Defender expert, fellow poet, and friend; to my family, especially my sister Bobbie, for her support from the beginning; and to my critique friends, Debbie Dutton, and the Mad Poets. A special thanks to my fellow writers and friends, especially Shirley Hailstock, who have welcomed me warmly into the sisterhood and who have offered their help and suggestions. Lastly, as always, for Ike, my husband, my love, and my fellow roadrunner.

One

"I don't see why I have to go in there acting all humble. I didn't do anything wrong." Linda Durard stared at the scuffed-up dirt-brown table she was leaning on. It looked like it had been here before Lenape Springs Prison had been built. The smells of pine and disinfectant mixed with the despair and hopelessness filling the low-security building. Building noises drifted in from the hall, but no voices mixed with them. Except for a few guards, everyone was in the yard. "Adult recess," one of the other inmates had muttered the first day that Linda joined the group shuffling out of the cell block to the large concrete area behind the building.

Linda had spent the whole time that first day with her back pressed against the corner of the tall chain-link fence as she watched the tired, angry, scared faces move around the yard.

For the first time in her life she wasn't sorry when recess was over. That feeling was still with her after more than three years. She blinked loose from her memories and glared across the table at Marian Green, her public defender.

"I didn't do anything wrong," she repeated.

Marian watched as Linda's face tightened even more than it was when she walked into the room. She looked ten years older than her twenty-four years. Marian wasn't surprised. She had seen it happen before. This place did that to women, innocent or guilty.

"That's not what a jury said."

"What do they know."

"They know what people tell them and the evidence presented to them. The prosecution laid out the case against you, and you didn't convince the jury that it was wrong."

"I never said I didn't deliver the packages. I said I didn't know what was in them. How could I prove I didn't know something? If I were going to lie I would have made up a better story."

The tears shining in Linda's eyes erased the extra years. She sniffed and wiped her eyes. When she moved her hand back to the table, the extra years were back on her face.

"Look," Marian said. "You've been in here three years, almost four. Do you like it in here or do you want to get out?"

"That's a stupid question. It's dumber than what I did." Linda pointed toward the door with its large pane of wire-clad glass taking up the top half. "Do you know what it's like out there on the cell block?" She shook her head and brushed her hands over the close-cropped curls that framed her face. "No, you couldn't. I wouldn't know if I wasn't in here. It's never quiet. Hear that?" She frowned. "All day, every day; 24/7; that buzz, that murmur keeps up. Every now and then somebody's voice breaks in and they yell at somebody or something or nothing. Then the sounds settle back to the usual droning. It's like that noise is part of the paint on the walls." She traced a gash in the tabletop. *How does somebody get something sharp enough to make that?* She blinked and went on. "Nights are worse. Every night you hear the sleep noises of so many people that, after a while, you can't tell which sounds are yours." She took a deep breath.

"Somebody cries. Every night. Not loud, but loud enough for me to hear. Maybe it's the same woman, or maybe they take turns." She shrugged. "I don't know who it is. I don't want to know. I just know it rides on the air every night. Every last blessed night that I've been here. It's gotten so I wait for it." She blinked hard.

"Linda . . ."

"Lenape Springs. It sounds like this could be one of those family vacation resorts with the unusual names that you find up here, doesn't it? Nestled among the pine trees here in the Pocono Mountains; if you didn't know better, you'd think people rushed up here with their kids to enjoy the fresh mountain air." She looked at Marian. "You've never been here on visiting day. It really tries to be a family getaway then."

"No, I haven't."

She didn't have to be here now. Lenape Springs had its own personnel to handle cases going before the parole board. One of them should have been in charge of Linda's case, but Marian had called in favors to get the case bounced back to her. There was something about this young woman that had stuck with her after she had represented Linda in court. She had done the best she could with what she had, but it hadn't been enough.

When she heard that Linda had been turned down for parole, she was determined to represent her this time. It wasn't uncommon for the first parole request to be denied. She just wanted to try her hand at getting it granted this second time. She had come up the previous evening and spent the night in a motel so she would be here for this.

She had to get Linda into the right frame of mind or this would be a wasted trip. She had to make the young woman believe that being released on parole was a possibility this time.

She let Linda talk herself out.

"I was in that visiting room one time, the only time I let my parents see me in here." She shrugged. "I figured they made the two-hour drive, may as well see them. That was a mistake I didn't repeat." She looked at Marian and blinked hard. "Do you know there are toys in that room for the kids? Did you know they let kids come here to visit? I don't think they should."

"Kids have to be allowed to see their mothers. Why punish them for crimes their mothers committed by keeping them away?"

"You don't think it's punishment for them to be torn from their mothers each time visiting hours are over? Buses from different churches all over the state pull up loaded with the relatives as if for a family outing." She shrugged. "I didn't see the buses, of course, but I heard some of the others talking about what happens with their families and how they get here." Her face hardened. "I did see the kids come in that one time. They came in laughing and running to their mothers and wrapping their little arms around them. Somebody spends a lot of time getting them ready, especially the little girls. You know how much time it takes to do the hair. Some of the little girls have heads full of barrettes or beads that click like castanets as they walk. It's as if somebody thought, if the kids look good enough, they can take their mothers home with them. After that one time, even if I came out to see my family, I would have refused to be in that room when they announced the end of visiting hours." She stared at the table. "The crying is really bad on the cell block on visiting day. I mean after the visitors leave. On that day the inmates don't wait until nighttime to start the crying."

"I can understand that."

Linda looked at Marian again as if she just realized she was still there. "Do I want to get out of here? You've been in my 'room.' How did you like the decor? One

wall of dirty scribbled-on concrete and three walls of
bars. Two of us share a space smaller than the closet in
my bedroom at home." She took a deep breath. "Or
what used to be my home. When you walk down the
hall, do you feel like you're walking past cages in a zoo
where all the animals are alike? I didn't do anything
wrong. I didn't break any laws. I don't belong in here."
She said the words again, but they had gotten weaker
over the years she had been here.

"That's what every woman in here says. Sometimes
it's true, sometimes it's not. Most times it's not." Marian
leaned forward and grasped the hand of the woman who
wasn't much younger than she was. "Look, Linda, You've
been convicted. You're already here. You had one parole
request denied. Fair or not, you can't change the past.
If you want to get out you have to do as I say." She
shrugged. "Of course, if you want to serve the more
than two years left on your sentence. . . ." She shrugged
again.

Linda took a deep breath of the old air filling the
room, the building, her world, for the past four years.

"Tell me what I have to do."

"You have to show you're sorry for what you did and
convince the parole board you've learned your lesson."

"I won't have any problem with that. I am sorry. Sorry
I ever met Jamal. Sorry I was dumb enough to believe
any word that came from his lying mouth. He asked me
to take those packages to his grandmother. He said they
were surprise gifts and that I should give them to his
cousin to give to her. I thought I was carrying presents
for a bedridden old woman. The packages were wrapped
up in pretty paper. I thought it was nice that he was
thinking about his lonely grandmom. The first wrapping
was red and gold. Another was royal blue and vivid purple. Expensive paper. Jamal never stinted on expenses.
The packages even had fancy gold bows on top." She

nodded. "Yeah, I'm sorry all right." Her face hardened and the added ten years returned. "And you better believe I've learned my lesson. I'll never trust another man as long as I live. I've proven to myself that I can't trust my own judgment."

Marian shook her head.

"Never is a long time." She sighed. "Look, I guess that will have to do. Just don't go into why you're sorry when you get before the board." She smiled. "We have a good chance of getting you out of here if you don't blow it. The fact that you turned Jamal in and testified against him will help. They've knocked sentences down to time served in other cases like yours."

"You mean there are other college women out there as stupid as I was?" She laughed, but there wasn't any happiness in it. "I guess that just goes to show you that intelligence and common sense are unrelated. Now there's a good subject for a thesis: 'The Correlation Between Innate Intelligence and Common Sense.' The researcher could publish it for the general public. Of course, it would only be a best-seller if the study showed how to strengthen that weak connection and if people with the deficiency realized they had it." She shook her head. "I shouldn't have gone to college a year early. I should have waited until I was eighteen. I should have given myself that extra year to get smarter."

"Linda, you have to stop looking back. It will drive you crazy if you don't."

"Tell me about it. Sometimes I think I'm already there." She grabbed Marian's hand. "Get me out of here. Please. Just tell me what I have to do to get out of here."

"Okay." Marian nodded. "Let's go over some things. Here's what will happen." She pulled a folder from her briefcase and opened it.

Soon two heads, Linda's with a cap of close-cropped

curls and Marian's with tiny braids pulled back into a French roll, were bent together over the table. Linda frowned in concentration as Marian explained the procedure. This was more important than any test she had ever prepared for in school.

"That went well." Marian smiled at Linda in the prison hallway after the hearing a few weeks later.

"The board members looked at me like I was dirt."

"They looked at you like you're a convicted felon seeking to be released on parole." She patted Linda's arm. "It doesn't matter. You're getting out. Let's go get your personal belongings. Then I'll take you home."

"I'm not going home. My family never believed I was innocent. I can still see Daddy's face when I tried to talk to him about this before the trial. It was as if he built a clear . . ." She shook her head. "I started to say plastic, but Daddy doesn't believe in plastic." She swallowed hard. "It was like a glass wall was between us. I could see him thinking, trying to decide what he should tell his friends. Not even Sheila believed me. As close as my sister and I are . . ." She swallowed again. "As close as we *were*, she never believed I didn't know what was in the packages." Linda stared at the cracked, beige tiles on the floor. "She wouldn't let me talk to her about it. She wouldn't even let me explain. I think she wanted to pretend that it never happened, that I didn't have a court date and might end up here." Linda wiped her eyes. "Afterward . . ." She shuddered. "After I was sentenced, she kept saying that she loved me no matter what. She still wouldn't let me explain. I guess she thought I was guilty just like the jury did." Linda looked at Marian. "Sometimes love isn't enough."

"They were in court every day during the trial. All three of them."

"Only because Daddy must have decided it was better for his image if he showed support for his wayward daughter than if he turned his back on her." She stared at the floor again. "I could have done without Mom's crying. The whole time I could hear her sobs and sniffling behind me. It was worse when I was on the stand and had to look at her." She shook her head. "She cried the whole time."

"What would you have done if you were them? You don't know how many women have no family show up for them in court."

"I'm just an embarrassment to them, now. I can imagine what Daddy's doctor friends think. They'll never allow their daughters to associate with me again. I've known them for years. Most of us went to the same private school. We used to hang out together. Pat, the daughter of Daddy's best friend from college, is . . ." She shook her head. "She *was* my best friend. We were in the same room all through school. We were even roommates in college, but none of that matters anymore. Her family will keep her away from me. All of my parents' friends will keep their children away from me. Stupidity might be contagious. Even the grown ones will avoid me. What would their new friends think?"

Marian wished she could tell Linda that it wasn't true, but she had seen it happen with other defendants. Their friends ignored what had seemed to be strong, old friendships and cut them loose without a word.

"You don't worry about them. You'll make new friends. You have your whole life ahead of you." She knew that was a lame cliché, but she used it anyway. "You have to put this behind you. You're not the only one to be in this situation. A lot of smart people have done some not-so-smart things because they were in love."

"I wasn't in love with Jamal." She shrugged. "I thought I was at the time. He was different from anyone

I had ever met. He was exciting. He was so sure of himself." Linda sighed. "And he was the handsomest man I had ever seen. He belonged on the cover of *GQ*. His eyes could see right into your soul. When he flashed his sexy smile on me, I felt like the most beautiful and most loved woman in the world. He had all these with-it women chasing after him, but he wanted me. Me. A shy little nobody college student with few friends, and he wanted me." She picked at a fingernail. "He was my first boyfriend." She gave a harsh laugh. "He needed somebody who was naive enough to be blinded by his flattery and dumb enough to deliver his drugs for him. Yeah, he wanted me. And he got me. Oh, yeah. He got me good."

"That's all over. You have to put it behind you. He has his own place at Graterford, thanks to you."

"It was the least I could do to repay the favor he did for me. He still didn't get what he should have. He got the same sentence that I got and it was all his fault."

"They didn't have as tight a case against him, so he was able to plea-bargain."

"Of course they didn't. He knew how to work his 'business' and how to manage the system. I was the one out there in the open."

Linda started walking. The musty smells in this part of the building, mixed with bleach and the smells of desperate people who usually had their hopes crushed, were too much for her.

She faced Marian. "I appreciate what you did for me. I really do. I know you did your best during the trial. I also know that you weren't supposed to handle my case up here." She wiped her eyes. "There is no way I can thank you. I'm not trying to still cause you trouble, but I'm not going home. I mean it. I don't know where I'm going, but I'm not going there. I can't. Isn't there a . . . a halfway house or some place like it where I can go?"

Marian sighed and nodded slowly. "I figured you wouldn't go home, although I think you should. Your family tried to visit you. Every week for months they made the long drive up here. The only reason you didn't see them was because you refused to."

"I didn't want them to have memories of me behind bars. And I didn't want to see the pity on their faces fighting with their belief that I was guilty. They need to forget all about me." She blinked. "They probably will. It doesn't matter. I will not go back to their house."

Marian shrugged.

"It's your decision. Your life. But I don't think a half-way house is the best place for you." She hesitated. "I know where I can get you a room. It's more modest than what you're used to, but it's clean and pleasant and the owner will wait for you to pay the rent until you get a paycheck."

"Did you ever believe me, Marian? I know you had to do your job regardless of whether I was guilty or not, but did you ever believe . . ." She shook her head. "No. Not *did*. *Do* you believe I was innocent?"

"If I didn't, I wouldn't take you to my Aunt Lorena's house." She smiled at Linda. "She's the one with the spare room."

The tears that had been trying to escape since before Linda could remember ran down her cheeks.

"You're . . . you're taking me to your aunt's house?"

"This isn't just any aunt. This is Aunt Lorena, my favorite. Now if it was one of my other aunts, especially the one who will remain nameless in order to protect me, it would be a different story. Sometimes I think I should take one of my hard cases to her." Marian laughed. "That might not be a bad idea. She'd straighten out that 'wayward child' as she'd call her, or kill her trying." She laughed again. Then it changed to a smile as she looked at Linda. "I know you're innocent. I've had too much experience not to be able to tell." Her words were soft. "In spite of being tempted in the case of my nameless aunt, I've never taken a defendant to meet a member of my family. I've always kept work far away from my personal life."

Linda wiped at her face, but more tears fell.

"I . . . I don't know what to say. You don't know how much it means to me to have someone believe me." She swiped at her eyes again. "But I can't pay your aunt. I don't know when I'll be able to. I don't have a job. And who's going to hire someone . . ." She shook her head. "Who's going to hire *me* with my drug conviction?" Her tears got heavier.

"Hey, don't fall apart on me, now." Marian patted the younger woman's shoulder. " 'It's all over but the shouting' as the old folks used to say." She took Linda's arm. "Come on. Let's go get your things so you'll be finished with this place. Then I'll take you home to Auntie. I already told her we might be coming so she's ready for you. We'll worry about getting you a job after we get you settled in. It shouldn't be too difficult. You finished your degree while you were here. Some of these women haven't even finished high school. You're way ahead. Besides, I'm pretty sure I know where we can find a job for you. They need somebody with computer skills for their program. I'll tell you more about it after I check with the man in charge of the place."

The processing to leave the prison went much slower than the one to get in, or at least it seemed so. The guard in the personal property room treated the procedure as routine, which it was to her—to Linda it was anything but. She was free. She'd never have to come inside these gates again.

"Don't come back, you hear? Get it together so we don't see you in here again." The guard slid a large envelope toward Linda. Then she showed a smile that was gone as soon as it appeared. "We're already overcrowded."

"Yes, Ma'am."

Linda lifted her purse from the counter. It felt strange having a purse again. She picked up her bunch of keys. Keys. She wouldn't need most of them. The keys to her house shouldn't belong to her any longer. The dorm room and exercise locker room keys from college didn't matter. The locks had been changed. She could throw *them* away like she had the past three years and eight months.

Out of habit she slid her appointment book back into the outside pocket. What good would a three-year-old calendar do? She fingered her wallet. She opened the bill section and slid in the three twenties, the ten, and the six ones. It was what was left of the money her father had deposited in her account during his first visit. She had spent the rest on the personal items she had needed. As soon as she could, she'd pay him back for what she used. She didn't want to owe her father for anything. Not after what she did to him.

She looked at her driver's license. She looked so young in that picture. She sighed. She had renewed her license just before she had been arrested, but it had expired a long time. It didn't matter anyway. Her car had been confiscated and sold and who knew when she'd have enough money to buy another. Were ex-cons allowed to drive? Could they get credit? She sighed. Nobody got credit unless they had a job. She had to get a job.

She didn't look at the packet of pictures before she tucked the wallet into the zippered section of her purse. As soon as she got a chance, she was going to weed out the pictures that didn't matter anymore. Probably most of them. Jamal's picture wasn't there. She had ripped that up as soon as she saw him for what he was, which wasn't soon enough.

She swept the rest of her things from the tan counter and into her purse. Quickly she signed the release form for her things and pushed the paper and pen toward the guard.

"I'm ready."

She followed Marian out of the building and never looked back. When they got to the car she stopped.

"Smell that?" She took in a deep breath. "That's free air. I know it's got car exhaust mixed with it and who knows what else, but it's refreshing. It smells different from the air in the yard. We're just on the other side of the fence, and the air smells completely different, sweeter." She closed her eyes and took in another deep breath as she stood in the May afternoon sunlight. Slight gusts fluttered her dark green skirt first one way and then another. She held down one corner of it. She'd have to get used to wearing skirts again. She'd have to get used to a lot of things again.

About three hours later Marian stopped the car on a wide street in West Philadelphia. Large, gray stone houses lined both sides. Built before row houses were renamed townhouses, these were larger than many newer single homes. The houses here all looked alike. Massive, round white columns sat on the same gray stone as that of the house. They supported the edges of the white porch ceilings and framed the steps leading up to the doors. Marian started toward the house she had parked in front of.

"Come on. Let's go on in."

Linda took a deep breath and followed Marian. The

columns with their fluted tops and the white trim on the porch looked as if they had just been painted that morning. The gray floor shone as if it had a fresh coat of paint on it as well. The swing hanging at the other end still showed its natural color, although something had renewed its shine, too.

"Looks like Auntie's been busy." Marian pointed around. "I never know what I'll find when I come here, and I stop by every week." She looked up at the ceiling. "I hope she didn't paint that herself, but you never know with Auntie. She's almost seventy, but I'm not sure she knows what that means. I gave up trying to get her to slow down. She said she'll slow down when she's gone." Marian laughed. "I doubt it. She'll probably be running all over Heaven when she gets there, trying to participate in all of the activities." Marian rang the bell.

"There you are, Baby." A small woman with a smile as big as she was opened the door. "I was wondering when you were going to get here. I left the center early so I could be here for you. I missed my favorite line dance song today." She hugged Marian. "But it was worth missing it for you. Besides, Lil will play it for me next time. That Lil is a nice woman. She shows a lot of patience for the rest of us old folks." She laughed. "Some like to be called senior citizens or seniors, but I believe in calling something what it is. Nothing wrong with being old if you consider the alternative." She laughed again and straightened the light blue blouse that matched her slacks. "Come on in. I don't want to spend the rest of the day chasing after flies." She stepped back and the two young women went inside.

"You must be Linda," she said after she closed the door.

"Yes, Ma'am." Linda wrapped her hands tighter around her purse strap and clutched her purse against her chest.

"You don't have to hang on to that handbag so tightly. It's going to be all right here." Her face softened. "And so will you."

"Yes, Ma'am."

"Linda, this is my aunt, Lorena Harris, but I think Perpetual Motion would have been a better name for her."

"I'm glad to meet you, Miss Harris. Thank you for letting me stay here."

"No problem. You all come on out to the kitchen. I was getting ready to make a pot of tea. You can join me. I think I can find a few cookies to go with it." Linda let out the breath she had been holding and followed her into the small living room. A rich, green sofa with a colorful quilt draped over the back gave the room a cozy feel. Matching chairs sat on the other side of a mahogany coffee table in front of the sofa. Quilts in different patterns were draped across them as well.

"These quilts are beautiful." Linda couldn't resist touching the edge of the one closest to her. "My grandmother used to make quilts. Did you make these?"

"Why, thank you." She nodded. "I did make them. When I first retired from teaching I thought I wanted to spend my time making quilts the way my mother and her mother before her did. For a while that's what I did. Then one day I picked up the quilt I had just started and looked at it. I had a little talk with myself. 'Lorena,' I said. 'Is this really what you want to do with the rest of your life?' I answered by folding that quilt up and putting it in a big plastic bag. I set that bag in the corner of the couch and made sure I saw it every time I came into the house and every time I went into the kitchen. I kept it around for a while until I was sure I didn't want to work on it anymore. Then I asked around until I found a church where they have a quilting circle. They were happy to have it and I was happy to be rid of it. At my age I don't need a load of guilt hanging around my neck. The first time I walked into this house and didn't find that quilt staring at me from the corner of the couch it felt like a heavy weight had been lifted off me." She laughed. "Now come on. We can talk some more over tea."

Linda followed her into the kitchen. White cabinets stood against the walls on two sides. Matching cabinets were fastened to the walls over them. The countertops looked longer and wider than they were because they were bare of the clutter found in most kitchens. A set of square, yellow-flowered ceramic canisters took up space but they were set back against the pale yellow wall. A basket of fruit sat on the counter next to the door.

"Now, before you sit, I have to tell you a few rules of this house."

Linda twisted her hands in front of her. The cozy kitchen now seemed as wide as the gym floor at elementary school. She felt as if she were standing in the principal's office, waiting for a lecture because she had done something wrong. Not that she had ever been in that situation. All through school she had been nervous just taking a message to the secretary in the office. That was the only reason why she went there.

The seconds before Miss Harris continued to speak seemed to take hours.

"There are only two, but they are important. Rule number one: You call me Auntie. Everybody does." She smiled. "Rule number two: I get a hug when you come in and, if I'm here, another when you go out. That will help me get my daily allotment. I read somewhere that four hugs a day help to keep you healthy." She shrugged. "I don't know if it's true, but why take chances?" Her smile widened. "Besides, it feels good." She opened her arms wide. "May as well start now." She wrapped her arms around Linda and patted her on the back. "There. Now you can sit down."

The friendly kitchen was back. Linda's face eased into a smile. It was still there after she sat in one of the four chairs that matched the round, dark oak table in the center of the room.

"Here. Try some of these." Auntie put a plate of cookies in the middle of the table and small dessert plates in front of each of them. "Tea goes better with cookies."

"You baked cookies." Marian took one and bit into it. "My favorite kind, too."

"It doesn't take any longer to bake shortbreads than any other kind of cookie. I made them because this special occasion calls for a celebration." She smiled at Linda. "It's not every day that Marian brings me a house guest."

Between sips of tea and bites of cookies, Marian and Auntie touched on a lot of subjects. Much of it was Auntie talking about the classes she was taking at the center that she attended five days a week. Then she mentioned the wedding she and Marian had attended at the church the previous Saturday. Auntie turned to Linda.

"Do you go to church?"

"I used to a long time ago."

She had belonged to the choir and the youth ministries all through school. When she went away to college she had decided that she was grown and didn't need church in her life anymore.

Would things have been different if she had found a church near the college? Would she have still hooked up with Jamal? She would have gotten her degree from sitting in a classroom on the college campus instead of in a room in prison.

Church didn't make everything come out right all the time, but if she had had an anchor back then, would she have gotten lost in Jamal's sweet talk? She sighed. *I*

*have to stop looking back. Marian is right. I can't change the
past.*

"Maybe you'd like to go with us to First African Baptist
some Sunday?"

"I think I'd like that." She nodded slowly. Maybe it
was time to get connected again.

Auntie turned the conversation to the planting the
Flower Guild had done at the church the previous weekend. Then Marian talked about the new doll she had
bought to add to the collection of African dolls she had
been keeping ever since she was given her first one for
her sixth birthday.

The conversation drifted to other topics, and Linda
was content to just sit back and listen. This was the first
time in three years that she had heard a conversation
that didn't have anything to do with the law or the court
system, or prison. It was good to know that other things
still existed.

Two

"Absolutely not." Avery Washington glared at the woman he had known since third grade when she moved in two doors down from him. "I won't have somebody like that around my kids. I won't have a little rich girl who got caught playing with fire in my center."

"You've hired ex-offenders before, Swifty," Marian said, using the nickname he had earned when he was on the high school track team. "What's the problem here?"

"Those others were foolish enough to think drugs were their way out of the 'hood. Your woman was looking for excitement. She probably did it just to tick Daddy off. After she got caught I'll bet she swore she didn't do anything wrong, right?" He glanced at Marian's face and nodded. "That's what I thought." He looked at his watch. "I have to go. The kids are waiting in the gym for me." He held the door open.

Marian glared up at him before she stepped out of his office. Others might be intimidated by his six-foot-five-inch height and the athletic body he maintained seven years after his days as a running back were over. To her he would always be the kid a few doors down the block from her house. One she used to hang out with. And she wasn't through with him.

"You're either prejudiced or a snob. Maybe a combination of both." Marian followed him down the hall.

Avery stopped walking and leaned against the wall.

"What are you talking about?"

"If this was a young woman from down the street you would have hired her before I finished telling you her story. If she were a young man from around here it would be the same. Even without her credentials the job would be theirs. If she were poor you would have been glad to give her a chance. You're holding her family's money and position against her. You're prejudiced, Swifty Washington. All the years I've known you and I never knew that about you." Marian crossed her arms and leaned against the wall opposite him.

"I'm not prejudiced. I'm not a snob, either."

"Then give her a chance. That's all I'm asking. You're always talking about how hard it is to find somebody to work with the kids who aren't into sports. Well, I found somebody for you. She finished three years of college in the field of education before she went to prison. She completed her degree while she was there. Her minor was computer science. She knows so much about computers she could design her own." Marian didn't know how close that was to the truth, but it sounded good. "Where else are you going to find somebody with her credentials willing to work for the small salary you can pay?"

"I pay as much as our budget will allow. One day I hope to pay my workers more. I also hope to expand their positions to full-time year round. Right now I'm doing the best I can with what I have."

"I know you are and I'm sure your staff knows it, too."

Everyone knew Avery was funding a big chunk of the expenses for the center he had talked about since grade school. Other kids from the neighborhood used to hang out on the corners every night. He and Marian and the others in their small group of friends used to complain about nowhere to go and nothing to do, but they weren't allowed to hang on the corners.

"The corner is not a place. It is not a destination. You will not waste your time hanging on the corner like you don't have a home to go to," Avery's mother said the one time he had asked to go hang out with some of the guys from his school. Then she found him something to do. Avery had grumbled to Marian and the others about it. Because of *his* experience, the rest of their crowd didn't complain to their parents.

During the school year any complaint of nothing to do brought them chores or activities planned by their parents. In the summer, any of them not lucky enough to have a grandparent or other relatives in the South learned something in every free class offered by every museum in the city. The kids whose families could afford it went to the Y on the other side of the city. When some of their friends couldn't afford the fees or the SEPTA bus fare, they all talked about needing a center close enough for kids to walk to. Avery was the one who remembered and did something about it.

He drifted away from their crowd when he was a sophomore in high school. One day he was pulling down A's and the next he was skipping school. That was about the time his brother, Denny, was killed in a drug deal gone bad. Avery hadn't gotten into drugs, he had just quit caring about anything.

Marian had worried about him. They all had. No one had worried as much as his mother had, though. She cared so much she sent him to a military school in Virginia to finish high school. It had turned him around. After college and seven years in the NFL as a Pro Bowl running back every year, he was the one who came back and did something about their childhood wishes for their neighborhood. The Grace Washington Community Center, named for his mother who had died six years earlier, was proof that he still cared. The three-year-old building was proof of his commitment.

"I could never pay them what they're worth. No amount of money would do that. They work so hard and they care so much. They deserve more."

"Sure they do." She touched his arm. "Nobody goes into this kind of work for the money. They knew that coming in. But it's also one reason why you're always shorthanded." She leaned back against the wall and crossed her arms again. "That's why I don't understand how you can turn down Linda. She deserves a chance just like everyone else. She did her time. And don't your other kids deserve somebody who can show them that there's something for them even if they're not into athletics? That's one of the things you always say you want."

"I don't want a junkie in my center. The kids see enough of them out on the street. Most of them pass at least one every day. These kids probably know more about drugs than we do. I won't have a junkie here."

"She's not a user. She never was. Even the prosecution admitted as much. The only thing she got hooked up with was the wrong man. Come on, give her a chance." She took a deep breath. "Hire her on probation. Let her work for two weeks. Then if you're not satisfied, let her go. If you want me to, I'll scrape up the money for her salary for those two weeks if she doesn't work out."

"You know I wouldn't let you pay for anyone who works here, Miss Moneybags. Your job as a public defender won't let you get rich any quicker than the jobs here would." He looked hard at her. "You really believe in this woman, don't you?"

"She reminds me a little of my roommate in college. Janice had been quiet and kept to herself. She never did fit in." Marian had never gotten to know her. Nobody had. The next semester she hadn't come back. Marian had asked around, but she never found out why. "Come on, Swifty. Don't make me beg."

"What do you call what you're doing now?"

"Using my persuasive skills on an old and dear friend."

"You always know when to pull out that nickname, don't you?"

"Whatever it takes whenever it takes."

"No wonder you went into law. I'd hate to oppose you in a courtroom."

"Does that mean 'yes?' "

"That means 'maybe.' I'll interview her."

"Thanks, Avery, you won't be sorry." She stood on tiptoe and kissed his cheek. "I promise."

"You better be right." He kissed her back. "I got to go to the gym. Who knows how many Allen Iverson wannabes I'll find hanging from the basket."

"I'll bring her by this afternoon."

"No, you won't. I don't hire on Saturday. I'll see her Monday morning. Nine o'clock sharp."

"Yes sir, Mr. Swifty, sir. Nine o'clock sharp it is." Marian flashed him a smile.

"Will you be coming with her?"

"I wish I could, but I have a full day in court on Monday."

"Good. You'd only be in the way. You'd probably try to take over the interview so much she'd forget who's hiring her." His jaw tightened. "She needs to know from the get-go who's in charge and what I expect."

"Avery, you'll give her a fair chance, won't you? Just think of how much she can help the kids."

"I promised to give her a chance and I will. She'd better not expect special treatment because you went to bat for her."

"She won't. She's not like that. You'll see."

"I hope so. We could use somebody around here who knows more about computers than the kids do."

"That's my Swifty." Marian gave him a quick hug and another kiss on the cheek. "I'll call you Monday to find out how things went."

"I'll bet you will."

"I love you, too, Swifty."

"Make sure she understands it's a part-time job with a small salary."

"I will. You won't be sorry."

She waved quickly and was gone.

"I better not be," Avery muttered.

Half an hour later Marian jogged up the steps to her aunt's house, still pleased with herself. It would be an adjustment from what Linda expected to do with her life, but, compared to prison, this wouldn't be hard at all. She'd have a long commute, but the job was hers and Marian didn't doubt for a second that Linda could handle it in spite of Avery's attitude. He must really need somebody badly to give in as quickly as he did. Linda just had to show that she could fill that need.

Marian pushed the bell twice and was reaching a third time when her aunt opened the door.

"I figured it was you. Linda offered to answer the door, but I told her I had to come so I could chew you out. Come on in."

"Hi, Auntie." Marian hugged her and got a hug back.

"It must be good news. You only lean on my bell like that when you have something good to share. I'm going to get you a bell for your handbag. That way you can pretend to be town crier without wearing out my doorbell."

"You always threaten to do that. You know you like my way of announcing good news."

"How did you know I wasn't taking a nap?"

"Because if you were, you'd be sick, and if you were sick, you'd have told me." Her wide smile was so like Auntie's that there was no mistaking that they were related. "Where's Linda?"

"We're out in the kitchen. You got her a job didn't you? I hope so. She's been worrying since you left her here yesterday afternoon." Auntie smiled. "All of a half day. Of course I could be selfish and say make her wait." Auntie chuckled. "That child has cleaned my refrigerator inside, outside and topside. She probably lifted it to clean underneath. I'm almost afraid to use it. She was finishing up the oven when I came down this morning. You know I'm an early riser, but that child beat me down today. If she's around here worrying much longer I'd be afraid to touch anything in my house lest I mess it up." Her face turned serious. "I'm glad you can ease her concern so quickly. I haven't known her long, but I can see she deserves for something to go her way. Come on out to the kitchen."

"I'd worry, too, if I were in her place. A lot of times my cases have trouble finding work. Most jobs open to them pay only minimum wages. Some folks take advantage of the fact that former prisoners have to get a job. It's even more pressing for those on parole." Marian set her purse on the coffee table. "Of course the fact that some of my clients are doing math and reading on a grade-school level makes it impossible to place them in better jobs. Linda's more fortunate than most. She was only one semester short of getting her college degree when she got into trouble." She shook her head. "Only one semester away." She waved her hand as if to chase away a fly. "Enough of that. She finished her degree at Lenape. As I told Linda, that's in the past." They walked toward the kitchen. "I have to tell her first, but I will tell you that she'll be happy with my news."

"You have good news for me?" Linda spoke as Marian's last words reached her. She met them in the doorway. "You got me a job interview? That fast? Already? No fooling? You really got me a job interview?" Linda's smile was the first Marian had ever received from her. For the first time she looked younger than her twenty-four years.

"Yes, I got you a job interview. I'm sure it will result in a job offer." Marian smiled at her. "Now quit swinging from Auntie's ceiling fan and sit back down. I'll tell you all about it." Marian sat across from Linda. Auntie handed her a glass of iced tea and joined them. "It's a long commute and you'll have to take two or three buses to work. It's only part-time. Sorry."

"I don't care. It's a job. I'll take any kind. In my situation I can't be particular." She leaned forward. "Uh, what do I do? What kind of job is it? When do I go? I guess it's too late to go right now?"

Marian laughed. She had never seen her so enthusiastic. She told her about the community center.

"The center has programs for all school-age kids, as I said, it's only part-time, but I think it's right for you. You'll get all the details from Avery on Monday when you go to meet him. He's calling it an interview, but it's just routine. The job will be yours." She set her glass on the table and frowned. "Listen, Avery and I grew up together. He can be . . ." She hesitated. "He can be gruff at times. Don't pay him too much mind when he is. He puts himself wholly into things he cares about, and I don't think he cares as much about anything else as he does about his community center. He had to cut through a lot of red tape to build it in a place zoned residential. He had to prove a center for kids would be an asset to the neighborhood and not a magnet for what the community organization called 'undesirables.' It took two years to build, but three years ago the center was finished. You should have seen Avery the day the mayor cut the ribbon and they were opened to serve kids. He was so pleased. He named the center after his mother."

"He didn't want to hire me, did he?"

"He's just very protective of his kids, that's all."

"And he doesn't want a pusher around them. I might be a bad influence, right?"

"Look, Linda, he doesn't know you yet. It will work out all right when he does."

"That's okay. I can understand that." Linda nodded slowly. "My own family's not sure of me and they've known me all my life." She blinked. Then she smiled. "Thank you for the job, and for bringing me here." She swallowed hard. "Thank you for everything. Don't worry. I'll be all right. I won't make you sorry for what you did for me."

"I didn't think you would."

"I'm glad about your job, too, Linda," Auntie said, "although this house will miss the best cleaner it ever had." She smiled and a twinkle showed itself in her eyes. "That's all right since it means I won't have to put up with a droopy face around here anymore."

They all laughed.

"I'm glad I can get rid of that face, too." Linda laughed again. "I guess it was wearing a bit thin."

"You got that right." Auntie nodded. They all laughed. Then Marian gave Linda the directions to the center in the section of town where Linda had never been.

When Linda awoke on Monday, the weak first gray light of morning had just started to filter through the blue and white curtains at the twin windows, and the really early birds had started their day. She smiled. This room was smaller than her room at her parents' house, but it was as friendly as Auntie was. Everything about this house was. Linda's eyes filled as she remembered how the older woman had greeted her as if she were family. She was going to be all right. Things were going to work out for her. She'd make good on this job. Marian had faith in her. She wouldn't let her down. And she wouldn't give Avery Washington any reason to regret hiring her.

She lay in bed a minute longer savoring her good fortune. Then, although she knew it was too early to go anywhere, she got up and tiptoed to the bathroom at the end of the hall to get ready.

Once back in her room, she was glad Marian had picked up her clothes from her parents' house. Marian had spent a long time trying to talk her into going herself, but finally her new friend went for her. Maybe one day she would feel up to facing her family. Maybe after she got a job and was working for a while. Maybe then she could prove she could make it on her own. Maybe then she could face them. Maybe.

She put on the two-piece designer pants suit she had bought just before she was arrested. She was happy the simple lines were still in style. She sighed. She doubted if what she wore would make Mr. Washington decide whether he was going to hire her. Still, she didn't want him to complain about the way she was dressed.

She fussed over her hair for five minutes, even though the short style didn't give her many options. She leaned closer to the mirror. The copper highlights had returned to her carmel-colored skin overnight. The dark shadows under her eyes would fade over time if she could stop worrying. If she got the job she could stop worrying. She closed her eyes. *Please let me get this job.*

She dabbed on her favorite perfume that her mother had sent with her things. Maybe it would bring her good luck. She could use some about now. She took a deep breath and tiptoed down the stairs.

The tall clock in the downstairs hall hadn't yet announced seven o'clock when Linda slipped out the door.

An hour and three buses later she was standing on a corner in North Philly. She had grown up just outside the city, but it had been a long time since she had been in the city.

When she and her sister, Sheila, were little her parents had taken them to the Thanksgiving parade every year. At some point in time, they had stopped going. After that they'd sat together and watched it on television. It wasn't the same, but she hadn't said anything. Her little sister, Sheila, was happy. She said she could see better and she didn't have to fight the cold. Linda missed the crowds and seeing the big floats and balloons up close, but she'd gone along with the rest of the family.

Her visits into the city had never brought her to this neighborhood before. She looked at the two women who got off the bus at the same time she did. They looked at her and then at each other, but kept on going around the corner. Linda wished she was going the same way. The eerie quiet pressing in on her made it feel like something was about to happen. How could there be such a heavy stillness in the middle of a city?

She looked at the drapes covering the windows of the house next to the bus stop and those in the house next to that and wished she was going to one of them so she wouldn't be out here alone. The porches that she could see looked like they had been swept this morning. So did the ones across the street.

She looked at the paper she held clutched in her hands. It was a good thing she knew the directions Marian had given her by heart. The way her hands were shaking, it was impossible to read the words she had written down so carefully. She took a deep breath and turned left at the next corner.

She looked down a street that was even narrower than the last narrow one. Here old, two-story brick houses lined the street as well. The picture facing Linda could have been used on a poster for urban pride. Not a piece of trash could be seen. The street and the sidewalks looked as if they had been cleaned just five minutes earlier.

Old tires, discarded by most people, had been turned inside out by the residents and painted sparkling white. The one closest to Linda spilled impatiens and pansies over the sides. More flowers shouted in a riot of color from the tiny yards beside steps leading up to tiny porches. The folks on this street could give lessons in keeping things clean and making do.

Linda let out her breath and felt her tension go with it. A street that looked like this had to be safe. The silence began to feel friendly.

She walked past houses and yards and porches that looked just as clean close-up as they had when she stood at the other end of the street. When she got to the next corner, she took a deep breath and turned left again.

There was no mistaking the Grace Washington Community Center. It took up half of the long city block, starting in the middle next to a small brick house that had stucco covering the side where an attached house had been torn down. The center didn't stop until it ended at the corner.

The center was the same two stories high as the houses around it, but that was where the resemblance among the buildings ended. The center's new red bricks contrasted with the dark red, almost black of its neighbors to the side and across the narrow street. It didn't look out of place, though. To Linda, it seemed to give hope for the future of the neighborhood. She grabbed some of that hope and walked briskly toward the center.

She took a deep breath and stepped up to the door, trying to ignore how her footsteps rang off the cement steps in the empty air. She reached the door, took a deep breath, and tried it.

It was locked. She looked at her watch. Eight o'clock. Of course it was locked. No one, no matter how dedicated, went to work an hour early, and on a Monday morning no less. She sat on the top step and waited for her future.

Avery looked at his watch as he walked from the parking lot around to the front of the center. A quarter to nine. Between the payroll to finish and the grant proposal he wanted to get to before the staff started arriving at noon, he had at least three hours worth of paperwork waiting for him. He shook his head. He'd meant to be in his office an hour ago. He found the only time he could get paperwork done was before anyone else got there or after they left. He sighed. He wouldn't get it all done this morning. He shook his head again. By now he should expect the unexpected to pop up at the most inconvenient times.

This wasn't the first time a frantic call at home from a mom with some crisis with her kid had thrown his schedule off. Today it was Roberto who had his mom upset.

"You gotta talk to him, Mr. Washington. I can't get him to listen to me. He says he ain't going back to school. He says he ain't wasting his time there no more. He's still laying up in the bed and won't get up. He's too big for me to drag out. You got to help me. I don't know what else to do. You gotta talk to him. He'll listen to you."

Avery told her to take the phone to Roberto. He hoped he could live up to her expectations.

"Get your butt out of that bed and get over here," he had told the sixteen-year-old when he was on the phone. "You and I are going to talk until you get your sense back where it belongs. Don't you let me have to come over there." Where had his mother's phrase come from?

After more than twenty minutes of lecturing and persuading and threatening, he had gotten Roberto to agree to meet him at the center. Before he hung up he added, "I mean it, Rob. If you're not at the center in an hour, I'm coming to get you and Heaven help you if I do."

Roberto had a lot of potential. Avery wasn't going to lose him. He stared at the phone after he hung up. Potential didn't always mean anything.

His own brother, Denny, had shown a lot of promise, too. If there had been a center for him . . . If there had been somebody to turn him around . . . He shook his head. What makes one kid turn things around and not others? Why hadn't Denny? Why had he thought he knew more than everybody who tried to talk to him? He had left home when he was seventeen. They hadn't heard from him for two months. Then his mom had gotten that phone call, and Denny had gotten three lines at the bottom of the page in the local section of the *Philadelphia Inquirer* where all routine overnight crimes, including homicides, are reported. Why had Denny thought he could beat the streets on his own terms? And how had he been suckered into the drug world after all he had seen in their neighborhood?

After he talked to Roberto, Avery, still thinking about Denny, had pulled on the green T-shirt with the center's logo above the word "staff."

Evidently hard heads ran in the family. He had never been involved with drugs, but he had thought he could beat the streets on his own, too. His mother, determined not to lose him the way she had lost his older brother, sent him away to that military school. How he hated that place at first. Then he discovered sports again and his anger burned itself out on the field.

Until the phys ed teacher had them run wind sprints he had forgotten the freedom of running track. The next thing he knew he was trying out for the football team as a running back. The day he ran in for a touchdown during practice he was hooked. Nothing compared to it. After he made the varsity team each touchdown brought the same high. He complained as his coach worked him harder than he had any of the others, but he stuck with it. He sent the coach a ticket to his first NFL game and thought of him when he ran in for his first pro touchdown. He presented him with that ball after the game.

Avery closed his eyes and remembered the feeling. Then he shoved the feeling back into the past where it belonged and finished getting ready.

Ten minutes later he was heading for the center. This was going to be a busier day than most and he didn't have time to waste on the past. The present needed every ounce of his attention.

Normally the staff would be coming in at noon, but today he had a staff meeting scheduled with everyone at eleven o'clock. They had to get the summer schedule in place. He had a week's worth of work to complete today. He thought he had put the paperwork in his briefcase on Saturday, but by the time he found out he hadn't, he was already home. If Marian hadn't come by pleading the case of her latest project, he probably would have double-checked when he went back to his office after he left the gym. He sighed.

With all of the other work that took up his weekend he hadn't had time to do anything else anyway. Nobody had told him about the paperwork involved in something like this. It took as much time as working with the kids. Maybe more. He was swimming in papers. He should have bought stock in a paper mill.

He didn't have time to waste this morning; especially this morning. Miss Society had better be good. She'd better be better than good. Although he did need another worker, with her history, it wouldn't take much to make him turn her down.

Three

Avery turned the corner of the building and stopped. That must be her. He looked at the young woman sitting on the top step, but he couldn't see her face. Her arms were wrapped tightly around her middle as if she was in pain. She was staring at the ground as if she found something interesting there to look at.

At least she's on time. Score one for her.

He walked toward her. Her head jerked up as she heard him. She looked his way and scrambled to her feet.

"I'm Avery Washington." He held out his hand.

She brushed hers down the side of her slacks and reached a hand toward him. It got lost in his. He saw her swallow hard. That didn't fit with the assurance her stylish suit should have given her. He frowned and she swallowed hard again.

"I . . . I'm Linda Durard. Marian Green told me you might have a job for me."

"Let's go inside."

Avery unlocked the door and stepped aside. He caught a whiff of gardenias as she passed by him. *If she needs a job so badly how can she afford perfume that would take a big chunk of the salary I can afford to pay?* He frowned. *Which designer perfume used gardenias as the dominant scent?*

In his other life he used to know things like that. The fashionable women who liked to hang around professional athletes always wore the latest, most expensive scents. One whiff was all he used to need to identify the perfume and often the regular who wore it. He shook his head. Things like that used to be important to him. That was a world ago, back before he got his priorities straight. What kind of priorities did this woman have?

"This way." His glare slid off her. May as well get this over with quickly so he could get to his work. Why had he let Marian talk him into this?

Linda followed him down the hall as he turned on lights along the way. It wasn't cold, but she shivered. His look said she was wasting her time even coming inside. Why had he changed his mind? What had she done wrong? They hadn't even talked about her skills and qualification yet. All she had done was introduce herself. He didn't know anything about her except what Marian had told him. What had changed his mind?

She took a deep breath and let it out slowly. *I just have to make him change it back. I have to have this job.* The center needed her. All she had to do was convince him of that.

"In here." Avery unlocked the door to his office and opened it. Linda stepped past him. This time she didn't look at him. She didn't want to see the look that said she may as well save her time and breath and go on home.

"Have a seat."

He went behind the desk and set his briefcase on the floor.

Linda sat on the edge of her chair, grateful to give her shaky legs time to regroup.

"Why should I hire you?"

Linda blinked at the abrupt question. Then she took in a deep breath and let it out slowly. Her mind swept through words, searching for the magical ones that would make him give her a job. She swallowed hard. Then she began telling him about her training, her qualifications, and her experiences.

"I was a secondary education major so I can tutor in all subjects. My minor was in computer science. No matter where the kids go when they leave here, they'll need computer skills. I also had a few courses in job skills training so I could work in that area." The whole time she was talking he just stared at her. *Doesn't he ever blink?* "I know this isn't a tutoring job, but if I see a need for it while I'm working with the computer program . . ." She shrugged. "Well, I have the skills."

While he stared at her she described in detail her classes that she thought would help her do the job at the center. She even told him about her grades and ranking in high school and her early college grades. Still he didn't answer, but let her ramble on. Finally her words died out. She waited for a response from him. For something. For anything. "If the job involves something else, I think I can do it." She blinked hard. "I'd be willing to try."

"Jane of all trades, huh?" His words, when they finally came, were as cold as the glare still on his face.

"No." She shook her head. "Just desperate for a job and willing to work where I'm needed."

"Look, Miss Durard. I'm not sure this is the right . . ."

"Hey, Mr. Avery. Here I am. I came just like I told you I would." A young man, squeezing the brim of an Eagles baseball cap between slender fingers, stood in the doorway. "I ain't changing my mind, though. I don't care how much my ma gets on my case. I ain't going back to school. I'm just wasting my time there. I'm tired of being broke. I'm getting me a j-o-b." He looked at Linda. "Sorry to interrupt." He frowned at her. "You don't look like you know nothing about being broke."

"Shows how little you know." Linda stared at him.

"Didn't anybody ever tell you not to judge a book by its cover? And those double negatives and 'ain'ts' won't get you much of a job. At least not any kind that would take you far from broke."

"Hey, you a pretty cool lady." He laughed and looked at Avery as he put his hat on. He snatched it back off when Avery turned his glare on him, but he was still smiling. "Where you find her, Mr. Avery? I like her. She gonna be working here? Seems like she gonna fit right in. I'll be here every day if she's here. You're gonna hire her, ain't you?" He looked at Linda. "I know it's 'aren't.' I know about double negatives, too." He shrugged. "I just don't want to sound . . ." He shrugged again. "You know what I mean?"

"Yes, I know what you mean." Linda nodded. "You don't want to sound like the ones in charge of hiring in the business world. The ones whom you want to give you a good job."

Roberto's answer was another shrug.

"You got enough trouble trying to mind your own business." Avery pulled Roberto's attention back to him. "You don't need to get into anybody else's. And you're here every day anyway." He looked at Linda. "I have to take care of some business with Roberto. That's how things usually are around here. There's always something to take you away from what you planned to do. It can be very frustrating. You want to wait for me to finish or do you want to go?"

"I'll wait." He wasn't going to get rid of her that easily.

"I don't know how long it will take. You sure you don't want to reschedule?"

"I'll wait. I don't have anything else to do."

"Suit yourself." He shrugged. "I'll come out to the lobby and let you know when I'm finished here." He glared at Roberto. "This shouldn't take long."

Linda left the office. In spite of not knowing whether

or not she had the job, she smiled. No way was he going to convince that kid of anything in a little while.

She went to the lobby. She spoke to the guard behind the desk and he introduced himself.

"I'm Bill. You going to be working here?"

"I'm Linda. I hope so, but I don't know yet." She settled into one of the brown plastic chairs for what she knew would be a long wait.

"If you got the qualifications, Mr. Avery will hire you. He's hard, but fair."

"So I've heard." She had seen the hardness for herself. As for the fairness, she'd have to take Bill's word for that and hope he was right.

"What do you do?"

She told him about her computer background.

"You don't have to worry about a job. Avery's been looking for somebody for that program since they put the equipment in. Bea Wilkerson's been helping out in there, but she's been grumbling about it as if that's part of the job. Of course, it is different from her usual job of helping on the playground." He smiled at Linda. "Don't worry. You got it made." He held out the morning newspaper. "Want to read a section?"

"No, thank you."

There could be a story about the mayor welcoming visiting aliens and it wouldn't register with her. She hoped he was right about her being hired. He began reading the paper, and she wished she could concentrate on the newspaper or anything else besides whether she'd have a job when she left here.

Much later, she was still wondering when people started coming in; probably staff. Some rushed past her as if they were late. Others seemed in no hurry to get where they had to go. All had pleasant words for Bill, the guard. Would she become one of them?

They threw curious looks at her. Some smiled. Some

didn't. A few stared longer than others. Their jeans, more eloquently than words could, told her she was over-dressed. Next time she'd fit right in. If there was a next time. She looked at her watch.

Two hours had passed since she came out of the office and she was still sitting. Her stomach was reminding her of how stupid she was to have skipped breakfast, but she didn't dare leave now to get something to eat. As soon as she did, he'd probably come for her and if she wasn't here he'd probably decide not to hire her. He looked like it wouldn't take much for him to turn her away. He had been ready to do just that when Roberto came into the office. She knew that. She might be wasting her time waiting, but she was going to stay here until they put her out.

She had once dropped out of a contest in school because she didn't think she had a chance of winning. Her father had sat her down and talked to her. Whenever things got rough in school, she remembered his words during that talk. She thought of them now.

"Never take yourself out of the running," he had said. "You won't get everything you try for, but if you don't try, you are guaranteed not to succeed. Never make it easy for someone to turn you down."

Linda sighed and reminded herself that Marian had said she'd gotten her a job interview, not a job. She blinked hard. What would she do if he didn't hire her? She had blown it with him and she didn't know how it had happened. She tightened her mouth. She wasn't leaving. She wasn't taking herself out of the running.

She paced as much as the small lobby allowed. She told her stomach to shut up. Then she sat back down in the chair to wait some more. She wanted this job. It was perfect for her. She could be an asset here. She had to make him see that, too. She needed this job. She threaded her fingers together in her lap and waited some more.

"Sorry I took so long." Avery's voice startled her. "Roberto was more stubborn than I've ever seen him before. If he could learn to channel that hardheadedness in the right direction, he'd succeed at anything he wanted to."

"Is he going back to school?"

He stared at her hard before he answered. "This afternoon. He tried to persuade me that tomorrow morning would be better, but I told him to go now. He'll only get his last two classes in, but that will make it easier for him to go back in the morning." He cocked his head to one side. "You knew what to say to get to him."

"I worked with a tutoring program for junior high kids in the neighborhood around my school." She shrugged. "Kids are kids whether they're in the city or in the suburbs."

"I guess so." He stared again. "You made an impression on Roberto. You've got a fan."

"I need all I can get. They're hard to come by about now."

He rubbed his jaw.

"Come on back to my office. Let's finish talking there." He looked at his watch. "I've got a staff meeting in less than half an hour. It was supposed to be almost over by now, but I had to reschedule it." He shrugged. "The staff all know how things go sometimes."

Linda followed, but she didn't see why he didn't just save them both time and tell her good-bye in the lobby. She pushed her purse back up on her shoulder. *I guess Mr. Avery Washington doesn't think it's professional to conduct business in the lobby.*

"I can do the job you want done," she said as soon as he closed the door to his office. She had sworn to herself that she wasn't going to beg, but she knew that's exactly what she was doing and she didn't care. She hesitated before she spoke. "I assume you're concerned about my criminal record. I can truthfully tell you that I was innocent, but I'm sure you don't believe me. Not many people did." She shrugged. "I probably wouldn't if I were in your place. Most people in prison claim to be innocent. You don't have any way of knowing the truth about me." She frowned as she searched for the words that would persuade him to give her a chance. "I'd never put anyone in jeopardy, especially kids. Life is tough enough for them without outside negative influences." When Avery didn't answer, she took a deep breath. Then she went on. "Let me show you I can do the job, Mr. Washington. Give me two weeks to prove myself. If you're not satisfied with my work, don't pay me."

"Did you and Marian get together on that?"

"On what?"

"Never mind." He stared at her. His jaw hardened. "So, you can afford to work without pay. What have you got, a trust fund?"

"No, I can't and no, I don't. I'm on my own. I'm counting on you seeing that I can fit in here and do the job that needs to be done. I'm counting on you letting me stay."

Her heartbeat throbbed so loudly she felt Avery must hear it, but she held her gaze steady on him. She finally blinked when footsteps and murmurings reached them through the door as people passed by in the hall. Had the staff left and come back? Her stomach growled. Maybe they went to get something to eat. She ignored her stomach. This was more important than food. Had she really been in here pleading her case for more than twenty minutes? She swallowed hard and captured the side of her bottom lip with her teeth. No matter. She wasn't leaving until he told her to.

Finally Avery blinked free.

"The staff meeting starts in five minutes. You may as well stay for it. That way you'll get to meet the others. I'll discuss your hours and what is expected of you after the meeting, if you can stay, that is."

"I can stay." No way was she going anywhere now.

He let his gaze slip from her to the pile of papers in front of him on the desk. Then he looked back at her. His voice wasn't soft, but it wasn't as hard as it had been.

"You've been here a long time. There are vending machines in the staff locker room across the hall. Somebody probably plugged in the pot of water for coffee and tea. Help yourself. The meeting room is over there, too, so you can wait with the others."

"Thank you." She blinked hard refusing to let the moisture filling her eyes fall. "You won't be sorry."

"I hope not." He stared at her. "I'm only giving you the two weeks you asked for to prove yourself. I'll be over there in five minutes."

Avery stared at the door after it closed. He had intended to turn her down. He had given her a fair interview just as he had promised Marian, but he had been convinced that Miss Linda Durard wouldn't fit in. Her designer clothes and her shoes that cost enough to buy food for a family in this neighborhood for a week would be out of place. What did somebody like her know about inner-city kids?

When he was young, people with more money than they knew what to do with came to his neighborhood, especially at Christmastime. They brought truckloads of toys and huge food baskets for every family on the block. They meant well. They just didn't know jobs would mean more than anything they could carry. They didn't know anything about people in neighborhoods like this. Neither did she.

One glance at her fresh-scrubbed face was enough to

convince him that he should do her a favor and send her away. She didn't know what she was asking for. He had decided that these kids would chew her up and spit her out before lunchtime on her first day.

He shook his head. Those wide brown eyes didn't belong to an ex-convict. She wasn't what he'd expected. He'd expected to see a hardened face. He had expected to be greeted with attitude big time even though she claimed to need a job. He hadn't expected her to look as innocent as she and Marian claimed her to be. How old did Marian say she was? She couldn't be as young as she looked and still have a college degree.

He looked at the paper with the information Marian had given him. Linda Durard looked closer to sixteen than the age twenty-four he had written down.

He let out a hard breath. Her innocent look was probably how she was able to get away with carrying drugs.

He had planned to tell her "Thanks, but no thanks." Then Roberto had come in. She had handled him as well as workers who had been here for years. Some of the staff still didn't know how to deal with Roberto. If Avery let her stay beyond her two weeks she'd have Roberto to thank for that. *If* he let her stay. That wasn't even close to a given.

He pulled together the papers he needed and went across the hall to the staff meeting room.

Linda swallowed hard when she got into the room. It wasn't really small, but it seemed so because she didn't know a single one of the others. A couple of them gave her looks that said they agreed with Avery that she was not dressed for a place like this. This was the first time she had heard of someone being condemned for being too dressed up. They spoke and then went back to their conversations.

She located the hot water and walked over to it, glad for a reason to leave the doorway.

"Hi, I'm Craig Daniels." A tall, thin man handed her a coffee mug and held out his hand. "I tutor the teens; mostly in science and math, but I can cover other subjects in a pinch."

Linda introduced herself and took his hand. She was glad for the warm smile greeting her after the chill in Avery's office.

"It's nice to see a fresh face around here." He still held her hand.

"You should know fresh, Craig," a woman seated near the machine said. She smiled at Linda. "I'm Cheryl Martin, the instrumental music teacher."

"You got that fresh thing right," another said and laughed. "If anybody knows fresh, it's Craig. He probably majored in it at Central State." She held out her hand. "I'm Roz. I teach music to the older kids, and I'm in charge of the choir."

"You ladies hurt me to my heart." Craig splayed his fingers against his chest. "You'll give Linda the wrong idea about me."

"We'll give her a true picture of you as a warning. If Casanova wasn't named 'Casanova,' he'd have been named Craig Daniels."

"What is this? Some charity for you?" A woman at the other end of the table spit out hard words that wiped Linda's smile away. The woman's narrowed stare traveled slowly over Linda's outfit. "You sure don't look like you need a j-o-b. Why do you want to work here if you don't have to? What are you doing here anyway? Slumming?"

"Don't mind Wanda." The smile from the short brown-skinned woman standing nearby wiped away some of the sting of Wanda's words. "I'm Bea Wilkerson. You should feel flattered by her reaction to you." She threw a hard look at Wanda. "She's always nervous about the possibility of competition for Avery's attention. She must see you as a threat to her plans." Bea laughed. "Not that Avery will ever see her as anything but another staff member."

Wanda glared as laughter came from the others, but she didn't say anything else.

"Listen to their warning about Craig." A man who looked like he belonged in the movies came forward. His soft, crooked smile and friendly eyes put her more at ease. "I'm Les Sherman. I work with the gym program." He held out his hand. "Welcome to the center. Let me know if I can help with anything. I've been here since we opened, but I still remember how it is to be new to a place."

Linda eased her hand from Craig's and said to this gentle man, "Thank you. I'll remember."

She moved away to sit in one of the chairs along the wall, but Bea urged her not to.

"Avery won't let you sit back there. That's what he calls hiding. Everybody sits at the table," Bea said. "I assume you'll be working with us?"

"At least two weeks."

"Two weeks? Why just two weeks?"

"Mr. Washington hasn't decided if he's going to hire me."

"Since when did Avery have a probation period?"

"Good morning." The conversations stopped. Everyone looked at Avery as he took his seat at the head of the table.

Linda's answer played in her head: Since me. She didn't think it was usual for a job like this, but she wasn't surprised. She'd just have to try harder to make it impossible for him to send her away.

"This is Linda Durard." Avery looked at her and the others did, too. "She'll be working with the teenagers in the computer lab. At least for a while." His stare hardened, but Linda didn't let hers waver.

"Hallelujah," Bea called out and let Linda blink free. "Now the kids will have somebody else's patience to try for a change. Honey, you don't know how welcome you are." She laughed and the others joined in. "You don't know what you're getting yourself into, either." The laughter got louder.

"You know you love them, Bea."

"Sure I do. I love my own three kids, too, but that doesn't mean they don't get on my last nerve sometimes. It will be good to spend all my time with the playground madness again."

"I know what you mean," Roz said. "I've been there too many times myself. It seems like when their bodies start doing that teenage thing, their brains go into reverse."

"Okay, folks," Avery broke in. "Let's finish this. I know you all have work you want to get to."

Linda looked around the table. There were eleven others besides herself and Avery. Then she put her full attention on Avery as he gave the report from the previous month. If she was going to work here, she had to know what was going on.

Avery opened each section of the report to questions and comments before he moved on. Then the discussion turned to the summer program that would start when school let out in six weeks. The department heads gave their reports and outlined what they had in mind for the summer. Workers commented along the way. They didn't keep their suggestions to their own departments.

Remembering how hard Avery was during the interview, Linda was surprised at how outspoken the staff was during the meeting and how receptive he was to their ideas.

She listened for where she could fit in. She noticed

that there was no mention of job training, and computers were only mentioned as an option for kids without
a scheduled activity. She couldn't ignore the excitement
growing inside her. She could do a lot here if he'd let
her. She bit her bottom lip. She'd have to make sure
that he let her.

Avery ended the meeting and she followed him back
to his office.

"That's the way things usually go around here," he
said as he shut the door. "Today was smooth with rela-
tively few snags, but most times problems come up that
we have to thrash out. That will probably come as we
get the details worked out for the summer program."

"I noticed that the others gave a lot of input."

"That's the way I run things. We use one another's
strengths. Nobody claims to know everything or how to
do everything." The hard stare of earlier was back.

"Neither do I."

"You know this is a part-time position. The hours are
four to eight Monday through Friday and one to seven
on Saturdays. I don't expect it to ever be full-time during
the school year and it would probably be difficult for
you to find another part-time job that would fit around
our hours. On the other hand, summer hours can be
grueling. We're open one to nine every Monday through
Saturday except on holidays. You get one evening off a
week. I decide which one so that our other programs
can pick up the slack. We also run a summer lunch program, but you won't be involved in that. We close down
from five to six for dinner. The only way to describe the
program is almost controlled chaos, with emphasis on
the 'almost.' In a crunch the staff is expected to fill in
for others." His stare dared her to accept the job.

She stared back and took a deep breath.

"Mr. Washington, the only way you're going to get rid

of me is to flat out tell me to go. I'm not any good at taking hints."

The silence grew. Stare met stare and held. Finally Avery spoke.

"Everybody calls me Avery. Did you get any ideas from the meeting of how we could expand the program?"

Linda nodded. She felt her excitement bubble up inside her. Did she dare assume she had the job?

"I noticed that computers were only mentioned as a sort of program filler."

"Yes, that's pretty much it."

When he didn't say anything else, she went on.

"I don't know how much you want from me, but I'd like to do word processing with them." She leaned forward. "It would serve several purposes. First, the kids will need that skill if they get any job using computers, and more and more jobs are using computers. Second, I could work on their writing and composition skills at the same time. Also, working with word processing could serve as an outlet for them to express what they're feeling. I'm sure they're like most other teens, angry a lot of the time."

"Were you?"

"Was I what?" A puzzled look covered her face as he pulled her attention from what she was saying.

"An angry teenager."

She shook her head and gave a little laugh.

"Me? Dr. Durard's daughter? Not by any standards. I was a good little daughter and an even better student. I had the family honor to uphold. Certain things were expected of Dr. Durard's children. I did what I was told at home and in school. The only anger I ever showed when I was growing up was when I was in a school play and the part called for it." She stared at the floor. "I've seen a lot of anger, though. I tutored sixth graders when I was a senior in high school and junior high kids when

I was in college." She gave another little laugh and shook her head again. "I thought what those kids had was anger until I volunteered to work with a group of women who were in prison with me." She blinked. "Then I realized I hadn't seen anything that came close to anger before. I found some anger of my own, too." She stared at him. "I'm still learning what an unproductive emotion anger is." She looked away and then back. "To get back to my ideas, I don't claim to be an English expert, but I think I could help the kids in that area, too. If we have kids interested in going further in the computer field, I could help them with that. I promise not to let them hack into any government computers."

Avery's face relaxed into an almost smile.

"Those sound like good ideas. You can start with your word processing plan and then phase in your other ideas where possible. That will be enough until we see how things go. How much time do you need to get your program going?"

"I could start with the kids tomorrow, if that's when you want me to start." She shrugged. "I'm not wasting one single day of my two weeks by using it for planning."

The lines around Avery's mouth deepened. In anyone else a smile would accompany the change. Not with Avery.

"If you need planning time, take it. I won't count it against your two weeks."

"I've done a similar program before." She nodded slowly. "I can start right away. Exactly what have they been doing so far?"

"Wasting time with games and junk. No government agents have come banging on our door, so I don't think they've hacked into any sensitive computer yet, but I can't swear to that." He looked sheepish. "I don't know much about computers and how they operate. I only use computers when I have to. They're like airplanes: good for getting you from point A to point B in as little time as possible. The computers here are just something for the kids to do when they don't have anything else to do. It's better than having them hang out on the streets." He cocked his head to one side. "Do you have any more questions?"

"Do I have your permission to make the computer games disappear?"

"If you're sure you want to do that. Don't you think maybe you should phase them out gradually?"

"No. May as well start off showing the new philosophy."

"Go ahead. I'll hang around outside the door the first day when they come in just in case they decide to revolt."

"I appreciate that." Did she imagine it or did he just joke with her?

"Any more questions?"

"What about the younger kids? Do you plan to have a computer program for them? I mean the kids who are ten and eleven years old."

"I haven't thought that far ahead. Let's get one thing going at a time. Anything else?"

"I know the job starts tomorrow, but is it okay if I have a look at the lab before I leave?"

"Help yourself." He gave her the keys and told her how to find her way to the room. "You may as well keep those. If you have any more questions before you leave, I'll be in my office. If not, I'll see you tomorrow at two. That will give you time to acquaint yourself with the center before the kids get here. They start drifting in around three. That's when we open, but if they show up early, Bea will supervise them on the playground. If the weather's bad we let them in. They wait in the gym until the programs start. On Wednesday, your hours will start at four. I'm not sure who you'll have your first day, if anybody, but I expect you might have kids coming to play the games. We'll play it by ear tomorrow. Probably the next few days, too. You have to go with the flow around here."

"No problem."

"Fill out the personnel form with Penny, our secretary. I'll see you tomorrow."

She got as far as the door before his words made her turn around.

"Dress is casual around here. We never know when we have to get dirty." His gaze traveled down her outfit. "Besides, we don't want the kids to think we're flaunting what we have in their faces." Any hint of warmth in his voice had disappeared. It had taken the softness from a few minutes earlier with it.

"I noticed how the others were dressed. I understand." Her face tightened to match his. Something had happened again to change his attitude toward her and again she didn't know what it was.

Avery seemed determined to make her show the anger she had found in prison. She took a deep breath. *I'm not going to let him.*

"If there's nothing else, I'll go check out the computers."

Avery stared at the door long after she had closed it. The work he needed to complete in a hurry was forgotten. He took a deep breath and caught a final whiff of gardenias. Or did it catch him? How much did it cost an ounce?

She didn't need to think her beauty would make him cut her some slack. The groupies who were drawn to professional athletes had tried to get next to him when he was playing football, but he always decided with whom he would spend time and it was always on his terms. Those women were considered beautiful by most people.

For a while he'd considered them beautiful, too. Many of them made their living because of their looks. Still, they hadn't been able to get to him.

Miss Linda Durard better not think she could be more successful with him than those other women had been just because she had a fresh and innocent look. His face tightened even more. She wasn't so innocent, anyway. If she had been she wouldn't have gone to prison.

He shook his head and tried not to think of prisoners who were released after it had been proven that they had been wrongly convicted. Those cases were so few they made national headlines and television specials when it happened. No, Little Miss Society Beauty had been guilty. He sighed. The operative words were "had been." She had paid for her crime. Maybe she was sincere now. It was obvious that she didn't come from a neighborhood where jail was a common thing. Her experience had probably scared her into doing right from now on. Or maybe not. Maybe she was one of those who craved excitement. Many of those rich groupies did.

Large, wide eyes in a perfectly formed face. Skin as smooth as a piece of tan satin with copper tones underneath and stretched over high cheekbones. What would a smile do to them? To her generous mouth? She would more than fit in with the women in his old circle. And her hair. Not every woman could wear her short hairstyle. She more than managed it. She could be the model enticing others to rush to the beauty salons to try to achieve her look. The cap of curls surrounding her face invited a caress. Was her hair as soft as it looked?

His face hardened. He wouldn't find out. It wouldn't be his hands testing it. He wouldn't have a thing to do with anybody who had been involved with drugs. He'd had more than enough of that experience with his brother.

She had better do her job without any suspicions

clouding her actions if she expected to stay at the center. She wouldn't get by on her looks, and her daddy didn't have any pull here. Avery's features tightened even more. There better not be any indication, not even the slightest bit, that she was up to her old tricks, or she was out of here before she could figure out what had happened. He didn't need for a court to decide her fate at the center. If she messed up, she was gone. His decision. No discussion required.

He leaned back in his chair.

So she'd gone to check out the computers today instead of waiting until tomorrow. Big deal. She was just trying to score points with him. His jaw tightened. No chance of that happening.

He shook his head. The center needed her expertise. Still, he wasn't sure whether he wanted her to succeed or fail. He shook his head again. He was being selfish and that wasn't the way he operated. He knew enough to keep his personal feelings separate from work. Even if he did dislike her he had to put the needs of the kids first. That's why he'd built this center, why he was here instead of someplace where he wouldn't have to work so hard.

He let out a hard breath and turned his attention to the papers on his desk.

He hoped she didn't come back to his office before she went home. He was having enough trouble keeping his mind on his work as it was.

Four

Linda's heels clicked down the hall to the stairs, punishing the floor as she went. Counting to one hundred hadn't helped. There weren't enough numbers in existence to help her get rid of her anger right now. She stopped at the door leading to the stairs.

How dare he insinuate she was insensitive to these kids' situations. Just because she hadn't grow up in a neighborhood like this didn't mean she wasn't aware of what life was like here. The younger kids in the after-school program she was involved with while she was in college lived in areas like this one. After a few weeks they had come to trust her. They talked about their problems; they told her about their situations.

Once she had taken a bag of groceries to a house because, during a conversation she'd overheard between two kids, she learned the mother's food stamps had run out before it was time for the next ones to come. Linda let a slight smile cross her face.

Professor Burke had railed at her when he found out she had gone into the rough neighborhood alone, but Linda had already done it and she wasn't sorry. After he calmed down he gave her a list of food banks. She had discretely referred other families to them when she learned of a need. She knew how important it was to be sensitive to the needs of others.

She had seen for herself a street that looked as if it had been transplanted from a war-torn country and plopped down just a few miles from her college.

Linda jerked open the steel fire door at the end of the hall leading to the stairs. It was a good thing it was fastened tightly to the frame.

Her footsteps on the stairs were as hard as they had been when she left Avery's office. Even if none of her contacts with this other world had taken place, she wasn't stupid. She could see. How dare he. Who did Avery Washington think he was?

She was smart enough not to make anyone feel uncomfortable by what she wore or by what she said. She didn't have to live in a particular area to understand that.

She watched the news, too. Every evening news broadcast reported something negative happening in areas like this. When she saw reports of trouble, when she learned of decent people huddled in their homes every night, afraid to go out and unable to relocate, she felt frustrated that there wasn't anything she could do.

She never saw a story about something like this center or its good programs. She frowned. How many other oases of hope were ignored by the news media?

Still fuming, she kept herself from slamming the door behind her.

She wasn't blind to reality. She realized the best center in the world and every social program in existence couldn't make up for all of the things lacking.

She located the lab. It was a wonder he didn't question her ability to recognize the words "Computer Lab" when she saw them. How did someone so young become so stuffy? This man had played professional football? He was probably one of those always-angry players who ignored the public and refused to be interviewed by the news media. She sighed.

She took a slow, deep breath and let it out even more slowly. Then she took another. She didn't have to like him to work for him. Her tension eased away.

She did like his no-nonsense hairstyle. No dreads, no head scarves; nothing but thick curly hair the way the Lord gave it to him. Her eyes widened, but her thoughts continued along the same track. No earrings either. Just him, pure and plain. She shook her head.

There was nothing plain about Avery, and it wasn't just his height that made him stand out. What would he look like if he smiled? What would a smile do to his strong features? How would his generous mouth curve up if he smiled at her?

No, no, no. She shook her head harder this time. She was losing it. The man hated her and she was daydreaming about him as if he were drawn to her. Deep inside she was wishing about a man she had just met. What *if* he smiled at her?

She wasn't going there. She didn't care about his smile or anything else about him personally. All she cared about was that he let her do the work she was hired to do. She was here to work and that was all. She didn't need another Jamal in her life. She was still paying for letting the first one in.

She found the right key and unlocked the door.

What kind of smile he had and how it affected her didn't matter anyway. The sky would fall down if he smiled at *her.* She was the last woman Avery would be interested in romantically. He might let her keep on working here if he needed her expertise for his program more than he needed for her to be gone, but if by some miracle he did let her stay, he'd be watching her so closely she would have to explain every breath she took.

What she had been convicted of was terrible. She admitted that. But she had a feeling his attitude wouldn't have been any more negative if she had murdered someone. Something was going on with him that she didn't know about. She didn't know if she wanted to know what it was, either. She had problems of her own. She didn't need to concern herself with someone who was more in control than she was. Maybe she'd better start looking for another job. She didn't expect this one to last more than two weeks.

She opened the door, turned on the light and gasped. She could be looking at the communications center of a prosperous business.

Computers lined two walls. More computers were placed back to back on tables in the middle of the room. Avery Washington and his two-week limit faded from her mind.

She walked closer to examine the equipment. Scanners and printers were hooked up to each computer. The computer stations along the walls had phone lines hooked up to the backs. This was way more than she had hoped for; much more than she ever expected. The kids could do a lot of research using the Internet. Electronic encyclopedias, print media, chat rooms just for kids, all were open to them on the Net. There was so much she could show them; so much she could teach them.

Ideas sprang up in her mind. She grabbed a piece of paper from a pack on the table and began to scribble them down.

When she finished she looked at the paper. It was filled on both sides. She had enough plans to last for the next five years. She sighed. She didn't even know if she'd still be here two weeks from now, let alone years. No negative thoughts. She remembered Marian's words to her . . . was it just a few days ago?

She booted up the first computer and started to dump the games, but she stopped. She couldn't do that to whoever would be in charge today. She'd do it when she came in early tomorrow. That way she'd be the one to bear the brunt of it when the kids saw that their games were gone. She smiled. Maybe, after they got used to being without them, she'd use a little playing time on computer games as rewards for completing the work she had planned. If she did it right, though, they'd be so caught up in their work they wouldn't think about the games.

She began checking the computers and the rest of the hardware and the software stored in cabinets beside the desk. There was more than enough here for what she had in mind. Somebody had stocked the lab well. She decided to check each station to see what was on every drive.

A while later she glanced at her watch. She had been in the lab for an hour and a half. In spite of the uncertainty of her future, she smiled. It was true. Time went fast when you weren't looking. Especially if you were interested in what you were doing.

She tucked her notes into her purse, secured the lab, and went downstairs. Her steps were so quiet that anyone just outside the fire doors would have to look to see if someone was really on the stairs.

She stopped walking when she got to Avery's door, but she didn't go in. The less she saw of him the better for her frame of mind. She was in a good mood now. She didn't need for him to change that. It had been a long time since she'd felt this upbeat and hopeful.

She said good-bye to the guard and went to catch her bus. The neighborhood seemed friendlier now. The few people she passed either spoke or nodded. She spoke and smiled back. Yeah, it was much friendlier.

The ride home went quickly. Few people were on the bus when she got on and few got on as the bus wound through its route.

She jotted down more ideas as they came to her.

There was so much she could do. She took a deep breath. She had two weeks. She'd do what she could in that time. If she had to leave after that . . . She shrugged. After that she'd share her ideas with whoever came after her, if they were interested.

She took the steps up to Auntie's house slowly. Her mind was still on the center. She started to unlock the door and go in, but she looked around. The day was too beautiful to go inside.

The porch swing fastened to the ceiling at the far side of the porch swayed gently as a slight breeze caught it. She sat on it and gave a little push to get it moving. Another breeze brought her the scent of roses. She wondered if Auntie ever cut them and took them in. She'd ask her when she came home. It would be a shame to enjoy them only in passing. The peach and red would look great with a few of the white scattered among them. The center of the dining room table would be the ideal place. She nodded. Yes, she'd ask Auntie about cutting some roses as soon as she got home.

Linda nestled back against the yellow-flowered cushion. When was the last time she'd sat in a porch swing? When was the last time she'd sat on a porch? She closed her eyes and let the quietness of the neighborhood seep into her.

"Child, why didn't you go on inside and take a nap? Did you forget your key?"

Linda looked up to see Auntie smiling at her.

"No, Ma'am. I just decided to enjoy the fresh air."

"I know what you mean. It's so quiet and relaxing out here. At least until the kids on the block get home from school." She put her bag on the wicker table and eased herself beside Linda.

"It's so relaxing out here I 'relaxed' myself to sleep." Linda laughed. Auntie chuckled with her.

"It's no wonder you fell asleep. What time did you get up this morning? I came down a little after seven and you were gone. Of course, you didn't leave any trace in the kitchen to show me that you had been there. You did eat before you left, didn't you?"

"I couldn't sleep." She didn't tell Auntie how she had lain awake waiting for it to get light enough for her to see so she could move around without making a lot of noise bumping into things.

"You didn't eat."

"I . . . I had a cup of tea."

"A cup of tea is not food."

"I . . . I wasn't hungry."

"I won't give you a lecture about breakfast being the most important meal of the day. I'll save that for another time. If you hadn't left your bedroom door open, I would have thought you were still in bed." Her face softened in a gentle smile. "I can understand how nervousness can block your appetite. I remember my case of nerves my first day of teaching." She laughed. "Actually it was too big for a case. It was more like a trunkload." She laughed again. "When I walked my third graders to the classroom that day and turned to face them after we got into the room, it was all I could do to keep from bolting and running home. Thirty little people were staring at me like I knew more about what to do than they did." She laughed and stared out at the street. "Most of those kids are probably parents by now, but I will never forget that first day." She looked at Linda. "If you could be relaxed enough at ease to sleep now, Avery must have hired you."

"Yes and no. He gave me two weeks to prove that I can be an asset to the center."

"Two weeks? What kind of time is that to show anything?"

"It's what I have so I'll make the best of it." She sighed. "I don't think he wants me there. I figured he just gave me that time while he looks for somebody else. I thought I'd maybe start looking for a different job in case this doesn't work out." She looked at the older woman then she looked away. "It's a shame, though. Those kids need a comprehensive computer program; not just something somebody put together as a fill-in activity for kids without something else to do. They use computers to keep the kids off the street, but if they're going on to college they definitely have to know what a computer can do. Even if they don't go on after high school, if they expect to find a decent job, they need computer knowledge to compete with the others out there trying to get the same jobs. Using a computer to just play games makes it nothing but a high-tech baby-sitter."

"If you show this much fire on the job, Avery will have a hard time letting you go." Auntie nodded. "That's good. You don't sound like you really want to go anywhere else."

"I don't. That center needs me. Those kids need my program." Linda sighed. "I hope you're right about him letting me stay." She smiled. "Now tell me about your day."

"Monday is always a full day for me. I had my keyboard lesson this morning. Then I played a couple of hands of pinochle before lunchtime. After that we had line dancing. We had a full room as usual. Some of the members find places to do line dancing five days a week. These young folks who think old folks just sit around and vegetate in front of the television all the time should stop by the senior center someday. Any day. They'd probably get tired just watching us do our thing."

Linda laughed with her.

"Tell me about what else you're involved in."

Auntie sat up straighter. She told about her other activities at the senior center and the church food bank where she volunteered on Tuesday evenings.

"Speaking of church, you going with us this coming Sunday?"

"Yes, I think it's time I get back."

Auntie patted her hand and smiled.

When a group of girls came out to jump Double Dutch rope the two women watched them practice their routines.

"They call themselves the Clayton Street Four. They won second prize in the competition last year. The whole neighborhood is so proud of them. Still, they're determined to take first place this year. They are out here for hours every day that it's not raining. They'd be out here then, too, if their parents would let them."

The girls were still practicing when Linda and Auntie went in to start dinner.

As they finished preparing the meal, Marian came in. She set the kitchen table and they sat down to dinner.

"Okay." Marian put a piece of chicken on her plate and looked at Linda. "I waited long enough. How did it go today?"

"Avery said he'd give me two weeks to prove myself."

"Two weeks? He didn't mention a trial period to me. That's not enough time to prove anything."

"That's exactly what I said." Auntie passed her the bowl of rice. "What's gotten into that boy?"

"He doesn't want me there. I got the feeling it's because of my record." She sighed. "I could do so much for those kids. They have a computer lab better equipped than labs at some colleges, but it's being underused. It's like having fifty channels on your cable and watching just the four local stations." She shrugged. "Two weeks will at least give me time to show the kids what they can do on the computers. Maybe whoever takes over after I leave will keep some of it in place." She pushed her carrots around on her plate.

"If he had anybody else he could hire, they'd already be working there. We touch base once a week. I know for a fact that he desperately needs somebody."

"Evidently not desperately enough to hire me." She placed her fork on her plate and fiddled with it. Then she looked at Marian. "I can understand. Really I can. I'm not sure I'd take a chance on an ex-con working with kids if I were in his place."

"He's hired ex-cons before. I didn't send them to him, but I know that for a fact, too. He's told me so." She hesitated before she went on. "Avery lost a brother to the streets. Denny had given his family grief since he hit his teens. He was determined to make big money and get his mother out of the neighborhood. He got involved with pushing drugs. No matter what his family said, he wouldn't listen. When his mother told him to straighten up or get out, he left. One morning he was found on the street shot to death. He was all of nineteen."

"I remember how broken up Avery was over that," Auntie said. "His mother was devastated. She blamed herself for putting him out."

Marian nodded.

"Avery blamed himself, too. He was only sixteen, but he came down hard on himself over it. He believed if he had only tried a little harder, he could have saved Denny. He lost interest in everything. For a long time Avery played the 'if only' game. His mother got him away from here in time to save him. Denny is one of the reasons why Avery came back here. He swore he'd keep the streets from claiming any other kids from the neighborhood." She shook her head. "Of course he couldn't do it. But he does manage to save a lot of them." She nodded. "A whole lot more of them would pass through our offices or end up dead in the streets if it weren't for Avery's center."

"I knew there was some other reason he didn't like me. What you just told me explains a lot." She stared at Marian. "I told him that the only way he was going to get rid of me was to tell me to go. I guess I have two weeks to make it impossible for him to do that." She stared at the floor. "And he has two weeks to try to chase me away." She looked at the two women. "I intend to dig in so hard a pit bull dog could take lessons. I want that job. He can't find anyone to do it as well as I can."

"I like your attitude. You hang in there, Honey. If it's meant for you to be there, that's where you'll stay." Auntie nodded. "I believe the Lord steps in whenever and wherever he's needed." She smiled. "Now, let's not waste any more energy on something we can't change. How about some pound cake? I have some leftover from yesterday and you know pound cake is always better the second day."

Tuesday morning Linda woke up with the birds again. She got ready. She smiled as she pulled on a pair of jeans and a loose shirt. This should be casual enough for Mr. Avery.

She slipped downstairs and went into the kitchen. She didn't feel like eating, but she forced some cereal and a cup of tea down. She needed a full supply of energy to face the unknown day.

She stepped out into a warm morning. A soft breeze carried the scent of roses from the bushes in Auntie's small yard. Linda inhaled deeply and let it out slowly.

She opened her arms wide. This was a gloriously perfect morning.

As she walked down the street, excitement replaced the case of nerves that had filled her the day before. She was on her way to work. She had a job. She controlled the urge to do a little dance on her way to the bus stop and instead walked at a pace only a little slower than a jog.

The only person on the bus was an older woman who had been sitting in the same seat the morning before. Linda guessed the woman had a job like she did. After only a few days out of prison, she had a job. She smiled at the thought. The tired-looking woman glanced at Linda from across the aisle. She lost some of her tiredness when she smiled back at Linda. Linda's smile widened.

"Good morning." She ignored the unwritten code about not disturbing invisible walls and not making eye contact with strangers. She felt too good to keep it to herself.

The woman hesitated before she answered back.

"I ain't seen you on this bus before. You new to the neighborhood?"

"Yes, Ma'am."

"What's your name?"

"I'm Linda Durard."

"Where you staying?"

"I'm staying with Miss Lorena Harris."

"Miss Lorena, the schoolteacher. I heard of her. She been in the neighborhood a long time." The woman nodded. "She's a right smart woman. She did right by the school kids, too." She nodded again. "I heard she didn't take any stuff from them." She smiled. "The children loved her, though." She looked hard at Linda. "You her niece or something? I heard she didn't have any children."

"I'm not a relative. I'm staying with her for a while."

"You on your way to work? You a schoolteacher like she is?"

"I'm on my way to work, but I'm not a teacher. I work at the Grace Washington Center and this is my first day on the job."

"I heard of that center, too. That football star built it, didn't he?"

"Yes, Ma'am."

"At least there's somebody who didn't forget his roots. I heard he's doing great things for the kids in that neighborhood, but you got your work cut out for you. I hear those parts can be rough at times. Course, every part of the city, and the suburbs too, can be rough." She shifted a tote bag on the seat beside her. "Ain't nothing we can do about it, though." She leaned toward Linda a bit. "I hope you'll still be smiling when you been on the job as long as I have." She shook her head. "Don't get me wrong, now. I appreciate having my job." She sighed. "I been working at the Smith Nursing Home for thirty years; longer than anybody else there. It just gets to be so tedious at times."

"Yes, Ma'am." *I hope I get to work at the center long enough for the job to get tedious.*

"Anyway, welcome to the neighborhood. I'm Willa Armstrong. I live three houses from the corner at the last stop. It's most convenient for catching the bus. I been riding this bus to my job at the nursing home for so long that the driver, Jesse, knows me; and he's my second driver. I had the first one, Sam, retire on me. But Jesse and me, we get along fine, don't we, Jesse?"

"Yes, Ma'am, Miss Willa."

"I'll let you in on a little secret." She leaned even closer. "When the weather's bad, Jesse toots his horn so I know to come out. Mornings when that wind starts to cutting and howling from all sides like it don't know where to go, it can rip through you if you're standing on the corner." She laughed and stood. "This is where I get off. I guess I'll be seeing you every morning." She smiled.

"I'll probably be taking a later bus. I wanted to go in early and get things set up."

"Well, you have a good first day on the job."

"I will." Linda meant it.

Other passengers got on and off, but her thoughts took all of her attention until she got off at her stop.

The streets that took her to the center were quiet again this morning, but she was more relaxed as she walked through them. She knew where she was going and what was waiting for her.

One thing waiting was a locked door again. She glanced at her watch. It was barely eight o'clock. She sat on the top step to wait as she had yesterday.

She had only been there five minutes when she heard a car pull into the parking. She stood. *Maybe Bill, the guard, starts early. Good.* She was anxious to get started.

Avery came around the corner and the smile Linda had been ready to give to the guard disappeared and a stare replaced it.

Avery stopped and stared back. His gaze traveled down her body pausing at her jeans, shirt, and sneakers. Then it settled on her face.

"You're early. I said two o'clock. I can't pay you overtime."

"I know I'm early and I didn't ask for overtime. I want to make sure I have enough time to do what has to be done before the kids get here. Besides, I'll probably be early every day for a while. I wasn't sure what time the bus would get me here; I have to work my way through the schedule to find the best one."

"You take the bus?"

"It's too far to walk." She stared. "They seize and sell assets of convicted felons. That included my car."

He stared long as if letting her words sink in.

"The bus is going to be rough going if the winter is bad. They can't make it down narrow streets in ice and heavy snow."

"If I'm still working here, I'll deal with it. You don't have to worry. I won't be late for work."

"That's not what I meant."

She shrugged. "I wanted to make that clear."

Avery unlocked the door.

"Go on in."

Linda stepped inside. She managed to avoid making eye contact. She tried but failed to ignore his spicy aftershave that floated to her as she stepped past him. It was a lot friendlier than the look on his face.

"Bill usually puts the water on for coffee."

"I can put it on, if that's all right."

"Help yourself." He stared at her after he unlocked the staff room door. "You still planning to get rid of the games?"

"If it's still all right with you."

"What will you do with them today?"

"I went to the public library last night and located some Web sites. I thought we'd explore some of those. And I figured I'd have them do word processing. I'm sure it would help with their assignments for the rest of the school year. I'll also find out what they're interested in and use those interests."

"Ambitious plans."

"I'm sure I'll drop some for lack of interest."

"You have a wide variety in mind. Many of them will be new to the kids. Good luck. They're young, but they can be set in their ways, too."

"I know."

He hesitated.

"Look, some of the boys might try to make a pass at you."

"I can handle them."

He shrugged.

"I just thought I'd tell you."

"Thank you."

"If you have any trouble, use the intercom on the wall."

"Okay."

"If you can't get to it, just yell for help. The art room and the music rooms are on the same floor. Somebody will come."

"Are you trying to scare me off?"

"I just want you to be aware of what you're getting into. Some of our kids come from rough backgrounds."

"I understand. My background's a little rough, too, now." She stared at him for a while. "If there's nothing else, I'd like to get started."

"Be my guest. I have work to do myself." He started into his office but turned back. "Make sure you have the kids sign in and out."

"I will."

"Good luck."

She stared at his back. He shouldn't say things he didn't mean. That would set a bad example for the kids.

She heated the water and took a cup of tea with her up to the lab. She unlocked the door, but didn't go in. Instead she walked down the hall, first one way and then the other. It didn't hurt to know where the other rooms were. She wasn't as sure of herself as she wanted Avery to believe. If he knew how apprehensive she was, he'd find a way to use it against her. She hoped she could fake her confidence for the next two weeks.

She took her time taking inventory of what was on the drives and in the closet. When she finished there wasn't anything about the lab and its equipment that she didn't know. She was going over her lists when the door opened.

"Hey, Miss Linda, I heard you was, I mean were, here, but I thought I'd come see for myself."

"Hi, Roberto. How was school today?"

"Aw, you know. Same old, same old."

"Do you usually come to the lab?"

"Sometimes. You'll be seeing more of me now that I know you're here."

Linda crossed her arms over her chest.

"We need to get something straight, Roberto. You're welcome here to work with the computers. But there's something you need to know." She pointed to a chair. "Sit down."

"Anything for you, Miss Linda." Roberto flashed a wide grin at her. Then he eased into the chair and slouched back.

"How old are you?"

"Almost sixteen. My birthday's in September."

"Do you know that when I was your age, you were in third grade?"

"No way."

"Yes way."

"You can't be that old." He sat up and frowned at her. Disappointment filled his face.

"It's the truth." She looked at him and smiled gently.

He stared at her for a while before he spoke. "I'm old for my age."

"I don't doubt it."

"But not old enough, huh?"

"Don't rush growing up. It's not all it's made out to be."

"Yeah, I guess." He nodded.

"I'll bet there must be at least one girl your age trying to get your attention."

"More than one." He sat up straighter. His smile was

more dazzling than before. "A lot more than one." He blinked hard. "I guess I have a better chance with one of them, huh?"

"I'd say so." It was her turn to nod.

He stared for a while longer. Then he shrugged.

"We can still be friends, though, can't we?"

"Definitely." She broke into a wide smile. "Now why don't you show me what you can do with a computer. You don't spend all your time playing games, do you?"

"Of course not. That's a waste of a good computer. May as well fill this room with quarter-eating machines."

"I agree with that. I took off all the games."

"All of them?"

"Every last one."

"I hope the fireworks won't destroy the center when the guys find out what you did."

"We won't worry about them, now. Show me what you can make the computer do."

Roberto turned to face the computer and began to access files. His fingers almost flew over the keyboard.

Linda pulled up a chair and watched in amazement. If he was any indication of the level of the other kids, she'd need more advanced activities than she had planned. She wouldn't mind that at all.

Roberto was still at the computer and Linda was still watching him when the bell sounded for the dinner closing.

"I'm going to the gym later, so I won't be back up here tonight. I'll probably see you tomorrow. Okay?"

"Okay."

"Miss Linda?" He hesitated at the door.

"Yes?"

"Welcome to the center. I'm glad you're here."

He rushed out before Linda could say anything else.

She smiled as she went to get her dinner from the lounge refrigerator.

"Where you going?" Bea's question stopped her at the large door.

"I have to revise my plans. I'll eat up in the lab."

"No, no, no." Bea shook her head. "That's one of Avery's first rules. That and no skipping dinner to keep working." She smiled. "I agree with him. You can't do it all at once no matter how much you want to. You have to learn to pace yourself or you'll burn out. You also have to take baby steps when you want to make giant leaps." Bea stared at the salad she had just pulled from her lunch bag. "You'll hear me complain about my job, but the hardest thing is knowing a kid is heading for trouble and not being able to convince him . . ." She looked at Linda. ". . . or her of it."

The others nodded.

"Been there, done that, much as I don't want to, I know I'll be there again," Craig said.

"We all have," Cathy said. She stared at the bare spot on the table in front of her as if something were there. "Eddie Allen." She shook her head. "He could capture an image in a few strokes. His use of color was amazing. I took a lot of art classes in college. No one in class with me ever came close to having his ability. I did everything I could think of to help him." She gripped her cup tighter. "It just wasn't enough. I can't help thinking that, maybe if I had had more experience in dealing with kids . . ." She released her cup and opened one hand. "Maybe I could have found the right words to save him."

"You got to try to let that go." Bea patted her hand.

"I try. I just haven't found a way yet."

"Some you can't save no matter what," Cheryl said. "I've had some talented kids in my music program. Some made it. Some didn't. There's no way of telling who will and who won't." She shook her head. "So you just keep trying."

"That's the truth," Les added. "You try with everyone. I've had some make it whom I didn't expect to and others with the best support at home and a scholarship practically in their hands slip away." He shook his head as if shaking away a memory. "You got to try to forget the ones you lose and remember the ones you help." He smiled at Linda. "And you got to take time out at dinner to rejuvenate."

"But not by talking like this." Craig unwrapped the white paper from the hoagie in front of him and laid the peppers from a separate pack on top of the tomato slices spread along the length. "You guys are depressing and you're dragging me down with you. Enough already."

"Somebody needs to tell Avery to follow his own rule." Wanda stared at Linda. "I try every chance I get, but he doesn't listen. Somebody needs to talk to him about taking a time-out. He eats at his desk every single night. Then he takes a full load of work home with him and he works there."

Wanda sounded as if she had a special right to be concerned about Avery. Linda blinked hard. Maybe she did. How else would she know what Avery did at home?

Linda took a bite of her sandwich. She frowned, but not at the ham and cheese.

Wanda and Avery. Why did the idea sadden her?

Five

From time to time, while Linda worked in the lab later that evening, the question—still unanswered—came back to her. She had to get her mind off the subject.

She revised her plans based on the way Roberto handled the computer. He couldn't be the only one with computer skills. The computer program in their school was more advanced than she'd thought. She was looking forward to helping them go further.

Les was waiting in the hall when Linda left the lab.

"Bea told me where you live and that you take the bus. You don't live far from my mom. I go visit her often and I'd be glad to give you a ride."

"Bea talked to you about me?"

"After I kept asking. I guess I wore her down." He smiled. "Look. I'm a pretty up-front guy. I know we just met, but I'm interested. Is there any reason why we can't go out and get to know each other better?"

"I'm not interested right now. I'm getting over something. I wouldn't be very good company."

"Don't be too sure. You have an occasional cup of coffee with me, we keep in touch here and at an occasional going out together, and I'll be the second one to know when you're over your 'something.' Who knows? It might be sooner than you think, and I wouldn't want to miss it." He smiled. "At the least you'll have made a friend." Linda had to smile back and his smile widened.

"No strings. No promises." Maybe it was time for her to take another step.

"No strings. No promises." He crossed his heart and lifted his hand up. "Come on. If you're ready, I'm going to pay Mom an impromptu visit."

He held the door and followed Linda down the stairs. Linda smiled as he told her about one of the kids.

"He tried to convince me that we should schedule a game in Arizona and Avery should fund a bus. He said he always wanted to see the Grand Canyon and this was the way for that to happen." Lester laughed. "I tried to convince him that it would never happen. Finally I just ended the conversation."

Linda laughed with him as they walked down the hall.

They were still laughing when they arrived outside Avery's office. The door opened and he stepped into the hall closing the door behind him. He looked from one to the other, but when his stare went back to Linda, it settled there.

"On your way?"

"Sure thing, Boss Man." Avery wasn't looking at him, but Lester was the one who answered.

"You need to be doing the same thing. You know what they say: all work and no play; you can't save the world in one day; he who fights and runs away . . ." He grinned. "Oops. That last one doesn't belong, does it? Anyway, you need to be heading out, too. You've slain enough dragons for one day."

"You're full of it tonight, aren't you?"

"Not full of *'it'*, full of *them:* sayings, platitudes, metaphors, similes, and so on." His grin faded. "Don't hang around here much longer, Avery. Like I been telling you since college: Not even you can do it all in one day." He turned to Linda. "When we were roommates I used to tell him he couldn't do it all, but there were times when he proved me wrong. Now I put it in a time frame." He looked back at Avery. "He's trying to make me revise my saying again." He touched Avery's arm. "Tomorrow's another day, Man."

"I know. I'm not far behind you."

"I'm going to call you later, Dad, and you better be home. I know you won't be on a hot date."

"Yes, son, I'll be home."

Les took Linda's arm.

"I used to call him Dad in college. So did the other guys who knew him. He was the oldest eighteen-year-old I ever met."

"Somebody had to use a little common sense," Avery answered.

"Yeah, well, now it's your turn to use some of it again. Just once you need to leave the job here instead of taking it home with you. A date, hot or otherwise, would be nice for you. Burn-out is not a pleasant feeling." He looked at Linda and smiled. "I guess I'll end the lecture for tonight. Ready?"

"Yes." Linda nodded. "Good night, Avery."

"Good night." Linda responded to the little tug Lester gave her arm. When she turned away, Avery was still standing like he had taken root in the hall.

Avery stared at the closed door to the entryway long enough to hear Les and Linda's laughter and their goodbyes to Bill. The outside door closed and he was still in the hall.

So, Les has latched on to Linda. That little pull on Linda's arm, and her following Les like she was eager, lingered in his mind. Why shouldn't he be interested? She was an attractive woman. His jaw tightened. She was a lot more than attractive. She was beautiful. His body tightened at the memory of her standing close enough for him to feel her heat and catch a whiff of gardenias. He swallowed hard. His gaze had followed the movement of her T-shirt as she gulped air. It had been hard for his mind to find words. He shifted his briefcase to his other hand. Hard was the right word to use. It was correct for right now, too. He took a deep breath.

What did he care about her and Les? What she did was none of his business. Neither was who she did it with. Maybe it was a good thing she wasn't attracted to him. He could never trust her. How could he be sure she wouldn't get involved in drugs again? The money in the trade was good, a whole lot better than what he was paying her here at the center.

He opened his office door to go back for his briefcase. Then he glanced at his hand, at the briefcase he was holding. *What is the matter with me?* He let out a hard breath. That was one question he knew the answer to. He didn't like it, but he knew it.

He locked his office door again and left the building with a beautiful, wide-eyed face with a full, soft mouth centered in his thoughts.

"Avery's not dating anyone?" Linda slid into the booth at the restaurant. Les had talked her into stopping for dessert. She asked the question she had been holding back since they left the center. The ride hadn't been long, but it had been long enough for her to curb her curiosity if that was all she felt concerning Avery. She didn't want to think about why he was still on her mind.

Les leaned forward and rested his arms on the table.

"Not that I know of. The center's business is the only thing he's interested in. Has been for a long time." He put down his cup and stared at her. "Why? You interested in the job?" His words were casual, but his look wasn't.

"Of course not." Linda frowned. What was that look Avery had given her when he saw her with Les? She almost believed he cared who she was with. She shook her head. No, when he looked at her all he saw was a pusher and all he thought of was his dead brother. She shifted her plate a bit to one side and then back. And all she saw when she looked at him was a man she wanted to get closer to.

She closed her eyes and inhaled deeply as an image came back to her: an image of thick eyebrows she longed to smooth into place, a strong jaw her fingers ached to brush along, a generous mouth she wanted to make soften before she touched it with her own.

Linda shook her head quickly from side to side. The image disappeared, but the longing stayed and hopelessness joined it. She'd never overcome her past as far as Avery was concerned.

She stared at the slice of sweet potato pie in front of her. It must be good. Lester had eaten all of his. She looked up at Lester.

"He wouldn't be interested in me, anyway."

"He's not blind and he hasn't lost his mind that I noticed. He's a little fanatical about his center, but Avery has been an intense guy since I met him in our freshman year at Ohio State. How could he not be interested in you?"

Linda glanced around the small restaurant. No one had bothered to hang pictures on the pale yellow walls, which showed the bumps and uneven surfaces old plaster develops over years. The scuffed-up tables, set with white place mats with no reminder of the restaurant name, had probably started life in a restaurant that hadn't made it. There was no danger of that happening here.

Bobbie's Kitchen's reputation for real soul food overshadowed the way it looked. The person responsible for what could loosely be called the decor knew to put all effort into the purpose of the place and not on the packaging. Tonight the effort was wasted on Linda. She glanced at Lester then at her plate.

"In your collection of sayings, you must have the old one about judging a book by its cover."

"What's that supposed to mean?"

"I have to tell you something about me."

She took a deep breath, let it out slowly and began talking.

"Now you know all about the life and crimes of the stupid and sorry." Linda hadn't looked at Lester the whole time she was talking. Now she dared to glance at him.

"No, I just heard the story of a vulnerable woman who was taken advantage of." He touched her arm and left his hand there. "You're through with that. You got to put all that away. You can't change what happened no matter how many times you go over it."

"That's what people keep telling me."

"Maybe it's time you listen to them."

"I guess so." Her face softened into a slight smile. "I'm sorry I wasn't better company."

"Next time you'll do better. There will be a next time, won't there?"

"Are you sure you want to?"

"Of course I do. They say there are no dumb questions, but you just proved them wrong."

He looked at the pie in front of her with just a small piece missing. "That is if Bobbie lets you back in here after what you did to her pie. Or rather what you didn't do to it." He switched his plate for hers and picked up his fork. "If I don't eat this, you'll have Bobbie changing her recipe and it's already perfect."

Linda laughed and watched him finish her dessert. In less than a minute the last bite disappeared. He paid the bill and they left.

On the way home he talked about his mother. When

he mentioned her activities at the senior citizen center, Linda mentioned Auntie.

"Auntie? You talking about Miss Lorena Harris? I know her. I met her at Mom's house one time."

"What's your mom's name?"

"Delores Jones."

"Miss Delores? I know her. She's a trustee at First African Baptist in Sharon Hill. Auntie introduced me to her one day after church. She was one of the first to congratulate me when I joined." Linda's eyes widened. "How about that?"

"Just more proof of what a small world we live in." He glanced at her. "And maybe it's a sign of our destiny."

"Les . . ."

"I know. No strings, no promises. I'm just expressing an opinion."

Before Linda could respond, he stopped the car.

"Here we are. Lester's door-to-door service." He got out and went around and opened her door.

Linda should have been dazzled by his smile. Maybe she would have been if she hadn't been thinking about that other face, the one without a smile. The one that closed against her every time.

"You didn't have to get out." She took the hand he offered.

"Of course I did. How else could I call it 'door-to-door' service."

They reached the door and Linda tensed.

"Good night." His soft words let her relax. "See you tomorrow."

"Thanks for tonight. It's been a long time since I've been out like this."

"Hopefully it's the first of many."

Linda held out her hand. He took it and held it for a few seconds. When he let it go, she unlocked the door and turned back to face him.

"Good night."

She stepped inside. He waved and went back to the car. She closed the door and leaned against it.

He's such a nice guy. Sense of humor, good-looking. There aren't many like him out there. Why don't I feel a pull for him instead of for someone who doesn't even like me?

The next morning the question was still with Linda, but she couldn't suppress a smile as she washed her breakfast dishes. Day one on the job had gone great. Of course, the test was yet to come. For some reason she had gotten a reprieve yesterday; the computer kids she had been warned about hadn't come in. She sent up a quick prayer of thanks. Roberto had been enough to deal with, although it had gone well with him. Avery had warned her about the boys trying to hit on her, but if Roberto was an example, she wouldn't have any trouble handling them.

That Roberto was something. If he set his mind to it, he could go as far as he wanted to in the computer field. She hoped Avery could keep him focused. It would be a shame for him to waste his talent.

Avery. The dish towel remained in her hand even though she was finished with it.

Before she'd gone to the center that first day, she thought her biggest challenge would be working with the kids. She let out a hard breath. Two days and two clashes with Avery. Would today bring clash number three?

How could someone so attractive be so . . . She frowned. So mean. She shoved his image from her mind. Oh no. She wasn't going to put Avery and attractive in the same thought. She wasn't going to notice him except as her boss. She dragged her thoughts back to what she was sure to face today. There were bound to be repercussions from the kids because she had removed the games from the computers. She'd have to figure out how to handle them.

She spent the ride to work trying out different scenarios dealing with the kids when they found out what she had done.

As she walked into the center, she was still running over different approaches in her mind, looking for the ideal one.

She glanced at Avery's office and let out a deep sigh when he didn't come out. She walked past softly. *I am not tiptoeing,* she swore as she slipped by his door. She didn't need him disturbing her train of thought today. She had to concentrate on what she had to face in the lab.

She heard footsteps in the hall and glanced at the clock. They must have been waiting for the door to open. The footsteps came closer and she tried to think of the ideas she had come up with. They had disappeared, every last one of them. She took a deep breath and waited.

Five boys came into the lab, spoke to her quickly, scribbled their names on the sign-in sheet and raced to the computers.

"I'm beating your score today," a tall wiry boy said. "Be prepared to meet your doom. I'll try not to hurt you so bad."

"Man, you ain't doing nothing but talking trash."

"That's 'cause that's all he can do," one of the boys said.

"Yeah? We'll see." He touched the keyboard.

" 'fraid not, fellas." Linda took a deep breath and refused to let her voice wobble. This was it. "The games are gone. I took them off."

"What?" The wiry kid turned from the computer. His eyes were wider than a small plate. "You did what? Who are you? Does Mr. Avery know?"

"I'm Linda and I'll be working here in the lab. And yes, Mr. Avery knows I removed the games."

"All of them?" A chunky boy next to him looked like this was Christmas morning and the space under his tree was bare. "You got rid of all of them?"

"Every last one."

"Oh, no, no." One of the other boys wrapped his arms around his middle and rocked back and forth like he was in pain.

"What you go and do that for? You're kidding. Right?" the first boy begged.

"All of them are gone." The chunky boy sounded as if he were still trying to believe it. "They're all gone. She wouldn't kid about something like that." He stared at her. "Would you?"

"No, I wouldn't."

"I didn't think so. That's nothing to joke about." The tallest of them looked as if he had just found out that the world outside the center had ended.

Linda let them fuss. She didn't interrupt until a curse word slipped out from the wiry one who had claimed to be the best player.

"What's your name?"

"Nathaniel. They call me Nate." He held out both hands. "Did you really dump our games? We've got a running contest going and I was gonna really pour it on them today."

"Well, Nate, I know you're upset, but I'm not going to have that language in here. And yes, the games are gone. All of them." She fastened him with a stare.

"I'm sorry, miss. I know Mr. Avery doesn't allow that language in the center, but I'm so p . . ." He stopped himself and took a deep breath. "I'm so angry." His frown deepened. "That's such a lame word for how I feel."

"I know the feeling. I've been there myself." Linda's face softened. "However, it will have to do."

"Yeah, I guess." He stared at her. "What we gonna do in here if we don't play games?"

Finally Linda smiled.

"There are lots of things we can do. To start with we're going to do word processing. Either school assignments or ideas of your own."

Linda looked at the slightly built boy who towered over her.

"What's your name?"

"My name is Tyree." He pulled himself up to his full height, but Linda could still look him in the eye. "About that writing. I got some ideas." He stuck out his chin. "I'm a rapper. Can I use the computers to write my raps?"

"I don't see why not." She frowned at him. "Mr. Avery didn't say you couldn't bring rap in here, did he?"

"No. he's cool with that as long as it's clean." He pointed a thumb to his chest. "Me and my homies, we got our own group going on." He pointed to the quiet boy beside him. "John here is part of my group. He don't talk much, but he can rap." The boy shrugged and ducked his head. Tyree went on. "Mr. Avery has a talent show here as part of the cookout before school starts up again. We always have a new rap for that. As a matter of fact, we're working on one now." He rubbed his jaw slowly. "If I type the words on the computer, my boys won't complain about my handwriting." He nodded again. "Yeah, that'll work just fine."

"Don't forget your school assignments. You must have essays or paragraphs to write for some of your classes."

"He usually does those in the hall before class."

"Shut up, Lamont. You do the same thing."

Linda looked at all of them in turn.

"Your grades probably show that the assignments were done at the last minute, too."

The boys got quiet. All of them avoided eye contact with her, except one. Finally Nate spoke.

"We get by."

"And you're satisfied with getting by?"

None of them answered, but they all shifted in their chairs, still not looking at her. Linda went on. "Do you know it won't take much more time to do a better job? If you do it earlier, you just have time to go over it and make changes, if you want to. The computer makes it easier than doing it by hand." She smiled. "Wouldn't you like to shock your teachers?"

"I'd like to do more than shock some of them," the chunky kid said. "They're always on my case. My name is Lamont."

"Well, Lamont, let's see if we can get them 'off your case.' Do you have an assignment due soon?"

"Tomorrow, third period."

"Thanks a lot, Alan." The others glared at Alan.

"Alan's what we call a nerd. He likes school." Nate shook his head. "I don't know what's wrong with him. We don't hold it against him, though."

Linda laughed.

"Are you all in the same class?"

Five heads nodded slowly.

"Okay, fellas. Fifteen minutes. Let's spend fifteen minutes on the assignment. That's all I ask."

"Fifteen minutes, tops. Then I'm gonna go hang out in the gym. Must be more interesting things going on down there than up here." Nate glared at her. "Now that you erased our games." He finally blinked when she didn't look away. "I had enough of school for today."

"Deal. Fifteen minutes."

Linda had them access the word processing program. She watched as they took out their assignment books.

She was counting heavily on them getting into their work so much they'd forget about stopping in fifteen minutes.

Forty-five minutes later, four of them held their finished papers in their hands. Alan was still working, unaware of anything else going on around him.

"I didn't know I could write this good." Tyree held up his paper.

"This 'well.' You didn't know you could write this 'well.' "

"You couldn't without Miss Linda's help," Lamont said.

"I didn't do that much. It's his work. I just made a few minor suggestions." Her glance swept over all of them. "All of you can be proud of your work. Your teacher will be shocked."

"Maybe she'll be shocked speechless."

"That will be a first. Miss Jones speechless." They laughed and Linda chuckled with them.

"What we gonna do in here after school is out?"

"You can still write, only *you* can decide what about. Maybe a story, maybe about something that makes you angry. Whatever you want to get out of your system. Writing is a good way to vent your anger."

"I don't know if I want to be doing any writing when I don't have to." Nate shook his head.

"You don't have to write. It's just a suggestion. Another thing you can do is try your hand at writing some computer programs. If you get good enough, maybe you can try to write your own game."

"You're kidding, right?"

"Somebody writes them. Why shouldn't you try?"

"Yeah." Nate nodded. "Why not?" He pulled out a sheet of paper and began taking notes as they discussed what kind of game they'd like to write. Their words tumbled together as each one added his ideas.

Linda watched them as they became involved. The gym was forgotten for the time being.

Finally they were satisfied with their work.

"Man, look at the time," Nate said as he glanced at his watch. "It's almost six o'clock. I can't believe we been up here that long."

"Me, neither," Lamont said. "But we got some good stuff done. Right?"

"Right, but after I go home to eat, I'm gonna come check out the basketball game. Crunch's team challenged Fred's. I got to see it."

"Good idea." Tyree looked at Alan. "You coming now, man?"

"I guess this is the best I can do." Alan glanced at the screen one more time before he sent his work to the printer."

"His 'best I can do' always gets an 'A,' " Nate shrugged as he looked at the paper coming out of the printer. "Ain't nothing wrong with that, if that's what he likes. He ain't hurting nobody being smart and everybody knows he's gonna get a scholarship after he graduates number one in our class."

The others agreed. They waited until Alan picked up his paper and gave it a final glance.

"Thanks, Miss Linda." Alan gave her a shy smile. "I'll be back to do some more writing, if that's all right with you. I like to write stories."

"His stories are good as some of those in the books. You should see them."

"I look forward to it. You can come up here and write anytime you want to. That's what I'm here for."

She relaxed as she watched them go. If this was the greatest challenge, she could make this computer program work. She smiled as she got her purse and went down to the lounge.

* * *

During the dinner break word had spread about Linda and the lab. So many kids stuck their heads in the door after they got back to ask if the games were really gone, that Linda lost count of them.

One girl didn't just peek in. She softly stepped inside and smiled shyly at Linda.

"Nate said you're doing word processing in here. Is it true we can come and do some writing of our own?"

"It's true. What's your name?"

"Helen."

"What do you write, Helen?"

"Just things." Her eyes widened. "But I don't show them to anybody." She shrugged. "I think they would look better if I print them out even though they are just for me."

"You can do that, and I promise I won't look at them if you don't want me to."

"Thank you." She hesitated. "Is now too soon to start?"

"Now is fine."

"Any special place you want me to sit?"

Linda shook her head. "Any place you want." She looked around. "As you can see you're the first. Sorry I don't have a prize for you."

"This is my prize. I wish I had a computer at home." She shrugged. "I didn't bring my notebook with me, but I have some ideas I can work on."

"Go ahead. I won't disturb you."

"Thanks, Miss Linda."

She worked at the computer for the rest of the evening. Several others drifted in, looked around, then told Linda they'd be back the next day.

Helen finally looked at the papers in her hand.

"I got a lot done. It's a lot easier making changes on the computer." She ducked her head toward her shoulder. "Is it okay if I do some more tomorrow?"

"Sure. I'll be here. If you know anybody else who wants to do some writing, tell them to come on."

"Yes, Ma'am."

Helen's smile as she left was much wider and more relaxed than the one she had when she first came into the lab.

Linda smiled as she watched her go. She was still smiling as she rode home. After today, the rest would be easy.

Her upbeat mode was with her when she slipped into bed that night. It was still in place the next morning. She was anxious to get to the center.

She walked toward the center determined to hold on to her mellow mood. She smiled at Bill and headed for the lab.

She got as far as Avery's office on her way upstairs when his door opened as if he knew when she would be passing at that time.

"Good morning, Linda."

"Good morning." She started past him. She didn't need his challenge first thing in the morning. She was feeling too calm.

"It was great the way you handled the guys yesterday."

"You were spying on me. I should have known."

"I wasn't spying on you. I wanted to make sure everything was all right. I didn't know how Nate and the rest would act when they found out their games were gone. They're in that lab every day. But they didn't throw you anything you couldn't handle."

"You sound surprised. Or are you disappointed?"

Avery sighed.

"I didn't know how they would react to you. Dealing with teenagers isn't the easiest thing in the world."

"You're right about that. Neither is having somebody not believe in your capabilities." She fixed him with a glare. "I thought I saw you lurking out in the hall."

"I was not lurking. I was not spying." His glare met hers. "I just wanted to make sure you'd be all right with the boys. As I said, I know teenagers aren't the easiest people in the world to work with."

"They're a lot more honest than some adults. They don't operate under hidden agendas like some people." Her stare grew hotter. "They let you know right up front how they feel."

"Yeah." Their stares remained chained together. The sound of the front door opening released them both.

"I have work to do." Linda turned her back to him.

"So do I." Avery took a deep breath. "I wasn't disappointed. You might not believe this, but I don't want you to fail."

"You're right. I might not believe that." She turned again and stalked out of his office.

Avery stared at her back as straight and stiff as his door. Every bit as rigid as his was right now. He still stood in the hall after he watched the fire door close behind her.

"I was not checking up on her or waiting for her to fail," he muttered as he moved into his office. "I wasn't."

The next two weeks was going to be longer than he thought.

He stared out his office window. *I don't want to think about how I'll handle it if I have to let her stay.* He sat at his desk. How did you ask somebody to change their perfume? He frowned. Was it really her perfume that was disturbing him? Could perfume jumble his thoughts until they didn't make sense?

She's not right for me, he told himself. *You know you could never trust her. She's nothing but trouble.* He shook his head. Beautiful trouble. He closed his eyes but that only made her image sharper in his mind.

Her big, brown eyes had flared in anger. Would they

simmer the same way in passion? Would their heat ignite a similar fire in him if she were wrapped in his arms? Would she feel as right pressed close to his body as he imagined she would?

He shook his head harder in an effort to drive that thought away. *Don't even touch that, Avery,* a strong voice in his head told him. Why hadn't he met her before she got tangled up with drugs?

He snatched a basketball from the box beside the door. Maybe he could work this craziness out of his system on the basketball floor.

He dribbled hard down the hall. If one of the kids did that they'd have the ball confiscated. The next bounce would have gone through a weaker floor. So would the one after that.

He entered the gym and drove for the far basket, trying to drive her from his mind.

Linda took a deep breath. What she needed was to jog a mile or ten to cool down. What she'd have to settle for was a dozen deep breaths. If she was going to work for Avery she'd better study relaxation techniques with a vengeance. She shook her head. No. She'd better master relaxation techniques. She didn't have time to study. And she'd better perfect them fast. Otherwise, her temper would burn out the motherboards in every single computer in the room faster than any power surge ever could.

She stored her purse in the bottom drawer of her desk. She pulled out the chair and forced her body into it when what she felt like doing was pacing her anger away. She would have sworn it was just about gone for good. Then she met Avery Washington.

She gave in and paced back and forth between the door and the windows. After a dozen times she went back to her desk.

She took out the notes she had made earlier during her phone conversation with the high school English department head, but she didn't look at them. She was still trying to convince herself that the heat inside her was only from anger at Avery and no other feelings.

Three days. She had known the man for only three days. This was not like her. She had to find the level head that, except for one time, let her keep things sensible. She would not allow herself to be attracted to this man. She wasn't a star-struck teenager. She knew better. She knew better than anyone else how important it was to get to really know a person before even considering involvement. And what happened to her vow not to let another man into her life? She leaned her head back and closed her eyes.

She would not imagine how it would feel to have his strong arms wrapped around her. She would not consider his body molded to hers. She wouldn't guess at how the thick curls at his neck would feel if she stroked her fingers through them.

She took a deep breath and tried to cool off her rapidly heating body. She did not feel drawn to him as she never felt to any other man.

Yeah. And Jamal didn't set you up, either, a voice inside her mocked.

What am I going to do? Every time she was near him her body tightened in anticipation. How could she break the attraction before it grew stronger? How could she keep from getting hurt again? She almost wished he'd let her go and solve her problem for her. Almost.

She sat staring at the paper in front of her, but no answers came. She was on her own. She'd better find a solution and soon. High blood pressure didn't run in her family, but she felt it was about to start with her. What was she going to do? How could she change her feelings? She sighed. Maybe Avery would solve her problems for her. If she could hang on for a few more days, maybe he'd tell her she wasn't right for the job. After all, so far they'd clashed every time they saw each other. The air was so tight with tension between them that a rubber band would have snapped from the stress.

A few more days. Then she'd look for a job as far from the center as she could get. After her two weeks were up she would place as much distance between her and Avery Washington as she could. Then maybe he'd stay out of her thoughts.

She dragged her attention back to her notes and picked up a pen. Planning computer activities was something she could do right now.

Linda walked up the steps to the house. She frowned. Why were so many lights on? Auntie was usually upstairs for the night by now watching television.

She opened the door, hoping nothing was the matter.

"Auntie?" She stepped into the living room.

"Hi, Linda."

A small, young woman stood and faced her. She twisted her hands in front of her the way Linda did, the way their mother did when she was upset. She looked a lot younger than twenty.

"What are you doing here, Shelia? How did you find me?"

Linda refused to let the flutter of happiness at the sight of her younger sister grow.

"I . . . I bugged Marian until she told me. Don't be mad at her. You know how persistent I can be." She blinked several times. "I came because I had to see you." She took a step closer, but she didn't touch Linda. "I missed you." Her voice wobbled and Linda watched her eyes fill. She felt her own eyes fill at the sight.

"Don't, Baby Sis. Don't cry. You know I could never stand to see you cry."

"I can't help it. I can't stand this and I don't know what to do to get things back to the way they were between us." She opened her hands toward Linda. "I don't know how to make things right."

Linda hesitated before she took Sheila's hands in her own. Suddenly they were clinging to each other as tears rolled down both faces that looked so much alike.

"You two have a lot to talk out. I'll leave you to it." As Auntie left the room, her smile covered both of them.

Linda led Sheila to the couch and sat beside her. She took a deep breath.

"Does Daddy know you're here?"

"No. I didn't want to get his hopes up." Sheila shook her head. She grabbed Linda's hand. "He's so torn up about this rift. You should see him. I don't know when I last saw him smile. Mom's not doing any better than he is. They're both so torn up over what happened."

"It's all my fault. I know it. I'm sorry I brought shame on them, on the family. I know it hurts them to have our, I mean their, friends know they have a daughter with a prison record. I can imagine how embarrassing it is for you. It must have cost you a few friends, too." Linda blinked away her new tears. "If I could undo it all I would."

Sheila frowned at her. A line that didn't belong on any young face appeared between her eyebrows.

"What you did isn't what has them so sad." She leaned toward Linda. "They talk about what they did wrong." Sheila wiped at her eyes. "Every day one of them mentions a new 'if only.' They said what happened was all their fault. They said they must have done something to make you keep them away after the trouble." She tightened her hold on Linda's hand. "You have to come see them. Please?"

"It's nobody's fault but my own."

Linda stared at their hands wrapped together. It reminded her of when they were kids and her little sister shared a problem with her. Now she was the one with the problem.

"Linda? Will you come?"

Linda continued her story. "Afterward, after I was arrested, I was so hurt. None of you ever let me explain what really happened. It was like you were all convinced that I was guilty and felt that not talking about it would make it disappear." She stared at Sheila. "Every time I brought it up, you said it didn't matter." She leaned toward her. "But it does. It matters to me that you believe I was innocent. After the trial I decided to quit trying to get through to you."

"Oh, Linda. I thought you felt you *had* to explain. I . . . I meant I love you no matter what." She wiped away a tear trailing down her face. "I'll listen to you, Linda, if that's what you want."

Linda pulled several tissues from the box on the table. She handed some to Sheila before she wiped her own eyes. Then she took a deep breath. "I need you to listen. To all of it. I need to tell you exactly what happened."

Sheila sat quietly while Linda explained how she met Jamal in one of her classes and how he involved her in something she hadn't been aware he was involved with. She explained that, until she was arrested and the police opened the package, she had no idea what she was carrying.

Several times her words faltered, especially when she got to the part about being arrested, but she didn't stop until the whole story was told. When her voice cracked, Sheila squeezed her hand in encouragement. Both of them wiped their faces as Linda's story unfolded.

Finally, Linda stopped. Relief flooded over her. She looked at Sheila.

"I'm so sorry you had to go through all that alone. I'm sorry I didn't better understand what you needed."

"No." Linda shook her head. "I'm sorry I didn't make you understand how important it was to me for you to listen." She swallowed hard. "If you think it would help, I'll come visit Mom and Dad. I don't get off from work until eight, though. Maybe we should wait until Sunday?"

"No way, I'll come get you tomorrow night. Just tell me how to get there."

"Afraid I'll change my mind?" Her smile was easy and her tone light. It felt good.

"No." Sheila shook her head. "I know how you are when you decide something. I just want to see things back the way they were as quickly as possible."

"They'll never be back the way they were, but they can be better than they are now. You sure they'll want to see me?" She pushed down the hope that tried to rise. "Daddy can be so, so unbending. You know how he is." She wiped at her eyes. "And Mom usually goes along with Daddy."

"I know, but I'm positive they'll be glad to see you." She pulled a pad and pen from her bag. "Tell me how to get to the center."

After Sheila tucked the pad with the directions back into her purse, Linda walked her to her car.

"See you tomorrow night, Sis." Sheila smiled and pulled away from the curb.

Linda smiled as she walked back to the house. It had been a long time since she had heard that. Too long. Maybe, just maybe, she had her family back.

That night she slept better than she had in a long time.

Throughout the next day she glanced at her watch every few minutes, but the time was moving in slow motion. Helen came back and one of her friends came with her, and Linda had something besides the coming evening to occupy her mind. It didn't take the girls long to get lost in their poetry, though, and Linda was soon back to time-watching.

From time to time a few other kids came, but they only took enough time to keep Linda from going out of her mind.

Later, after much whispering between them, Helen and her friend, Kira, approached Linda about the possibility of doing a newsletter. Helen nudged Kira forward.

"I don't know if we can do it here," Kira said, "but The Smith Center has a paper they put out every month. It's usually only one page on both sides, but it lets all the kids know what's going on. You know: games and stuff. We could even include stuff about school. You know, awards and things like that." She frowned. "We don't have a school paper anymore. The budget for it was cut. Mr. Riley, our sponsor was so . . ." She stopped and took a deep breath. "He was so mad. Some of the kids heard him fussing about it with Mr. Casey, the principal." She shrugged. "But Mr. Casey didn't change his mind."

"I guess it takes a lot of money to print a paper." Helen's soft voice faded to nothing. Her look said she didn't expect the paper to happen.

"I can't promise you a paper, of course, but I can promise to talk to Mr. Avery about it." She smiled at them. "If we can have a paper, what do you have in mind? Let's sit down and talk about the details."

Linda sat with them as they threw out ideas. By dinnertime they had a list of what they wanted to include and who else might be interested. Linda hoped Avery would find funding somewhere. The kids weren't asking a lot, and developing a newsletter would help them with so many skills.

She locked up the lab, got up her courage, and decided to approach Avery right away.

"Excuse me." She entered his office. He looked busy, but he had told staff members that, if his door was open, they could come in.

"What is it?" He looked up from the papers on his desk. The serious look that seemed permanent, at least around her, was in its place.

"I need to talk to you about an idea the kids came up with."

He waited without commenting, so she explained what they had in mind. She didn't let the fact that his frown hadn't smoothed out stop her. She ended with her sales pitch about how many skills the paper would help the kids perfect.

"These things are just off the top of my head. I can come up with a list, if you want."

"That's not necessary. I'll see what I can do. I think I know where we can get funding. I . . ." He leaned on his desk. "You better go eat. The kids will be back before you know it."

"Yeah. Thanks for listening."

"No problem. That's what I'm here for."

"I guess I'd better go."

"Yes, I guess you better."

She stood there a few seconds more, then she broke free. She was still trying to regain her composure all through dinner in the lunchroom with the rest of the staff. Not once did she think about Sheila and their parents.

After dinner, when she went back to the lab, time went back to moving at a crawl.

Finally the day was over and she rushed out of the center. She stood in front, realizing she had no idea what Sheila was driving, now. Cars lined the street. A horn blew from a car parked at the corner, and Linda dashed to it. She was so anxious to go she never looked back. She didn't see Avery watch her get into the car.

Who's she meeting this late? Avery frowned deeper than he usually did when he thought about Linda. Who did she know with enough money to drive a new sports BMW? Avery's face tightened. He could think of one way to get a lot of money, fast.

It hadn't taken her long to hook up with her old life. His face tightened even more. Guess she got tired of riding the bus already. *She hasn't even gotten her first paycheck and already she's decided it won't be enough. Now, with her new old job, she can buy more perfume when hers runs out.*

He shook his head. She wouldn't be around the center when that happened. He knew, from the minute he saw her, that he couldn't trust her. People don't leave the trade. Yeah, she was innocent all right. He just saw for himself exactly how innocent she was.

He had been right about her all along. He clenched his teeth. Why didn't he feel happy about that? He could fire her; he could let her go tomorrow. He had a reason to get her out of his life forever now. Why wasn't he raising his fists in victory? Why did he feel as if he had lost something precious? Something that comes only once to a person?

He got into his car, fumbled with the ignition before he finally got the key in. Still he didn't start it.

Why did tonight have to be the one night he didn't stay late to work?

Six

"How was your day?"

Sheila broke the silence after she and Linda had ridden for fifteen minutes in silence.

"Okay." Linda continued to stare straight ahead.

"What did you do?"

"Helped some kids with the computer programs."

"You don't feel like talking." It wasn't a question. Shelia knew something was on Linda's mind. Ever since they were little she would shut down when something was troubling her.

"No, I don't. I'm sorry I'm such poor company, Sheila." Linda shook her head. "I'm worried. I don't know how Daddy will act toward me after what happened."

"I can understand your feeling that way, but it will be okay."

"Are you sure about this? I mean really sure that I should do this? You know him better, now, than I do." She sighed. "It's been a long time." Linda let go of the words that had been filling her mind since she got into the car. "Maybe we should wait until another time. Maybe you should ask Daddy if he wants to see me. I probably should have asked you to tell him I was coming. I shouldn't go home like this. He never did like for anything unexpected to happen." Linda twisted her fingers through her purse straps. "He doesn't always welcome surprises. Remember that surprise birthday party Mom held for him? He didn't smile the whole evening."

"That had nothing to do with the surprise part. He was just trying to deal with being fifty. That 'Over the Hill' T-shirt that Uncle Buddy gave him sure didn't help." She laughed. Finally, Linda joined in.

"If Uncle Buddy hadn't been Grandmom's brother and so old, I don't know what Daddy would have done when he insisted that Daddy was going to put that shirt on and he was going to help him do it." Linda laughed again at the memory.

"Thankfully, Mom took the shirt and said she'd put it away so it wouldn't get messed up."

"Since she didn't let them finish their reverse tug-of-war it's still in one piece in a drawer where she put it 'away.' "

"Or else Mom donated it to the thrift shop and some-body else was forced to wear it." Sheila's words started them laughing again. "Bet no one gives him one for his sixtieth birthday in four years."

The laughter bubbled and then faded. Linda sighed.

"I still don't know about this surprise visit. Maybe it's not the timing or the surprise part of it that he'll object to. There's a good chance that he doesn't want to see me ever again. I wouldn't blame him. I can't imagine what I did to his reputation, to his standing in the com-munity. You know how everybody looks up to Daddy." She stared straight ahead. "Or at least they did until I messed up." She swallowed hard. "His friends must be having a good time laughing at the prominent doctor with an ex-con for a daughter."

"His real friends are supportive. Maybe this helped him see just who his real friends are."

"I wish he could have found out some other way without me being involved. I just don't know that I'm doing the right thing."

"I do." Sheila glanced at Linda and patted her hand. "It will be fine. If Daddy knew you were coming he'd find a fatted calf somewhere. Although the grill's too small and the weather is too hot, and it would take too long to cook something that big, he'd find a way to have it cooked." She patted Linda's hand again. "He'll be glad to see you."

Sheila didn't try to carry on any further conversation and Linda was grateful. She needed all her efforts to think of what she would say. *What will I do if Sheila is wrong? What if Daddy doesn't want to see me?*

For the rest of the ride Linda tried to convince herself that her parents would be glad to see her. She didn't know how she would cope if they didn't make her feel welcome back home.

It was true she had shut them out, but she had done it to keep from hurting them any more than she already had. If they didn't let her back into their lives . . . She stared straight ahead. She refused to think of that "what if."

Half an hour later, Sheila pulled into a wide, gently curving driveway and turned off the motor when she reached the doors to the triple garage. The split-level ranch home sprawled on the two and a half acre lot. Except for the fuller trees and the new height on the trees Linda had watched the gardener plant, things looked just as she remembered. The real difference was what had happened to her. She brushed her hand across a peach rose on her favorite bush.

"It will be okay." Sheila smiled at Linda. "Let's go in."

Butterflies hovered in Linda's stomach. She forced her shaky legs to take her up to the door.

"Maybe I should wait here while you go and check with Daddy." Linda stopped just inside the door.

"Don't be silly." Sheila smiled. "Besides, if I leave you here, you look like you'll try to run home." Her face softened. "And you already are home."

She took Linda's hand and tugged her along toward the family room, four steps down at the side of the front hall. Soft music floated in the air. Linda smiled. Mom and Daddy still listened to the Mellow Oldies program that came on the radio on Saturday nights. She relaxed her hold on her purse. Some things hadn't changed. Maybe others hadn't either.

The couple, reading as they listened, looked up.

They don't look much different, was Linda's first thought.

"I thought I heard you pull up, but you didn't park in the garage. Is something the . . ."

Linda watched her father's eyes widen at the same time she heard her mother.

"Oh, my." The book tumbled from her mother's hands and the thud, as the book hit the floor, was the only sound to intrude on the music still wafting through the air.

Linda stared at her father, trying to see what he wanted her to do. As he stood his surprise gave way to a smile.

"Welcome home, baby," he said as he opened his arms.

Tears tumbled down Linda's cheeks as she stumbled to him. Then she closed her eyes and let his hug soothe her.

Her mother found her way to them and added her arms to the pair already enfolding Linda.

Linda glanced at Sheila and watched her come to them. The circle was complete.

Finally, as if on cue, they each relaxed their holds, but

their hands still remained joined until the end of the song that no one noticed.

Her father led her to the sofa and her mother followed. When they sat, Linda was still between them.

"I've missed you." Her father's voice was rough. He cleared his throat as he gazed at her.

"My prayers have been answered." Her mother stroked her cheek as if afraid Linda would be frightened away if she touched too hard.

"I told you it would be all right." Sheila wiped her eyes.

"Why wouldn't it be?" Her father frowned.

"Linda wasn't sure you'd want to see her."

"How could you think that?" His frown replaced the smile that had been on his face before Shelia's words.

"Daddy, I know how important reputation is to you. Ever since I can remember, you were telling us that, giving us different examples. I know what happened with me must have brushed off on you, affected you."

"You're my child. That's more important than anything else."

"Linda wants to explain what happened."

"That's not necessary."

"Your mother's right. There's no need for . . ."

"Daddy, she *needs* to explain." Sheila patted her father's shoulder. "You have to let her do this. I'll go make some coffee and tea. I don't think anybody's going to be able to sleep any time soon anyway."

She left the room as Linda clasped her hands, leaned forward, and began the story she would tell for the second time in as many days.

When Sheila came back into the room, Linda was ending her story by telling them about Auntie. Sheila set the tray on the coffee table.

"We didn't mean to deny you the chance to explain," her father said.

"No," her mother added. "We only meant that we love you no matter what. We didn't want you to think that our continued love was based on your explanation. I'm so sorry."

"No, Mom, I'm sorry for not telling you how I felt. The misunderstanding is my fault."

"We won't talk about fault or being sorry ever again. We'll go on from here." Her father patted Linda's hand.

Sheila placed a cup and a slice of sweet potato pie in front of each of them. The pie and the cups remained untouched until Linda finished talking.

The room was quiet, except for the radio. All four of them were wiping their eyes; the tissue box was almost empty.

"Have some pie." Her mother swallowed hard. "I . . . I know you missed my pie."

"I sure did." Linda took a taste. She licked the fork. "Better than I remembered."

Her mother smiled. "Take a piece to have with your breakfast tomorrow."

"Mom." A surprised look covered Sheila's face. "You never let us have cake or pie before lunch."

"It's all right this one time." Their mother reached over and patted Linda's face. "Linda has some catching up to do."

"Thanks, Mom." Linda stuck her tongue out at Sheila as she cut another slice. She ate it then glanced at her watch. "It's after one. I can't believe I talked for so long. I'd better go."

"You had a lot to say." Sheila smiled.

"Why can't you stay here tonight?" Her father asked.

"Why can't you come on back home, period?" Her mother asked.

Linda smiled. She had worried for nothing.

"I joined a church near Auntie's. It's my choir's turn to sing tomorrow, so I have to go back tonight." She squeezed her mother's hand. "I'm settled in at Auntie's and it's an easy commute from there to work."

"We can get you a car. The lack of transportation isn't a good reason to keep you from moving back home."

"Daddy, that's generous of you, but I have to work my way back on my own. I let myself get into a mess and I'll get myself out." She kissed his cheek. "Thanks for the offer, though."

"Can you come for dinner tomorrow?"

"I'd love to, Mom." She squeezed both hands still clasped in hers. "You know, I'm not that far away. You'll be seeing so much of me, you'll get tired of me."

"Sweetheart, you know that could never happen." Her father's quiet voice was sure and steady.

Linda stood and they did, too.

"I think I'd better get back."

"Okay." Sheila picked up her purse from the end table and started for the door.

"I'll take her back," their father said. "It's too late for you to be driving around the city."

"I'll go with you to help you find the way." Their mother wrapped her arm around Linda's shoulder.

Linda smiled. It was true that her dad could get easily lost when he went somewhere for the first time, but it was also true that once he went somewhere he could find his way back with no problem.

"Maybe I should go, too, to make sure both of you get back all right." Sheila smiled at her father. "Daddy, I've been out later than this, and you know it." Her smile widened. "But if you want to take Linda back, that's fine with me."

They all laughed. Their father shrugged and looked sheepish. Then he lifted his chin.

"Okay. There's nothing the matter with me wanting to take my little girl back to where she lives now." He looked hard at Linda. "But it will never be her 'home' as long as her family is here. This will always be her home and she'll always be welcome here."

"That's right, Daddy. There's nothing wrong with it." Sheila unfastened the angel pin from her blouse. "Here." She pinned it on Linda's shoulder and gave it a pat. "This is so, when you wake up, you don't think this was all a dream."

Linda squeezed Sheila's hand and nodded at her.

When they were young and something really good happened, and especially on Christmas nights, they took something to bed with them so when they woke up they'd know they hadn't been dreaming.

Easy laughter followed Linda and her parents to the car.

During the ride back to Auntie's house, Linda listened as her parents filled her in about what had happened while she was away. Two sets of friends had gotten married and one couple was already divorced.

Linda asked about Uncle Buddy and the incident with the T-shirt came up.

"He never gave me another 'old' gift again. Mama always said he had a mean streak." Her father glared when the others laughed at him. "He had some nerve. He's twenty years older than I am and he gives me some shirt talking about 'Over the hill.' "

He laughed with the others. Laughter continued to fill the car as they made their way to the West Philadelphia neighborhood where Linda now lived. Easy, warm, family laughter. Family. She had her family back.

"What time should I pick you up for dinner tomorrow?"

"I could take the bus."

"You'll do no such thing. You know how the schedule is on Sundays. You'd spend half the day on the bus. What time?"

Linda told him, then kissed his cheek and got out the

car. She leaned in and kissed her mother good night as well, then started toward the porch.

"Wait a minute. I'll walk you to the door."

"Daddy, I'll be all right. It's right here." She pointed to the house.

"Nothing wrong with a father walking his daughter to the door, is there?"

"No, Daddy. Nothing at all."

"Good, because I was going to do it anyway."

Linda chuckled and he did, too.

When they reached the door, she kissed his cheek again. He waited until she was inside before he went back to the car.

After she locked the door Linda wrapped her arms around herself and waited until she heard the car pull away from the curb.

Then she tiptoed upstairs, looking forward to the next day.

Linda awoke early, afraid the meeting with her family had been a dream. Then she looked at her shirt draped over the chair. A ray of sun glinted off the angel pin perched on the shoulder. She smiled and stretched. She hadn't realized how good it would feel to be back in touch with her family.

She put on her robe, the one Sheila had given her before she . . . She shook her head. No negative thoughts. Not today.

She walked softly downstairs, made a pot of tea, and sat at the table smiling.

"Morning, Linda. You were late coming in last night." Auntie came into the kitchen and poured a cup of tea.

"I should have called you. I'm sorry."

"I'm not fussing at you. I'm not your housemother and you're a grown woman so you don't have to account for your coming and going to me." She smiled. "But I was worried." She looked sheepish. "That's why Marian won't stay with me. She said I go gallivanting all over the place without so much as a 'by your leave' and then I worry if somebody is two minutes late." She sat across from Linda. "What you do with your time is up to you." She stirred sweetener into the cup. "You still going to church this morning?"

"Yes, Ma'am. We sing this morning." Linda leaned forward. "You'll never guess. You know that Sheila picked me up and I went to see my parents. We sat and talked for half the night."

"From the look on your face I'd say things went well."

"They went better than I could ever expect. We cleared up a lot of misunderstandings."

"Things have a way of working out when you talk them through."

"Daddy's picking me up after church. I'm going over there for dinner." She touched Auntie's arm. "I can't believe it. They weren't angry. They listened to me. They listened to my whole story, and they believed me." Tears filled her eyes. "That was so important."

"I know." Auntie patted her arm.

Linda fixed the pancakes for their usual Sunday breakfast. They were light, but not as light as she was feeling.

Throughout church service Linda had to make herself pay attention instead of letting her mind race ahead. Once or twice she missed a cue in a song.

As she stood for the benediction, she promised herself she'd get a tape of the service so she could listen when she could concentrate. She couldn't remember a word of the message. She sighed and smiled. She was going home to dinner with her family.

Sunday dinner had always been special at their house, but today it was more than what Linda had expected.

The meal centered around a crown roast, but it was as if it were a fatted calf.

Conversation around the table flowed easily. They asked Linda about the center and the rest of the meal was spent talking about it and her job. Her eyes sparkled when she talked about the kids.

They finished dinner with her mother's coconut cake, Linda's favorite.

"This cake is every bit as good as I remember. Everything is." She slid another slice onto her plate.

"Tell us something we don't know." Sheila pretended to glare. "I was counting on a piece of that cake with my lunch tomorrow."

"I'll be considerate. This is my last slice."

"Only because you're about to burst."

"I'm making up for lost time. Besides, I left you some."

"I'll have to battle Daddy for what's left."

"It's your fault, you know. You're the one who insisted I come home."

Sheila smiled. "Mom's disappearing coconut cake notwithstanding, I'm glad I did."

"So am I." Linda blinked hard. "It's good to be back." She stood. "To show you how good it is, I'm going to do something I never thought I'd do. I'm volunteering for clean-up duty." She laughed. "I must be getting old. Not long ago I would have done everything I could think of to get out of that job."

"It's a good thing I'm sitting down," Sheila said. "Many times I had to do some quick thinking to keep from getting stuck with the kitchen every night." She stood. "To show there are no hard feelings, I'll help you. Before you say anything, I know that's a first, too."

Their parents went into the kitchen to keep them company.

Linda glanced as the two of them stood, her father's

arm around her mother's shoulder, holding her close to him, the way she remembered seeing them stand so many times before when she was growing up. She had missed that. Funny the things you can miss and not realize it until they are back.

After the kitchen was clean, and the dishes were back in the china closet, her parents made Linda promise to make Sunday dinner with them a regular thing.

This time her father let Sheila take Linda back to Auntie's after he found that he couldn't talk her into staying. Linda kissed them good-bye and hugged them before she left.

During the ride home, she thought about what had happened to her in a short while.

Auntie has welcomed me into her home as if I'm a member of her family and it is good, but it's also good to have my own family back and to know that they're still there for me.

Linda sang one of her choir's songs as she walked into the center on Monday. Today she included the words she had forgotten the previous morning in church. She smiled. All was right with her world again.

"I need to see you."

Avery was waiting outside his office. The look on his face said he was about to unleash a cloudburst on her parade. *Now what?*

"I saw you get into that car on Saturday."

"So?"

"It was a new car, a very expensive one."

"I repeat: 'So?' "

The elation that had filled her over the weekend fizzled. She glared at him. "It was well after closing time when I left. Nothing in our agreement says that I have to explain to you what I do on my own time."

She continued to match his glare. Then her eyes widened and she gasped.

"I see where this is going." Her mouth tightened. It was true that anger made you see red. "My sister met me to take me home." Her words were slow and distinct. "What you saw was not a drug connection from what you think is my past. My sister, Sheila, took me to see our parents." She lifted her chin. "Do you want their phone number so you can verify my story?" She shifted her weight. "If you talk to Marian, maybe she can arrange to have me wear one of those ankle manacles and give you the tracking device so you'll know where I am at all times."

"I . . ."

"I don't want to hear it. I don't want to hear anything from you." She continued to glare at him even though his matching glare had disappeared. "Unless you tell me I no longer work here, I'm going upstairs to get ready for the kids."

She stared at him a few seconds longer. When he didn't say anything, she whirled away. Her feet pounded the floor all the way to the lab.

"I don't need this." It took a great deal of effort not to slam the door. She had work planned, but she had to walk off the anger first.

She went into the hall and locked the door behind her. Then she began walking up and down the hall. She was still walking when she heard kids on the stairs. Her anger wasn't gone but it was under control.

The first chance she got she'd look for another job. There had to be somebody who could use her skills even though she did have a record. She'd ask Marian about firms willing to take a chance on people with her background. It was obvious things weren't going to work out here. She'd never have Avery's trust. It was a shame. She loved working with the kids.

The kids came in to work on the newsletter. Linda

helped them, but from time to time her thoughts strayed to leaving.

Before she left tonight she'd compose a general letter requesting a job application. She'd try the government offices first. Maybe she could get a job with the post office. She sighed. Marian would know what places would be a waste of her time.

The last kid had left and Linda was on her way out the door when Avery came in.

Linda felt her anger creep back.

"I came up to apologize." He rubbed the side of his face. "I'm sorry. You didn't deserve the way I acted with you when you came in. I . . . I jumped to conclusions and I shouldn't have. I know I do a lot of that where you're concerned. I know I have a lot of baggage and it comes out with you. I also know that's no excuse. I promise to do better." He took a deep breath. "The look on your face when you left the hall led me to believe you plan to leave the center. I hope you'll stay to finish out the two weeks we agreed upon."

"I keep my promises. I asked for two weeks and you gave them to me. I intend to stay for the rest of the time."

"Good. Truce?" Avery held out his hand.

Linda hesitated. Then she held out hers.

"Truce."

"Good," he said again. "I'll walk down with you."

Linda walked beside him in silence. She was more tense than before. With her anger faded, she felt vulnerable. She was glad when they reached his office door.

"I have a few things to finish up. I'll see you in the morning."

He watched her go. The slight sway in her walk was much more disturbing than the usual angry pounding of her footsteps when she left him.

Seven

A few days passed and the truce was still in place. Avery came to the lab several times. The first time Linda braced herself for a verbal attack, but Avery only walked around and asked the kids about their projects.

"Look at this, Mr. Avery," Tyree called him over. "We got a new rap almost finished. Miss Linda said she might let us put it in the center paper, I mean newsletter."

Avery listened as Tyree gave an impromptu performance.

"What you think? I know it still needs work, but it's almost done. I should'a used the computer before. Sure saves a lot of paper."

"We're working on a write-up about the game last week." Kira attracted his attention. "Want to see it?"

Linda watched as Avery gave the kids his full attention and made suggestions. He had a way with the kids. It was easy to see that they not only respected him, but liked him as well. The last was especially understandable.

He left and she couldn't explain her feeling of loneliness.

The next couple of times he just peeked in, spoke, and moved on. One morning he actually smiled at her. That day it took her five minutes to access a file that usually took five seconds.

Linda was surprised she wasn't more at ease around him now, but she shouldn't have been. With the anger between them gone, how was she going to deal with this new and more disturbing dilemma? Why couldn't she find him repulsive? Why was life so complicated? Why wasn't the sky green with yellow stripes?

She was relieved when Lamont asked her to help him and she had another problem to occupy her. For a while.

Dinnertime came and she counted on conversations with the others to pull her back into focus. It worked for a while, too. Then Avery came in and scattered her all over again.

"Sorry to interrupt, folks," Avery said, "but I thought I'd better remind you about the date for the annual dinner/dance fund-raiser held by The Friends of the Center." He sat at the table and opened a file. "Last year some of you didn't remember . . ." He stared at Craig, ". . . and it was embarrassing to explain to all of his female fans why he was missing. I wouldn't want to witness any hearts breaking again this year."

The staff laughed. Craig's laughter was the loudest.

"I'll do what I can to prevent that." He shrugged. "But I'm only one man. Some of the women are bound to be disappointed."

The laughter got louder.

"Do your best. Anyway, I know you have all circled the third Saturday in June on your calendars. Here are your tickets." He handed them to Roz who passed them along. "As you can see, they're worth their weight in gold. The public will be paying one hundred bucks for the privilege of dining with us."

"A hundred dollars?" Bea held her ticket closer. "Wow. Inflation really kicked in this year."

"We have a couple of big projects planned for the coming year. One is the refurbishing of the playground. They also want to increase scholarship help to our kids.

You know how tuition keeps going up. We don't want anyone to have to drop out because they don't have money." He looked at Linda. "I hope you'll be able to make the dance."

She managed to nod, but still he pinned her with his glance. Finally he stood. "I'll leave you folks to your meal."

"Wouldn't you like to join us?" Wanda's question attracted everybody's attention.

"No, thank you. I have work to do."

"Girl, you need to give it up," Bea said after Avery left.

"Amen," Cathy added before she opened her salad container. "That horse has been dead so long there's not much left to bury."

Linda wondered if that was true. Then she wondered why she wondered.

The rest of the night and the rest of the week were routine. Linda was thankful.

Monday morning was too beautiful to pull out "maybe" problems. She would not let her mind focus on having only one week left before she'd know if she had a permanent job. She told herself that whenever the possibility of working somewhere else slipped into her thoughts, pulling Avery with it. One week and one day was what she had left, to be exact.

The fact that he specifically mentioned her attending the dance didn't mean she should get her hopes up. It could be that he forgot she might not be here then. It was true that things had been going smoothly between them, but she didn't want to read too much into that. It could be that Avery was letting her alone because he knew he wouldn't have to put up with her much longer. Whatever his reason, she wasn't going to make it easy

for him. She started on a Tuesday and she was going to
make Avery wait over the next weekend to fire her on
the last day of their agreement. Let her be on his mind
the way he was on hers.

She stared into the backyard from the window over
the sink, but she wasn't seeing the small garden.

She had promised herself to never let another man
get to her. Yet, here she was, after only one week, letting
her thoughts get tangled up by him, letting him wrap
around her emotions. How could she have let a man
back into her heart so soon? Especially one who thought
so little of her? He hadn't hidden his feelings of distrust.
More than once he had condemned her without even
talking to her.

She sighed. At least he didn't have ulterior motives
like Jamal had. Avery was up-front with his opinion of
her. In anyone else she would have appreciated it. In
Avery it just hurt.

How could she be so stupid again? She blinked. And
why hadn't she met Avery first?

She wasn't in love. Love didn't happen so fast, but
she was getting there. The job was going well. She'd miss
it when her time was up. The kids were great. She shoved
Avery from her mind and tried to figure out how to keep
him away.

"Hey, Miss D." Two boys and a girl sprawled in the
reception area spoke together as if they had rehearsed
the greeting.

"Miss D.?" A puzzled look crossed Linda's face.

"Yeah. It sounds better and is easier to say than Miss
L. My name is Michael. You know, like in Michael Jordan
the great NBA star?"

"You don't mind us calling you that, do you?" The

other boy pushed his glasses up on his nose. "I'm Evan." He shrugged. "I don't know no NBA star named Evan."

"Evan's a fine name. Were you named after your father?"

"Yes, Ma'am, and my grandfather, too."

"A name is what you make it." She smiled at him. "And a family name is something to be proud of. It lets you know where you came from. As far as calling me 'Miss D.' is concerned, no, I don't mind." She looked at their faces. "Now, what's up? You three look like somebody just gave you some bad news."

"You got that right. We just found out that Mr. Les won't be in today and Mr. Avery will be late," the girl said. "I'm Dawn. You know like in Dawn Staley, the great gold-medal-winning Olympic female basketball star?" She glared at Michael. "They won't let us use the gym without a staff person with us."

"I guess they think we might jump from the bleachers or dunk each other or something crazy like that." Michael's frown deepened. "If it wasn't raining, we'd be on the court outside. We wouldn't need anybody with us out there." He shifted the basketball he was clutching to his other hand. "The weatherman didn't say nothing about no rain today."

"You don't know anything about basketball, do you?" Hope was evident in Dawn's voice.

"I might know a little something."

"It don't matter whether you do or not." Michael shifted the ball again. "We just need a staff person in the gym." He sat up straighter and the chair looked too short. "Will you go in with us? I mean to show these two a thing or three."

"In your dreams." Dawn leaned in closer to Michael.

Linda looked at the guard. She raised her eyebrows in a question.

He shrugged.

"Sometimes the staff members covers for each other if they're not too busy. Usually Avery covers for Les in the gym. It's unusual for both of them to be out at the same time. Les called and said he forgot he got called for jury duty today." Bill looked at the kids. "To tell you the truth, nobody else will go in the gym to work. They said too much can go wrong in the heat of the game. You know how these kids can be when they get to playing." He shrugged again. "It's up to you."

Linda chewed on her lip. Then she looked back at the kids. They looked like she had already said "no."

"Will you let Avery know where I am? And if anybody comes for the computer lab, tell them to come to the gym and get me, please."

"Will do."

"You'll go in with us?" Dawn's eyes widened.

"For real?" Michael's voice sounded younger than his teenage years.

"For real." Linda smiled. "I don't know how long I can stay with you, so I don't want any moaning and groaning if I have to leave and lock up. Deal?"

"Deal." Evan looked hard at her. "I don't guess you know how to play? If you did we could play a little two on two."

"She can't play," Michael said before she could answer. "She's more the cheerleader type."

"You think so?" Linda fastened him with a stare. "Probably too old, too, right?"

"Well, you ain't as young as we are."

"That's true."

"He thinks females can't play." Dawn glared. "He forgets all about Dawn Staley."

"Let's see if we can make him rethink his chauvinistic opinion."

"All *right.*" Dawn's eyes lit up.

Linda hoped she didn't let Dawn down too hard. She

also hoped Evan and Michael weren't as good as some
of the other boys she had seen playing a pick-up game
on the outside court. If they were, she and Dawn were
in trouble no matter how good Dawn was.

They went to the gym and moved onto the floor where
they set the ground rules. They gave her first out. She
shifted the ball to her left hand and forgot everything
except the game.

The play and the score went back and forth as time
was held back. Everything—the center, the city—everything outside the gym was erased as the game continued.

The game was tied at thirty. Two more points. The
next team to score had bragging rights. Linda tried again
to catch her breath as she had been doing for . . . For
how long? Forever? Why hadn't she insisted the game
end at twenty points? Then she wouldn't have been in
danger of dropping dead and proving Michael's belief
that she was too old.

She watched as Dawn reached in, swiped the ball from
Evan, and drove down the floor in a hard dribble. Dawn
shot, but her shot hit the rim and bounced off. Michael
came down with it.

"Get ready, Y'all." The game slowed as he dribbled
at a walk. "This is it. Big Mike is gonna deliver."

Linda gulped in the deep breaths of air that her lungs
were screaming for as she matched her pace to his slow
movements down the floor. She shut her eyes hard for
a few seconds. *Thanks for small favors.* Then she opened
them again and watched Michael.

They had all been missing their shots for what seemed
like a week. Whoever scored next was winner. She'd like
it to be them for Dawn's sake, but right now she just
wanted it over while she was still alive. If Michael mentioned her not being young right now, she'd be the first
to agree with him.

She looked at his chest heaving in and out and smiled.

He isn't doing much better than I am. Then she glanced at the other two. Neither were they. If they kept on playing much longer, Bill would have to call the paramedics for all four of them.

Her smile disappeared as Dawn darted over and stole the ball. Linda raced back down the floor the other way. Michael was guarding Dawn so close she couldn't get a shot off. She didn't try.

The next thing Linda knew the ball was in her hands and Michael was so close that, if she wanted to, if sweat wasn't burning her eyes, she could have counted the threads in his T-shirt. A smirk spread over his face as he looked down on her. How tall was this kid, anyway? And how did he get down the floor so fast?

She pivoted under his arm, slipped around him and let go with a one-hand shot. The ball rolled around the rim slowly for about a year before it plopped in.

It wasn't pretty, but it was effective. Then everything happened at once.

Dawn grabbed her in a hug and swung her around at a dizzying speed. Then, still holding Linda, she jumped up and down all the time yelling: "We did it. We did it. We beat them."

Applause, foot stomping, and whistles filled the gym. Voices burst out all around. Linda spun around to face the bleachers.

"All right!" somebody yelled.

"Go, Miss D. Go, Miss D. Go, Miss D.," a group of girls chanted from the bottom bleacher.

"Way to go," somebody else yelled.

"Go on with your bad self."

It had been years since Linda had heard that expression. It must have come from a staff member.

She looked around. The bleachers were crowded. When had all these people come into the gym?

Staff members were scattered among the kids. A few

An important message from the ARABESQUE Editor

Dear Arabesque Reader,

Because you've chosen to read one of our Arabesque romance novels, we'd like to say "thank you"! And, as a special way to thank you, we've selected four more of the books you love so well to send you for FREE!

Please enjoy them with our compliments, and thank you for continuing to enjoy Arabesque...the soul of romance.

Karen Thomas
Senior Editor,
Arabesque Romance Novels

Check out our website at
www.arabesquebooks.com

3 QUICK STEPS
TO RECEIVE YOUR "THANK YOU" GIFT
FROM THE EDITOR

Send this card back and you'll receive 4 FREE Arabesque novels! The introductory shipment of 4 Arabesque novels – a $23.96 value – is yours absolutely FREE!

There's no catch. You're under no obligation to buy anything. You'll receive your introductory shipment of 4 Arabesque novels absolutely FREE (plus $1.99 to offset the costs of shipping & handling). And you don't have to make any minimum number of purchases—not even one!

We hope that after receiving your books you'll want to remain an Arabesque subscriber. But the choice is yours to continue or cancel, anytime at all! So why not take us up on our invitation to receive 4 Arabesque Romance Novels, with no risk of any kind. You'll be glad you did!

Call us
TOLL-FREE
at 1-800-770-1963

THE EDITOR'S "THANK YOU" GIFT INCLUDES:

- 4 books absolutely FREE (plus $1.99 for shipping and handling)
- A FREE newsletter, *Arabesque Romance News*, filled with author interviews, book previews, special offers, and more!
- No risks or obligations. You're free to cancel whenever you wish... with no questions asked.

BOOK CERTIFICATE

Yes! Please send me 4 FREE Arabesque novels (plus $1.99 for shipping & handling). I understand I am under no obligation to purchase any books, as explained on the back of this card.

Name _____

Address _____ Apt. _____

City_____ State_____ Zip _____

Telephone ( ) _____

Signature _____

Offer limited to one per household and not valid to current subscribers. All orders subject to approval. Terms, offer, & price subject to change. Offer valid only in the U.S.

AN082A

Thank you!

Accepting the four introductory books for FREE (plus $1.99 to offset the cost of shipping & handling) places you under no obligation to buy anything. You may keep the books and return the shipping statement marked "cancelled". If you do not cancel, about a month later we will send 4 additional Arabesque novels, and you will be billed the preferred subscriber's price of just $4.00 per title. That's $16.00 for all 4 books for a savings of 33% off the cover price (Plus $1.99 for shipping and handling). You may cancel at any time, but if you choose to continue, every month we'll send you 4 more books, which you may either purchase at the preferred discount price. . . or return to us and cancel your subscription.

THE ARABESQUE ROMANCE CLUB: HERE'S HOW IT WORKS

ARABESQUE ROMANCE BOOK CLUB
P.O. Box 5214
Clifton NJ 07015-5214

PLACE
STAMP
HERE

faces were turned down in frowns, but most were showing the joy Dawn was still yelling.

"Good game, Miss D." Evan offered his hand.

"You, too, Evan." She patted his shoulder. She looked
at Michael.

He stood staring at her. Then he took a deep breath
and walked slowly toward her.

"You're pretty good." He held out his hand and the
noise from the crowd got louder.

"Not too bad for an old cheerleader, huh?"

He shrugged. "Guess I was wrong."

Linda took his hand. "You've got a wicked hook
shot," she told him.

"It's all right."

"It's more than all right."

"Thanks." He frowned at her. "You played in high
school, huh?"

She nodded. "The Lady Tigers were state champs
three years in a row."

"College, too, I bet." It wasn't a question.

"State champs too, but only twice."

Michael grimaced.

"I guess I picked the wrong person to play against."

"You know the story of the Three Billy Goats Gruff?"

He nodded and she went on. "I'm just the little Billy
Goat Gruff. There are a lot out there way better than I
am." She gulped air and wiped her forehead on her
sleeve. "A little longer and I would have passed out."

"I was sucking for air, too." He nodded. "You're still
good at doing your thing." He shook his head. "I didn't
expect you to be so good. I figured you . . ." He hesitated.

"You figured I'd be too old."

"I know the pros are older than you, but they practice
every day. I ain't never seen you on the court outside or

on the floor. You got some secret place where you practice?"

"Luck and determination is all I had." She cocked her head sideways. "You do a lot of mouthing off, you know?"

"Yeah, I know." He shrugged. "That's part of me. They expect it." He nodded toward the crowd. "Sometimes it makes them so anxious to prove me wrong that they make dumb mistakes when they go up against me."

Linda laughed.

"You know Dawn scored most of our points."

"I know—she's good." Finally he smiled. "As good as me. I just don't want to admit it to her. Don't tell her I said so."

"Hey, Miss D., that was cool. Totally awesome." Roberto hesitated, then he hugged her quickly and pulled away. "I knew you was . . ." He stopped. "I knew you *were* somebody special." He looked at Michael. "Maybe now that you taught him a lesson he'll stop bragging about how good he is."

Michael stopped walking and stared at Roberto.

"I can still take you anytime you say."

"I know you can, Bro," Roberto smiled.

Michael stared a few seconds more. Then he shrugged and walked away.

"Catch you later, Miss D.," Roberto said before he joined a group of his friends.

Linda followed Michael toward the hall. They could barely move. Everybody wanted to comment on the game.

She stepped out of the middle of the crowd when they reached the door. Avery leaned against the wall. People passing raised their hands in high fives and she returned them. Others patted her on the back and complimented her. She thanked them, but her gaze never left Avery's face.

What was he thinking? His face didn't give a clue. His jaw was determined, but she had seldom seen it any other way. His gaze skimmed her heaving chest, but settled back on her face. He'd make a good card player. She took another deep breath. *Why didn't he say something and get it over with? Why doesn't he tell me how wrong I was to embarrass one of the kids?*

He stood looking at her as if he were in no hurry to say or do anything.

Linda used the sleeve of her tee to sop up the sweat dripping in her eyes. Avery's gaze followed her hand but returned to her face.

Do I have some kind of a homing device embedded in my face? she wondered. *How do I get rid of it?*

She wiped her face again and glanced at her watch. They had played for more than an hour.

Finally the gym was empty. She couldn't stand the suspense any longer.

"I . . . I'm sorry I wasn't in the lab where I belong."

"No need to be. Nobody was up there. Everybody was in here 'watching Miss D. teach Michael a lesson.' That's what Jimmy told me when I came in to see what the noise was all about."

"Were you here long?"

"Long enough. About half an hour. I was late getting in because I had to take care of something that came up with one of the kids."

Linda grimaced. He had been here for most of the game. Why didn't he stop it? Maybe he'd wanted to find out just how irresponsible she was? She looked down at the floor. And he found out, didn't he?

Avery finally pushed off from the wall.

"Can I see you in my office?"

Here it comes. He wasn't going to give her the other week. Why was it so hard to get a job and so easy to lose it? She should have been in the lab. That's what she was hired to do. She didn't have anybody to blame but herself. She'd miss this place. She hadn't been here long, but it was long enough to learn to like the job, the staff and, of course, the kids. The ones who used the lab regularly were doing better in school. Their attitudes had changed. They were learning to ignore the stigma many of the kids attach to getting good grades. Her kids had begun to show her their papers when the teacher returned them. They were proud of their marks.

Her kids. Not much longer. And it was her own fault. She hadn't been where she belonged. She had told Michael she'd stay in the gym just until she had to go to the lab. She blinked hard. She'd still be on the basketball floor if the game hadn't ended.

She watched Avery's shoulders as he led her to the end of her job. She should be worrying about being jobless. And she was. But that wasn't occupying her whole mind. She was noticing how his T-shirt molded to his back and shoulders as if it were made just for him. She saw what was meant by muscles rippling. How could his attitude be so unyielding and his body so attracting? She felt her temperature rising and her heart speeding up when she should be at the cooldown stage.

How would those muscles feel if she brushed her hands over them? She opened and closed her hands to make the itch go away. It changed to an ache and spread through her body. What if he held her against his chest in a tight caress? Would those muscles soften to accommodate her? She wanted to look away but she couldn't. She watched him take in a deep breath. She didn't think it possible, but his shoulders expanded even more. He took out his keys and his arm muscles looked like a photograph used in an anatomy book. Every part of him that she could see looked like an example of a perfect specimen.

She took a deep breath and released it slowly. Maybe

that would leave room for some common sense to find its way to where she could use it.

All of my vows to keep away from men forever have disappeared and it hasn't been a month since I made them. She shook her head.

It's bad when you can't keep a promise to yourself. Maybe it would be good for her if he fired her. If she stayed here she might do something stupid. She sighed. Not that he would ever feel anything but contempt for her. If the center didn't need her she would have been gone that first day. Center needs aside, she'd be out of here anyway after what she did today. She couldn't be trusted. She almost bumped into him when he stopped.

"Go on in." He stood to one side and let her pass.

She took a deep breath and stepped inside the office. She looked around. She hadn't been in here since that first day. The same neatness greeted her. Avery wouldn't have to look for anything. He'd be able to put his hands on anything he needed. Her body tightened. And what he didn't need, too.

The first time she had come into this office she had hoped for a job. This time she was going to lose that job and she deserved to lose it. Why didn't he just get it over with? Would he let her say good-bye to the others?

She watched him open a closet.

"Here. You look like you could use this."

Linda stared at the T-shirt he held out.

"You're not firing me?"

"Why would I do that?"

"I wasn't in the lab."

"We cover for each other."

"That's what Bill said."

"It's unusual for me and Les to be out at the same time. Bill said Les called after I did. They'll probably keep him for a case. They have every year for the past three years. When we're both out, we usually shut down the gym. If it hadn't been raining this morning, the kids would have been outside." He let out a hard breath.

"I embarrassed one of our kids. I wouldn't blame you if you let me go."

"Do you want me to fire you?"

"No." She shook her head. "Of course not. I just want to make sure you considered everything before I get my hopes up only to have you change your mind."

"Michael will get over it. He's been asking for this for as long as he's been here, always running his mouth. He's never been in trouble and he can play basketball, but it did him good to get beat."

"Especially by an old woman."

"Old woman?" Avery frowned. "Is that what he called you?"

"Not in those exact words, but yes. He also said I was more the cheerleader type."

"He hasn't learned not to judge by how things look." He shrugged. "I'm still working on that myself."

Linda let his words sink in. Did that mean she was past the point of having to prove herself to him?

"There was nothing normal about this morning," Avery went on. "One of our kids got in trouble last night." He named a boy Linda didn't know. "He got picked up for fighting. Luckily, no weapons were involved, but after the police picked him up, he mouthed off and then wouldn't tell them his name. They let him cool off all night and called me this morning on a chance that he might be one of ours. Sure enough, he is." Avery shook his head again. "One thing we need around here is an anger-management program. I don't suppose you know anything about that, do you?"

"Sorry. That's not one of my trades. I'm still working on that myself." She smiled. She still had her job.

Avery blinked. He looked puzzled; like he couldn't

find his next words. Then he shook his head rapidly and continued.

"You want to sit down and catch your breath?"

"It will take more than a few minutes for me to recover, but I'm all right standing." She pulled her shirt away from her body. "Besides, I'm all sweaty. I don't want to mess up your chair."

"Where'd you learn to play?"

"High school." She shrugged. "And college."

"You didn't put your sports background on your application."

"I didn't want to look like I was superwoman." She stared at him as she wiped her face on her shirt. "Or a Jane-of-all-trades."

He stared back. Then he rubbed the side of his face.

"You can use my bathroom to clean up, if you want to." He pointed to the door between the cabinets. "You'll find towels and washcloths on the shelf in there."

"Thanks. I won't be long. I know the kids are probably outside my door waiting for me."

Avery stared at the closed door. She was the last person on staff that he would have picked as an athlete. He swallowed hard.

He closed his eyes and pictured her driving for the basket for a lay-up. Her T-shirt, damp with sweat, had tightened across her breasts and his body had tightened at the sight. When he should have been looking at her hands and following the ball, he couldn't pull his eyes away from her shirt. Or rather, what was under her shirt. What other things was she good at? His body tightened again at the memory.

He shifted in his chair. If only her past were different. He could forgive almost anything but drugs.

He let out a hard breath. Denny had been dead for over eight years, yet he was still affecting Avery's life.

His jaw tightened. Not again. He might have to be involved every now and then when one of his kids got sucked in by the drug world, but never again would he personally have any emotional ties to anything to do with drugs. He continued to stare at the bathroom door.

He was still staring when she came out. His gaze transferred to her. He was glad dry shirts didn't cling like wet ones. He took a deep breath and tried to gain control. He took another. It wasn't working.

Her face looked fresh, kissable, waiting. For him. His vow of a few minutes ago was fading fast.

"Thank you for—" She gestured toward the bathroom. "I left the towel and washcloth in there." She shrugged. "I didn't know . . ." Her words trailed off. "I didn't know what else to do. To do with them, I mean." Again she shrugged. "I hope . . . I hope that was all right. To hang them on the rack, I mean." She ran out of words. She didn't seem to be able to find any more. Finally it dawned on Avery that it was his turn to talk.

"That's okay. That's fine. The rack is fine." Why did her eyes have to be so warm? Why did her skin seem to beg him to see if it was as soft as it looked? Why was the sun hot? He knew why he was getting hotter the longer he looked at her, thought of her. He didn't like it, but he knew.

"I . . . I'd better be going. The . . . the kids are probably waiting for me upstairs."

The door opened after a quick knock. "Hey, Mr. Avery, guess what I . . ." Roberto looked from one to the other. "Sorry if I interrupted something." He broke into a wide smile as his gaze settled back on Linda. "You sure shut Michael up, Miss Linda. He won't be walking around here bragging no more. I mean anymore." He looked back at Avery. "Maybe I'll come back later."

"No, no. I was just leaving." Linda thanked Avery again and hurried out.

"Hey, Mr. Avery, you got a thing for Miss Linda?"

"Roberto, what I have or don't have is none of your business, is it?"

"No, sir." His smile was back. "I can understand it if you do. I kind a got a thing for her myself, even though she is a lot older than me." He shrugged. "She thinks I'm a kid."

"You are a kid. Now what's on your mind?"

"I got me a job. At least I will have if you give me a good reference. The manager at the video store said I can work part-time until school is out and then, if it works out okay, he'll let me work full-time. But I got to have a good reference from you. Will you do it?"

"Sure. Where's the paper?"

Roberto pulled the paper from his back pocket and tried to smooth it out before he handed it to Avery.

"Come back before you leave tonight." He looked at the form. "I'll make a fresh copy and put it in an envelope for you. You want it to look good when you give it back."

"Thanks. I'll go so you can have enough time to work on it. Make sure you tell them how faithful I am coming here. And tell them I never get into trouble. And don't forget . . ."

"Maybe you should do this yourself?"

"No, sir, I can't do that. I just want to make sure I get the job. I mean, I know I haven't been perfect, but I've been better since you talked me into going back to school, haven't I?"

"Yes, you have. Now, good-bye, Roberto. Let me get this done."

"No problem." He opened the door but didn't leave. "About me barging in here. I'm sorry if I interrupted something between you and Miss Linda."

"There wasn't anything to interrupt."

"Okay. If you say so. See you before I go home. Right?"

"Right."

Avery chewed on his lip. He didn't know how he felt about Roberto's interruption. Would she still be here if it hadn't happened? Would he have gone over to her? Would he have found out if her perfume was still on her?

He hadn't even touched her and here she was filling his imagination, making him want things he shouldn't want. Things that could only mean trouble for him.

He walked over to the copy machine and automatically put Roberto's paper into it.

He felt like he was slowly sliding down a slope and he didn't know where he'd end up. What was worse, he wasn't sure he'd stop if he could.

Eight

Linda was fixing her cup of tea when Bea came in the next morning.

"You're early."

"So are you."

"I have some sample software I want to look at. I want to see if it's something we can use in the lab. What about you?"

"My daughter, Ellie, had a big bulky science project to take to school. She put a lot of work in it and was afraid it would get broken on the bus." Bea took her coffee to the table and sat across from Linda. "It has something to do with genetics: DNA or RNA or something like that." Bea smiled. "She explained it to me and I nodded and said, 'Uh-huh' at the right times, but I have no idea what she was talking about." She laughed. "She wants to be a doctor."

"You must be proud of her."

"I am. She's only a junior at Central High, but already she's had scholarships offered based on her PSAT scores." Bea sighed. "A good thing, too. My oldest, Rodney, has another year to go at Temple. David is two years behind Ellie. It's hard enough now. There's no way, even with scholarships, I could swing her full tuition for all those years. I'm proud of all three of my kids." She wrapped both hands around her cup and stared at her coffee. "Walter, their father, would be proud, too, if he were still alive."

"I thought I remembered you mentioning you have three kids."

"Yeah. I've been blessed. They've never been in trouble." The pride was evident in her voice.

"That is a blessing considering how things are nowadays. Kids have so much temptation coming at them, I don't know how any of them manage to turn out all right."

"That's right. I wouldn't want to be young nowadays." Bea set her cup down. "Enough about me. I have been using more restraint than I thought possible by waiting a week, but I can't hold back anymore. What are you doing here? Wanda's dumb comments when you first got here aside, how did you find a place like this? We're not exactly in the mainstream, and I doubt Avery put an ad in the newspaper."

Linda rolled the palms of her hands back and forth around her cup as she stared at the tea inside. She blinked several times.

"If I'm prying, just tell me to mind my own business," Bea said. "You won't hurt my feelings."

"It's not that." Linda took a deep breath and looked at her. Then, avoiding making eye contact, she told her about her stay in prison and how she ended up at the center.

Bea was the quietest Linda had ever seen her. She still didn't react after Linda's words stopped. The only sound in the room was the *click click* each time the second hand on the wall clock moved her life forward.

Finally, Linda took a deep breath and looked at her.

"I don't blame you if you don't want to have anything else to do with me." She steeled herself for the rejection she knew was coming from her new friend.

"That's over and done with," Bea said, touching her

hand. "If we had to keep paying for our past mistakes, nobody would get to move on in life." She smiled. Linda felt the tension leave as Bea continued. "You have to quit beating up on yourself."

Linda blinked away tears that filled her eyes.

"Thanks, Bea. I . . . I wasn't sure how you'd take it. I—" She wiped her eyes. "Thanks."

"Try to put it behind you, okay?"

"Okay." Linda finally smiled. She wiped her face. "I'm going up to the lab. I want to do some things before the kids get here."

"Did I mention how glad I am that you're up there with those computers instead of me?"

Linda laughed. "Every day."

"I want to make sure you know how much you're appreciated so you won't think about leaving."

"I'm not going anywhere but upstairs. At least not until after next Tuesday."

"What's next Tuesday?"

"The end of my two weeks."

"Girl, please. You know you're not going anywhere, but upstairs like you said, even after next Tuesday. Avery's not going to let you go. He knows how we need you and he knows I'm not going up there on a permanent basis." She held up her hands. "I'm not being uncooperative; those machines intimidate me and they know it. I can almost hear them snickering when I come near." She leaned forward. "You can just put leaving out of your mind."

"I hope you're right." Linda stood. "I better go do what I came in for."

Alan, Tyree, Lamont, and John came in as soon as the lab opened to work on their projects, just as they did every day. After the first few days, they hadn't mentioned games. They were working on a graphics program.

Word about what was happening in the lab had spread among the kids and anybody with the slightest interest in computers had to see it for themselves. Linda wondered if a center paper could spread news any faster than the kids were already doing.

Other kids formed groups to see who could design a program that would perform the most operations. Linda had to designate some of the computers for word processing only, after a big argument broke out between the writers and the programmers.

Afterward she smiled at the idea of kids arguing over who would get to do something so educational.

The first edition of the *Grace Washington News and Views* was almost ready when Helen approached Linda after everybody else had gone. She clutched a copybook in her hand.

"A lot of what I write is poetry." Her words sounded like she was sharing a secret. "I mostly keep my poems to myself, but maybe we could use one? I don't mean in the first edition, but maybe later?"

"I think we can find space for one in the first edition, if you want."

"I'd like that." She held out the open book to Linda. As she waited she shifted her weight from one foot to the other and back. "Maybe it's not good enough." She held out her hand to get her book back. "It's a dumb idea. Forget I asked, okay?"

"Not okay. This is beautiful. I know we'll find space for it."

Helen's smile filled the bottom half of her face.

"For real?"

"For real."

"Thanks, Miss D." She reached for Linda, but pulled back. Linda drew the girl to her and hugged her.

"I'm going to be published. Wait 'til I tell my mom."
She almost floated from the room.

Linda looked through the copy to find a space for
Helen's poem. She smiled as she remembered the smile
on the girl's face.

The paper was ready. What had started as a one-page
edition had grown to ten pages. Stories and poetry
shared space with the interviews the kids decided to include. Roberto wrote a report on what the kids were
calling *the* basketball game. Linda showed it to Michael
and Evan before she approved it. Sometimes she felt she
was watching the tail wag the dog, but it was fine with
her. She'd give it a final read-through that night at home.

That night, as she did every night, she went home
exhausted. And she loved every day of it.

The next morning she took a deep breath and took
the finished copy to Avery to take to the center's sponsor
who had agreed to print it. Avery wasn't in yet, so she
gave it to Penny. She went to put her lunch in the refrigerator in the lounge, wondering why she wasn't relieved she hadn't had to face him.

After dinner Avery came to the lab. Linda let herself
fill up on his image. It had been too long time since she
last saw him.

"I read the paper. It's great."

"It's longer than I planned."

"That's okay."

"It won't be a problem?"

"No problem."

He had gotten a haircut. Was he going somewhere
special? Who was going with him? Did he really not have
a life outside the center? He was too virile not to have

a woman in his life. What kind of woman did he find attractive?

"Hey, Mr. Avery. Come look at this."

Avery walked away from her and Linda was wondering how she could thank Alan for freeing her.

He bent over Alan's station listening to him and asking questions.

Linda sneaked a look at the way his pants fit. Didn't the man look bad in anything? She forced herself to look at a poster on the wall away from Avery, but, if someone asked her, she couldn't have described it. His image still filled her mind.

"I'd better get back downstairs."

His husky voice pulled her back to him. How could he make those innocent words so sexy?

He threw her an intense look and Linda blushed. She hoped he didn't have a hidden talent for mind reading.

She tried to convince herself she was glad to see him go; that she didn't want to get a glimpse of the more relaxed Avery he had once showed her. She told herself she should be satisfied he trusted her enough for him to stay away. She should be glad not to see more of him. That's what she told herself. But her heart didn't believe any of it.

If hearts could really ache, that's what hers did whenever she admitted that nothing would ever come of her growing feelings for him. She was in trouble. She felt like she was in quicksand and couldn't do a thing to pull herself free.

She knew exactly how Wanda felt, although she hoped she could keep from being as obvious and pathetic. She didn't handle humiliation well at all.

When Linda stepped inside the center two days later Bill handed her a bulky envelope.

"Avery told me to give this to you."

Linda tensed her hands so they wouldn't give her nervousness away. Had he decided not to wait until Tuesday to fire her? Is this how he decided to do it?

She opened the envelope and slid out a stapled packet. The first copy of *The Grace Washington News and Views* lay in her hand. It was beautiful. Bill read over her shoulder until she handed him a copy of his own.

"My interview is on page five." He leafed through until he found his page. Then he held the booklet out for her to see.

Kira had suggested they interview Bill for the first edition since he was the one person that everybody saw every day. She had done a good job.

Linda said good-bye to him, but only silence answered her. She hoped nothing needed Bill's attention for a while. She watched him turn the page. He was seriously lost in the paper.

The lab wasn't any busier than usual, but it seemed that way because of the kids who kept poking their heads in to comment on the paper.

As she walked to the lounge at dinnertime, every kid she saw in the hall had a copy. Many of them were reading as they walked. Snatches of discussions reached her. A few mentioned wanting to work on the next edition. Who said kids didn't read anymore?

The staff had nothing but praise. Even Wanda, though she had a pained look on her face, gave her a "nice paper" comment.

The Tuesday morning sun promised a perfect late-May day. Linda awoke as early this last day as she had the first time she went to the center. She had managed to survive the rest of the two weeks without doing or saying anything stupid mainly because Avery stayed out of her way.

No more popping out of his office as if she wore a

homing device and he had the detector. He hadn't come into the lab after the day he came to talk about the paper. He was avoiding her just as she told herself she wanted. It made her job easier. Didn't it? Wasn't not seeing him what she had hoped for? Then why had she found herself looking at the door whenever it opened or whenever footsteps in the hall got close to the lab? Why had she been disappointed whenever they kept going? It was so bad that a couple of times the kids noticed.

"You expecting somebody?" Tyree asked the previous day when she had been more distracted than usual.

She got a better grip and managed to stay focused on the task at hand the rest of the time the lab was open.

She sighed and slipped out of bed. *I guess it's fitting. Nervous the first day, nervous the last.* She shook her head. *I can't believe two weeks have passed already.*

She let out a hard breath. Her plans for the lab were falling into place. It was too bad she'd have to trust somebody else to continue the programs she started.

She pulled the blue T-shirt with the center logo over her head. Somebody else would decide whether there would even be any more editions of the newsletter. Probably not. No one else had time for it. They were busy with their own work. Maybe the new person Avery hired to work in the lab would keep at least the newsletter idea.

In spite of what she expected to happen today, she smiled. *I'd love to be there when Avery tells Bea she has to go back to working the computer lab.* She blinked. *I'd love to be there, period, after today.* The program was running smoothly, but her past hadn't changed. She was still who she was. No matter how good her program was, her past would always be true.

She rode the bus to the center wondering if Marian had any more magic up her sleeve, some trick that would let her find a job Linda could keep.

She spoke to Bill as usual and walked through the lobby. *Should I go up to the lab and wait for Avery to come looking for me or should I see if he's in yet and save myself a trip?*

Her question was answered when Avery's door opened as she reached it.

"I need to see you. Come into my office, please."

Linda stiffened and let out a long, slow breath. No smile this morning. So what else was new?

She stepped past him and wished he had forgotten his aftershave this one time. She was going to have enough trouble forgetting him as it was.

"Sit down, please."

She perched on the edge of the chair in front of the desk and waited as he sat facing her.

"Two weeks are up today."

"I know."

"How's it going up there?"

"I think it's going well."

He stared at her.

"I got a call from the English teacher at the high school."

"I've just been having the kids use standard writing rules when they do their school assignments. The writing is their own. I only help them clean it up. I don't know what there is for her to complain about." She sighed. "I talked to her once about what they're doing in school. Maybe I should have called her before I did anything."

"The teacher didn't call to complain. She wanted to know who was the miracle worker over here."

"She didn't complain?"

"No. She asked me to thank you for making her job easier."

"Oh." Linda chewed on her lower lip. "I don't suppose she has a job for me over there? Or at least a reference?"

"Why? Are you planning to leave the center?"

"Not unless you tell me I don't have a job." She shrugged. "I just assumed."

"The kids need what you're doing up there." He leaned back.

Linda's gaze flew to the way his T-shirt molded to his hard chest. *Either he uses the center's gym after we leave here or he has his own at home.* She blinked free and made herself listen to his words. This was her future he was talking about.

"I never would have believed you could get the kids to accept life without those games. I heard that they're taking more interest in their school assignments. Nate showed me one. He never showed me his school work before." He shook his head. "That's a miracle. And the newspaper has kids who never pick up anything in print unless it's for an assignment reading."

"So I get to stay?" She let out the breath she had been holding and grabbed a fresh one. "I have a permanent job?"

"If you want it."

"I want it." She nodded and allowed herself to smile at him. "Thank you."

"You're welcome." He smiled back and the temperature in his office shot up ten degrees. A tropical beach didn't have anything on him.

She should get up and leave. There was no reason for her to stay here staring at him and forgetting her vow to keep herself free of any involvement. How he felt about her had shrunk until it had all but disappeared from her mind. Still she stayed fastened to her chair. So did he.

Penny opened the door. "Avery, I just wanted to . . ." Linda tore her gaze from Avery and looked at Penny who stared from one to the other. "I . . . I just want to let you know I'm here." Her stare moved from Avery to

Linda and back. "Yeah, well, I'll be at my desk if you need me."

"Okay." His words escaped but his gaze didn't.

Linda shook free, glad for Penny's interruption.

"I'd better get upstairs."

She found some strength hidden inside her somewhere and followed Penny out the door. She ought to thank her. If she hadn't come in, Linda would still be sitting there staring at Avery and getting lost where she had no business being in the first place. She'd have to work on that. Real hard.

You got your job. You got your job, she kept telling herself as she went to the lab. The same sentence skipped through her mind as she checked the printers to make sure they all had paper.

Happiness battled the apprehension inside her. A strong face with piercing eyes and a sensual mouth bubbled up in her mind. Where was she going to find the strength to continue to fight the attraction that was growing within her?

At dinner, Les helped her out with that one.

"You are now looking at the newest permanent staff member," Linda announced when she joined the others gathered in the staff room.

"Hallelujah," Bea yelled as she looked up. "You don't know how scared I was that I'd have to go back to that computer room."

"Bea, you know it wasn't that bad."

"Easy for you to say, Wanda. All you deal with is a dance floor. You don't have to face a room full of machines smarter than you are."

They all laughed. Roz looked at Linda. "Congratulations." She rushed over to her and gave her a warm hug. "I'm not surprised."

"I'm not either," Wanda said. "Not one bit." Her eyes reminded Linda of a snake about to strike. "I guess Avery goes for fluff just like all the other jocks do." She stamped from the room and slammed the door behind her.

Linda stared openmouthed at the closed door.

"Don't mind her," Cheryl said. "She's probably been hoping you'd be gone by now. She thinks Avery is her territory."

"She and Avery have a thing going?" Linda didn't look at Les as she asked the question he hadn't really answered when she went out with him the first time. She hadn't asked it again the following week when they went for dessert again. She hoped she didn't sound as disappointed by the possibility of Avery being involved as she felt.

She remembered that the day she started they said Avery wasn't interested in Wanda, but things can change in two weeks. She knew from her own experience that feelings can develop that quickly. Maybe the same was true in Wanda and Avery's case.

"Only in Wanda's dreams," Bea said. "Like I said two weeks ago, she's an employee to Avery, nothing more. That's still true. If she didn't do her job so well, she'd have been out of here long ago, the way she keeps trying to attract him." Bea shook her head. "I don't think he's the kind of man to be interested in a chaser. Avery probably figures if he keeps her at a distance, she'll get the message." Bea leaned her arms on the table. "I think I have a better chance of winning the lottery than that happening." She let a glance sweep over everybody. "And I don't even buy tickets."

The room filled with laughter at Bea's last words. Linda laughed with them.

"So, are we going to go out and celebrate tonight?"

If somebody was awarding points for persistence, Les would have a bunch.

"I'm not much for partying. I told you that. Besides, we just went for dessert yesterday."

"What does yesterday have to do with today? I'm not suggesting anything big. Let's just go out to grab something to eat." He frowned. "I had to twist your arm last week and again yesterday. You sure you don't have somebody special?"

"Positive." *At least nobody interested in me,* her mind added.

"Good. Let's go to Not Just Salad. They serve a mean shrimp scampi."

"I don't think so. . . ."

"Let's all go," Craig added.

Les's hard look matched Craig's. Linda thought they looked like two male animals trying to expand their territories.

"I'm in for that," Bea said. "This isn't my night to cook."

Linda listened while each of the others said whether or not they could make it. When they had finished, she still didn't know who was coming.

"Should we invite the boss?" Roz asked as the group got ready to go back to their rooms.

"No," Craig said. "He might cramp our style. What if I want to talk about him?"

"Since when did you let whether somebody was around decide whether you talked about them?"

"Tell it like it is," Bea said.

They were still laughing as they left the lounge.

By the end of the day Linda was looking forward to the evening. She had a bunch of new friends and a job she loved. So what if the boss disturbed her whenever she saw him? She'd just stay out of his way. Maybe Les could help her break free of the pull toward Avery. She'd keep reminding him that friendship was all she was interested in. Nobody could ever truthfully accuse her of using people.

Craig offered her a ride to the restaurant before Les had a chance to.

Linda was in an awkward position. If she refused, Les might read something into her preferring to ride with him over Craig. Which she did. Craig came on too strong. But if Les knew she'd rather ride with him, he might read something more into it.

She sighed as she got into Craig's car. May as well make it clear to him that she wasn't interested. If she were looking, she wouldn't pick somebody like him. He was too . . . She searched her mind for the right word. He was too slick. She'd had more than enough of that type.

It took a while, but by the time they reached the restaurant he seemed to have gotten the message.

The food was great and the company was just as good. Wanda was the only one missing. And Avery. Linda took a deep breath. She had forgotten how great it was to relax with a group of friends.

Craig told about chorus rehearsal that night. "Tyree spent twenty minutes trying to convince me that we should do a rap as part of the concert in June. When I told him 'no,' he insisted that I hear it before I decide. It wasn't too bad." He looked around the table. "But there is no way my chorus will ever do a rap." He laughed. "He'd still be pleading his case if I hadn't ended it." He shook his head. "I have to give him points for persistence."

Cheryl had a story of her own to tell, and they laughed with her. When the laughter faded, Bea spoke.

"I hate to be the first to leave, but with kids in the

house, mornings come early and I am not a morning person."

Linda looked at her watch.

"Midnight? What time does this place close?"

"I think it's open all night."

"I'm a morning person, but not after staying up this late." She stood. "I'm with you, Bea."

"No, you're with me," Les said. "I'll take you home." Linda glanced at Craig who only shrugged. She was glad he had gotten the message. Everyone said their good-byes, and they all drifted to the cars.

When they were on the expressway, Linda took a deep breath.

"Les, do the others know about my background?"

He shrugged. "Yeah, they all do. I didn't tell them," he added quickly. "Some kind of way Wanda found out. Less than a week after you got to the center she made sure we all knew." He glanced at her. "As you can see, it doesn't make any more difference to them than it does to me." He took her hand in his.

Linda smiled, but gently pulled her hand away. Why couldn't she feel something for him?

"You're a nice guy, but as I told you last week, I'm not interested in a relationship." She lifted one shoulder. "I . . . I just thought I'd better remind you."

"How about a friend? You could always use a friend."

"That's true. You can't have too many friends."

"Good. I'm cool with the friendship thing. At least for a while. You can't blame me if I hope something further develops. Now that we got that out of the way, do you like to dance?"

"I'm not sure I still know how."

"It's like learning to walk. Once you know how, you don't forget. My fraternity's having a fund-raiser a week from Saturday. Will you go with me?"

"I don't think I . . ."

"Just as my friend," he added before she could finish.

She took a deep breath. "I think I'll pass on this. Maybe another time."

"If I thought I could change your mind, I'd keep trying." He stopped the car in front of her house. "You're not going to change your mind, are you?"

"No, sorry. Let's just stick with dessert, okay?"

"It's got to be okay."

He turned off the motor and opened her door. He took her hand to help her out, but she let it go as soon as she was standing.

She unlocked the door to the house and turned to face him.

"Thanks." She smiled at him nervously. "Tonight was great. I appreciate the ride. I have to get some wheels as soon as I can."

"I'm glad you enjoyed it. And you can count on me for a ride anytime. 'Mi coche es su coche.'" He smiled back. "See you in the morning."

"Your car is mine, huh? Just don't try to sell it, right?"

They laughed.

Linda relaxed as she watched him go back to his car. *Nice guy,* she thought again. *Why not him?*

She went upstairs thinking that fate must love practical jokes.

The sun had come up and settled in by the time Linda awoke on Wednesday morning from the first good night's sleep she'd had in a long time. The previous night had been fun. Plain, old, harmless fun. She had forgotten what that felt like.

She twirled around on the porch after she locked the door. If the girls had been out jumping rope, she would have joined them for a turn or two. She let a wide smile cover her face. It was still there when she got off her last bus, in spite of the drizzle that had started. She opened her umbrella and kept smiling. She felt like Gene Kelly in his famous scene.

Two weeks ago she was worried about her future. Now it looked better than ever.

She would not let her hopeless attraction to Avery dampen her spirits.

Nine

Over the next few weeks, Linda realized things would never go any further between Les and her and she told him so. She didn't think their regular evenings out should continue. They felt too much like a date and she knew, no matter what Les said, that's the way he viewed them. He wanted more and she wished she could give it to him. She had known him for a while and her opinion of him hadn't changed. He was a nice guy. Why couldn't people have more control over who they were attracted to?

"Maybe you want to spend your time with somebody else." They were at Bobbie's Kitchen, what had become their usual restaurant. She sighed. It wouldn't be theirs after tonight, though. "I feel like I'm just wasting your time."

"You don't like my company? Is that it?"

"Of course not. I enjoy your company." It was true. No matter what else, she had made another friend; but friendship was all she wanted from him and she knew he hoped for more. "If you weren't spending so much time with me, you might find that special someone you were meant to spend your life with." She shrugged. "I feel like I'm blocking that opportunity."

"You're beginning to sound like Mom, nagging me

about finding somebody. You been hanging out with her at church?"

Linda laughed.

"You know what I mean. No strings between us, remember? I know now that there won't ever be."

"I remember our no-strings clause." He smiled, but there was a sadness in his eyes. "But you can't stop me from hoping."

"Les . . ."

He cut off the rest of Linda's words.

"Looks like you found your groove at the center." He reached over and patted her hand.

She hesitated. She'd tell him later that this was the last time she was coming here with him.

"Seems like it."

"Good. That means you'll be with us for a long time." He pulled his hand away from hers. "Can I give you a ride to the dance on Saturday?"

"Les, weren't you listening to me?"

"Of course I was. I'm not asking you for a date. I'm just a friend offering a friend a ride. You are going, aren't you?"

"Yes, I'm going."

"You're not taking a bus. It's too late and too complicated. Besides, you don't want to ride the bus all dressed up in your partying clothes." He leaned forward. "I know you said you don't party, but you have to make an exception this one time. Everybody parties at the annual fund-raiser. Even Avery comes out from under the mountain of paper he's always working on and puts on a tux."

Linda got lost with the image of Avery in a tux. What he did to a T-shirt was awesome. What he would do to a tuxedo must be illegal.

"So what do you say? Are we on?"

"No, we're not on and, no, I'm not taking a bus either.

I don't need a ride because I picked up tickets for my sister, Sheila, and her date today. I'm going with them."

"You did some arm twisting, did you? Anything to keep from catching a ride with Les's Door-to-Door Service."

"That's not true. First of all, I didn't have to twist her arm. I told her about the center and the work we do there. She thinks it's a worthy cause. My parents would be coming, too, but they're in Africa." She gave him a hard look. "As for not wanting to ride with you, that's how I got here tonight, isn't it? 'No strings' doesn't mean avoiding a friend. That's what we are. Friends. I know we won't ever be anything else. I'm just pulling back from making this a regular thing like a date. I think this is it for a while. Okay?"

She smiled and hoped it would ease the hurt she saw on his face.

"I guess it has to be okay." He stared at her for a few seconds. "Never let it be said that Les Sherman can't take a hint." He held his stare for a few seconds longer. Then he blinked loose. "Let's do justice to our dessert before Bobbie comes over and questions us."

Linda savored a bite of the coconut cake. Now they both knew it would be a while before they came back here together.

Linda still arrived at the center early, although it wasn't necessary. She had just arrived when Bea came in.

"Since school is almost out, I know you didn't have a project to deliver this morning," Linda said.

"No, that would have been easy compared to what's on my mind." She frowned. "Look, I can't find a tactful way to do this, so I'll just blurt it out like I do everything else." She took a deep breath.

Linda watched her struggle for words. It was unlike Bea not to just speak her mind, no matter what. This must be serious.

Linda waited. Finally, Bea, after letting out a long breath, started talking.

"I was hoping you still came in early. I need to talk with you privately." She put her spoon down and stopped pretending she was interested in her coffee. "I'm worried about one of our girls. Until a little while ago, she's showed a lot of promise. Lately . . ." Her words trailed off and she sighed. "Tamika's lost interest. This last report period her grades started slipping. If school wasn't almost over she'd probably fail this last semester, that's how bad it is. She's an A/B student. Or at least she was. She's just finishing her sophomore year, but if she had continued making good grades and stayed involved with her school activities, she was sure to win a scholarship after graduation. Now she's thrown it all away for some man." Bea glared. "And I do mean *man*. Sloan's a lot older than she is, and everybody around here knows how he gets his money. Tamika knows it, too."

Linda felt a chill. She knew this story. She had *lived* this story.

Bea went on. "I've known this child since she used to run to me every day and tell me about school. She'd let me see her report card before she showed her mother. Her mother and I talked every so often, but not much for a year or so." She shook her head. "She called me two weeks ago. She tried to talk some sense into Tamika, and when she couldn't, she came to me." Bea stared out the window with unseeing eyes. "Her mother remembered how close Tamika was to me and thought maybe I could get through." She sighed. "I tried to talk to that child more times than I can count, but she tells me I don't understand, that she knows what she's doing." Bea leaned forward. "I don't know what else to do. I thought maybe you could try to make her see that she's making a mistake." She shrugged. "I thought . . ."

"You thought that, since I've been there, maybe I can get through to her."

"I don't mean to throw your past in your face. And you know I'm not trying to insult you or hurt your feelings, but I was hoping you'd agree to talk to her. Not to tell her your story, but, as you said, you've been there. Maybe she'll listen to you better than she did to her mother or to me. I thought you might have an understanding of what's going through her mind and how to get through to her." She opened her hands. "I don't know what else to do. I hate to lose her."

"I don't feel insulted. I do understand what's going through her mind. I'll see what I can do." She stared out the window, but she didn't see any more than Bea did. "Maybe if someone had talked to me when I got involved with Jamal things would have been different. You say you think Tamika knows what her boyfriend is doing?"

"I know she knows. I talked to her about it as soon as I found out."

"I'll try my best. I don't want anyone else to go through what I did."

Two days later Linda got her chance. She was on her way from the lounge when she saw Tamika coming toward her in the hall. The lab would wait.

"We need to talk."

"I'm on my way to see the game. Some guys from my school are playing guys from Franklin. What do you want to talk about?" Her face tightened. "I bet Miss Bea's been putting my business out to you."

The glare thrown at Linda would have made anyone else back off. Linda met it with a stare of her own.

Tamika looked away.

"Look, Miss D., I know what I'm doing. You don't have anything to say to me I haven't already heard from Miss Bea and my mama. My counselor even got on my case."

"Let's not talk out here."

A girl passing by in the hall smiled and spoke. Linda spoke back and, even though she didn't feel like it, smiled, too. Then the serious look came back on her face.

Kids were on their way to various rooms, but most were on the way to the gym. The official basketball season was long over, but there was always a pick-up game going on, especially on Friday nights. Most of the time no one came to the lab during a game. She hoped tonight was one of those times, but it didn't matter. This was more important than any computer work.

"Come with me, please. Just hear me out." She pulled Tamika toward a room away from the flow of kids streaming toward the gym, not giving her a choice. She was glad Tamika didn't pull away.

As soon as they were in the room, she let go and faced the young woman.

"You need to cut him loose."

"Who?"

"Don't give me that. We both know who and what we're talking about. This is too serious for game playing, Tamika. You know I'm talking about Sloan."

The girl stepped back.

"Miss Bea has been talking about me. I knew it. First, my mama gets on my case, then she goes to Miss Bea, now you got your nose in my business." Her glare was as hard as the one she'd given Linda earlier. Linda matched this one, too.

"They care about you. They're worried about what you're doing with your life."

"I'm not doing anything wrong. Besides, it's my life.

I'm tired of people badmouthing Sloan. I love him and he loves me. I know what I'm doing."

"You're sixteen and he's . . . what? Twenty-five? What's he doing messing with a high school kid, anyway?"

"He's twenty-seven, and I'm mature for my age." She glared at Linda. "He loves me. He said so." She shrugged. "I know what he does. We talked about it. He said he's not going to do it much longer. As soon as he makes enough to move his family into a nice house, he's gonna quit. He promised me. Besides, like I said, I'm not doing anything wrong."

Linda shuddered as she listened to Tamika utter the same words she had used with Marian in her other lifetime. She remembered how little that had mattered. She had to make Tamika realize it, too. She hesitated as she searched for the right words. When she found them, her voice softened.

"Sit down, Tamika. Let me give you the *real* facts of life from someone who knows."

An hour later they came out of the office. This part of the building was quiet. The only sounds were faint ones coming from the gym at the other end of the hall.

Linda saw Avery standing at the end of the hall. She stared at him for a few seconds. Then she turned her attention back to the girl with her. She put her arm around Tamika who was unaware of the looks exchanged by the adults. Her eyes were dry, now, but it was obvious she had been crying.

"Are you going to be all right?"

"Yeah." She nodded slightly.

"Are you're sure Sloan won't hurt you? Do you want me to go with you when you tell him?"

"I don't need anybody with me. I've known Sloan since I was in grade school. He lived down the street from us in my old neighborhood. I had a crush on him, then, but I was just a little kid and he barely looked at me." A slight smile found its way to her face. "I was so flattered when he noticed me." She sighed. "A while ago I went back to my old street to my girlfriend Val's birthday party. Sloan wasn't at her house, but he was coming out of his house. We stood there on the sidewalk talking for so long I almost missed the cutting of the cake." She laughed. "Val didn't speak to me for days." Her sigh chased the laughter away. "It was worth it. When I saw Sloan and he finally noticed me, it was just as I had always imagined." She dipped her head to her shoulder and stared at the floor.

Her story stopped, but Linda didn't say anything. She'd give Tamika as much time as she needed.

Finally Tamika looked at her.

"My mom remembers April fifteenth as Income Tax Day and Val remembers it because it's her birthday." Her smile didn't look at home with the tears in her eyes. "I'll always remember it as the day Sloan noticed me." She wiped the two tears that left her eyes and slid down her cheeks. "I felt like I'd been waiting forever for him to look at me like he did that day. Like I was somebody he had been looking for forever." She stared at her hands wrapped around each other in front of her. "Now that he's finally seen me as all grown up and decided we are right for each other . . ." She looked at Linda. "This is like killing a dream. You know?"

"I know." Linda nodded. "I know." She took a step closer. "I'm not going to tell you that you'll forget him, because you probably won't. You never really forget your first love. But I *can* tell you that, over time, remembering will get easier." Linda patted the girl's shoulder. "I know what you're feeling. Believe me, I do. But you have so much of your life ahead of you."

"I guess." She took a deep breath. "Sloan won't hurt me." She blinked hard. Her eyes filled again and she wiped them. "He's not really a bad person, you know. He just wants something better." She shook her head. "He won't like me breaking up with him, but he'll let me go." Her voice softened. "He really does love me." She sighed and stood straighter. "If he quits pushing today I'll go back to him tomorrow. But he won't quit. He'll never quit. I've been fooling myself. He's probably been fooling himself, too." She took a deep breath and wiped her eyes again. "Thanks, Miss D. for telling me about . . ." She glanced around and saw Avery for the first time. Then she looked back at Linda and leaned toward her. Her voice was low. "Thanks for telling me what you told me about yourself."

Linda hugged her and held her for a long time.

"Remember, it's going to hurt bad for a while, but you'll be okay. Trust me. I know."

"I do trust you." Tamika took another deep breath. "Let me go home and get this over with. I don't feel like watching a game tonight."

"If you need to talk to me, you know where I'll be."

"I know." She wiped at her eyes. The look on her face was too old for someone only sixteen. She ducked her head and walked away. "Bye."

Linda watched her leave the center. She hoped Tamika was right about Sloan's reaction. She hated to let her go see him alone, but she knew she had gone as far as Tamika would let her. She'd get her number from Bea and call when she got home that evening.

She walked toward the steps. She had to go to check on the lab. Even if no one was up there, she didn't feel like watching a game either.

"Linda."

Avery's rumbling voice made her turn around. The way his presence always affected her, how had she forgotten he was in the hall? She must have been more wrapped up in the conversation with Tamika than she thought.

She watched as he came toward her. Caught again not being where she should have been when she should have been. Maybe this was where he'd let her go. At least, if she left, she wouldn't see so much of him. Then maybe she could get him out of her mind and keep him from moving further into her heart.

"I'm sorry I'm not in the lab. I know this is the second time I've been irresponsible about my job. I'm on my way up now to make sure everything is okay." She took a deep breath and let it go. "Unless you would rather I leave now."

"Why are you so set on having me fire you?"

"I'm not." She shrugged. "I just know how you feel about me."

Avery hesitated. An intense look crossed his face and then disappeared.

Linda tensed and waited.

Finally he spoke. "Thanks for talking to Tamika. Bea told me what's going on with her. Maybe she'll listen to you. Nobody else could get through to her."

"You mean you don't think I'm trying to recruit her for the drug trade?"

Linda watched Avery swallow hard. She saw his mouth soften. She was so lost in the action that she almost didn't hear his words.

"I'm sorry for the way I've acted toward you, for being so suspicious of you. I'm sorry I—" He opened his hands toward her. "I'm sorry." His gaze bored into her.

"I am, too." She turned away but then turned back to him. "Do you know how sorry the word 'sorry' is? I'll be in the lab."

Avery watched her go. He tried to ignore the slight wiggle in her walk that she probably wasn't even aware of. He imagined his hands wrapped around her hips, imagined easing her close so her breasts were pressed against his chest. He closed his eyes and the memory of her perfume flooded back to him. The first day he met her, though he struggled against it, it grabbed him. Now it held him even tighter.

He opened his eyes and watched as she opened the fire door to the stairs. He wished the hall were longer.

She never looked back at him. He wasn't sure how he felt about that. He wasn't sure of a lot when it came to her.

He went back to his office, but just stood inside the door. Her hair was a bit longer, her curls a bit fuller. Was she letting it grow out? He never had a chance to touch them, much less let his fingers get lost in them. Would the curls disappear if she did let her hair grow? Were they as soft as they looked? Would he ever have the opportunity to find out?

A vision of Linda, her eyes heated with passion instead of anger, planted itself in his mind. The passion would be for him and it would match his for her.

He shifted his stance, trying to get more comfortable. His loose pants were not loose enough as his body reacted to her the way it always did.

Even as he tried to cool off with one deep breath and then another, he knew it wouldn't work. Air cold enough to have an effect on his heated body hadn't been discovered yet. He shook his head.

She had no idea how he felt about her. How long could he keep it that way?

Ten

Before she left the center, Linda called Tamika. A sobbing Tamika assured her that she had broken up with Sloan.

"He didn't take it any better than I did." She sniffed. Then silence hung in the air. "He tried to act casual about it, like he didn't care, but I saw through him. He wiped them away real fast, but I saw tears in his eyes. A lot of tears." She sniffed again. "Of course, I had to look through my own tears." Her voice trembled. "Then he kissed me softer than he has ever kissed me before. I knew it meant good-bye." Her sobs reached Linda. "I miss him so much, but you were right. I had to break up with him before I got pulled in like you did." Tamika was quiet. Linda waited. "I'll be okay. I don't know when, but I'll be okay some day."

She hung up. Linda knew that, in spite of the crying, Tamika would be all right in time.

The next day Tamika came to thank her in person. The sadness in her eyes was too old for a teenager, but no tears showed.

"Why don't you hang around here for a while?"

"I'm not into computers."

"That's okay. You can look at what the others are doing. Besides, it's not just about computers. A lot of the kids use them to write stories and poems. You might find it's something you want to do. It might help you get over this rough time."

Tamika sighed.

"I don't think I want to write, but I may as well hang around here. It's not like I have anything else to do or anybody waiting for me."

She stopped at each station, listened to a sentence or two as the other kids explained what they were doing. Then she moved on. When she had circled the room and reached the door again, her thin "good-bye" told Linda she was leaving.

"She just broke up with her boyfriend," Kira said. "They were real tight for a long time. She was talking about getting married after graduation." She glanced at Linda. "He wasn't any good, he was into all kinds of stuff that can get you in trouble." She shrugged. "We couldn't tell Tamika anything, though. She was in the Honors Program with us until she hooked up with Sloan. Now that they broke up, maybe she can get herself together and get involved again." She turned back to her computer. "Some people just have blind spots about other people."

Linda didn't say anything. She knew from firsthand experience about blind spots where a man was concerned.

After thinking about her own dumb mistake for a few seconds more, she turned her attention back to the kids in the lab. Maybe something good finally came out of her relationship with Jamal.

School let out and Linda was busier in the lab than before. The kids had decided that they needed a magazine so they could share more of their poetry and short stories than could go in the newsletter. When Linda explained how expensive it would be to print enough copies for everybody at the center, they came up with an alternative plan.

"E-publishing is a big thing now. It goes with publishing on demand, but it starts on a disk," Kira said. "If we can't get any money to print it when we finish, we can always leave it on disk and anybody who wants to can read it on the screen."

"We can print out one copy to keep here, can't we?" Helen asked. She and Kira were selected by the others to be coeditors.

"Sure. We won't have a problem with that. But let's not give up yet. We might be able to distribute it. I just didn't want you to be disappointed if it doesn't happen."

Linda smiled as she thought of the changes that had taken place in Helen. Not only did she share her writing freely now, but she encouraged others to do so as well. She had become the leader of the poetry group and was thriving in that capacity. Gone was the timid young lady who had approached Linda so shyly that first day. In her place was a self-assured person to whom other kids came for advice. The least Linda could do was try to get them financial support.

She steeled herself and approached Avery the next day about the kids' ideas. She was determined not to let her mind drift from the reason she was with him into some fantasy world that could never be real.

"It's important to them to have other kids see their work. Leaving it in electronic format is the cheapest way for them to share their writings. I think we'll end up with a good-sized book, though." She frowned. "It will, I mean we can, I mean we . . ." She took a deep breath, but it didn't help. "That is, we won't use the paper it would take to print out copies. That would take reams and reams of it and be very expensive." Her frown deepened. "I had no idea so many of our kids wrote poetry and stories. Some of them have been writing since they were in the early grades." She chewed on her lip, hoping it would help her regain the control she had before she came face-to-face with him. What had happened to her determination to stay focused on her purpose for being there and not on Avery? "Think about it, okay?"

She fled from his office without waiting for an answer, trying not to take thoughts of him with her.

Avery came into the lab the next day and it took all of Linda's effort to focus on her work. He was probably here to ask about the journal. He never came to the lab without a reason. She tried to force herself to concentrate on what he had to say so that she could answer intelligently, but it was hard. How could she keep her mind on words instead of on the stalwart man towering over her, standing close enough for her to touch, if she dared? His solid chest, molded to perfection, beckoned to her hands, her body. She tightened her grip on the papers in her hand, knowing she was wrinkling them and would have to make more copies, but that was the last thing on her mind right now. She needed a serious reality check.

She yanked her gaze from his body and moved it to his face. Stupid mistake.

His mouth, even more sensual than she had imagined, seemed like a perfect fit for hers, now that she gave it her attention. He seemed to be waiting for her to see if this was true. She shook her head. Her hormones were raging, and she had no idea how to control them. She forced her gaze up higher, but there was no safety there, either.

His dark chocolate eyes pulled her in and she was lost in their sweet, promising depths. His look showed her the way she felt. Or did it?

Longing filled her, swiftly followed by regret heavy enough to bring her back to her senses.

Now she knew firsthand what unrequited love felt like. *Love?* She felt her eyes widen as she took a step away from him. Oh, no. Uh-uh. She would not allow that to happen. No one was supposed to ever reach that deeply into her heart again, especially not someone who didn't want to be there.

She stepped back again until a table stopped her escape.

"What do you think about our idea for a journal, Mr. Avery?"

Like the answer to the prayer Linda hadn't made, Helen rescued her.

Linda was grateful for the day Helen set foot into the lab. She was more than grateful for her self-confidence at this moment. She didn't want to think about what stupid thing she might have done if Helen hadn't saved her.

Avery pulled his stare from Linda. That allowed her brain to start functioning again.

"I think the idea of a journal is a good one." His gaze darted to Linda and then back to Helen. "I think I might be able to find funding to print copies for everyone. I have a couple of possible sources I can check."

"For real? Enough money for us to give everybody a copy of the journal like we do the newsletter?"

"Don't get too excited yet. I'm not sure I'll be successful. It will be expensive, but there are several places I can try."

"Thanks, Mr. Avery. Everybody's going to be so excited."

"Helen, I said I'll try. No guarantees."

"Right. I understand." Her enthusiasm said otherwise. She rushed back to the group waiting for her at the far table covered with papers. The smiles on the others' faces widened as Helen continued to talk. Avery shook his head.

"I hope I don't have to disappoint them." He looked from the kids to Linda. "I have to get back to the office. I have a desk full of work waiting for me." He didn't move.

Linda wasn't sorry. She wasn't anything but lost. Helplessly, hopelessly, desperately lost.

"Mr. Avery, Helen said we're going to get to print our journal for everybody. Is that right? You gonna let us do that?"

He smiled at Kira.

Is he as grateful for the interruption as I am?

"I said I'd try to get funding so we could print it. I didn't say we had it."

"I know you can do it, Mr. Avery. I got faith in you." Avery laughed.

"Let me go work on this and see if I can live up to Kira's faith. See you later."

He smiled and Linda realized she had been waiting for it again since the first day she saw it. It had been worth the wait.

Three days later Avery came into the lab. He spoke and the kids stopped keyboarding and turned toward him immediately.

"I have some news to share."

"You got the money for our journal. Way to go, Mr. Avery. I knew you could do it." Kira danced around the room.

"Is that right?" Helen stood. "Are we really going to get to print out our journal?"

"We aren't that far yet. I got a strong 'maybe,' but they want more details. I came up here to ask Miss Linda to explain the project to the company representatives."

"When?" Kira asked the question, but Avery looked at Linda.

"Is tomorrow too soon?" he asked her.

"Tomorrow is fine," Kira answered. It was a good thing she did. With Avery standing so close, Linda wasn't even sure of his question.

"Is it?"

Avery's stare deepened and drifted to her mouth. It was all she could do to keep from touching her lips to feel if his gaze had left a mark.

He blinked and looked back into her eyes. That was even more disturbing for her.

"Is tomorrow okay? I made a tentative appointment for them to come here before we open."

"Yes. That's fine." Her answer would have been "yes" no matter what he was asking.

"Can we talk to them, too?" Kira looked at Linda. "I know you can do a good job of explaining to them by yourself, but I thought maybe Helen and I—" She shrugged. "Maybe we can make them see how much we really want this."

"What do you think about that?"

Linda made herself concentrate on his words instead of on the mouth that released them.

"I think it might be a good idea. Maybe Kira's and Helen's enthusiasm will sway them if they haven't made up their minds by the time I finish explaining what we have in mind and why the kids need this."

"Okay. I'll set it up for tomorrow morning at eleven. That will give us plenty of time before the rest of the kids get here. We don't want anything to disturb us. I'll see you then."

Linda may as well have closed up the lab for all the work that got done right after Avery left.

The kids sat around celebrating and dreaming about seeing their names in a journal. Linda didn't remind them that it might not happen. They wouldn't have heard her if she had. She let them dream.

Then they got to work planning the layout. Sometimes the discussion got heated, but it always ended in agreement. Then they moved to the next item.

Finally, they decided to print out a copy and work from that. They were still moving writings around when the bell rang to signal closing time.

The next morning Linda arrived before ten o'clock, but Helen and Kira were already waiting on the steps. Linda sat beside them and waited for Avery.

Linda felt her heart speed up when she saw him come around the corner.

He stopped in front of them and smiled. Linda thought her heart was going to burst through her chest.

"Did you three spend the night here?"

"Mr. Bill wouldn't let us." Kira laughed. The others laughed with her.

"Let's go on in. You can chew your nails more easily sitting in a chair."

They followed him into the meeting room.

"Hey, Helen. Look at us. We're big time: in the staff meeting room and all." Kira looked around the room. "This isn't what I thought it would look like in here."

"What did you expect?" Linda put water on to heat.

"I don't know. Something fancy. Meeting rooms in the movies and on television are always big and fancy." She touched the back of one of the plastic chairs around the table. "And these chairs are supposed to be soft and cushiony."

"You watch too much TV," Linda said.

"Yeah," Avery said. "Besides, you're a writer. You know the difference between real life and fiction. This is real life."

He set the bag he was carrying on the table. He smiled and Linda had trouble remembering why she had opened the cabinet. She blinked and took out a cup, then went back for another.

Avery took a carton of juice from the bag.

"Natural sugar to get the brain cells working. Let's go over our final strategy."

Linda filled the cups and soon the four of them were reviewing their presentation.

"Thank you for explaining the project," Avery said when Linda and the girls had finished.

"It's very impressive," a board member said. "I believe we can fund your project. We'd like to meet with Mr. Washington to finalize things."

"Thank you. We really appreciate your help."

Linda took Kira's hand in one of hers and Helen's in the other. Gently she pulled them from the room. They followed her up the steps in a daze. They didn't snap out of it until they were inside the lab.

"We got it. We got it." Kira and Helen danced and skipped around the lab. "We're gonna have our journal. We're gonna have our journal."

They each grabbed one of Linda's hands and pulled her with them as they circled the room again bouncing and twirling.

"I don't need to ask how you feel. It's obvious." Avery entered the lab, and Linda stopped where she was. Color swept over her face. Suddenly she felt foolish. She straightened her T-shirt and smoothed her jeans.

"Don't stop because I'm here. There's nothing wrong with celebrating something like this. You just got a big commitment from the Johnson Corporation. Not only will they print the first edition, but they're willing to print future issues as well. They want a copy to show to the rest of the board. Congratulations to all three of you. Your hard work paid off."

He shook each of the girl's hands and received a hug from Kira followed by one from Helen. Then he turned to Linda. He held out his hand to her and she had no choice. She had to take it. Her mistake was looking into his face when she did.

"Okay," she answered Kira's question and then hoped it was. She had no idea what she had agreed to. Warmth from Avery's hand was seeping through her body, settling in places ignored for a long time. Still she stared at him. And still he stared back.

What had that child just asked? He hoped it wasn't something that should have been answered with a "no."

Linda's hand was as soft as he remembered from that first day, but warmer. Or was the heat coming from him? She looked cool, a lot cooler than he felt. The boiler on a January morning would feel cooler than he was feeling right now.

He had to pull away from her before his body sent out smoke to let her know what he was feeling. He had to let her go. He had to. But not yet. He wasn't ready to let her go yet. He felt himself lean toward her, but he couldn't stop.

"Here." Kira stood beside them.

Avery finally broke free. He looked at the folder the girl was holding out. How long had she been standing there? Had she said anything before he had escaped from the hold that had taken over him? If so, he hoped it wasn't important.

"I put it in a nice folder for you. I know they already agreed to print it, but it won't hurt to have the copy for them in a pretty folder. Whenever we wrap a gift at home, my grandmom always reminds us that the Bible says, 'Never put new wine in an old skin.' " Kira laughed. "Not that she put wine or any other alcoholic drink in anything." She laughed again. "Anyway, I wanted to make it look good for them."

"It never hurts to dress something up."

Linda sounded as if she had just run a marathon. Avery felt the same. He left while he still could.

Linda didn't move from the spot where Avery had fastened her. She couldn't. What would have happened if the girls hadn't been there? Had he really moved toward her or was it just wishful thinking on her part? Had he gotten over her past? Had she proven herself to him? What did it mean if he had forgiven her? What if he did no longer associate her with drugs? Would something develop between them? *Am I ready for it?*

Whether she was didn't make a bit of difference. She swallowed hard. Avery felt the pull between them just as she did. She could tell. He hadn't tried to hide it just now.

What would it feel like to have his arms wrapped around her? To have his lips on hers? To return his kiss? To get lost with him and found by him?

She looked around. She was glad the girls were busy on their own. She wasn't in any frame of mind to help them with anything. She couldn't even help herself.

Linda's journal project and its funding had been fully discussed at the staff meeting, and she had been congratulated by the others. Wanda even managed to mumble her congratulations.

Avery ended the meeting and went back to his office. After he left, the conversation turned to the dinner dance. It was still the topic of interest the next day.

"I pulled out my sequined dress," Bea announced from her place at the table in the lounge. She looked at Cheryl who was about to say something. "Don't even start. Anybody who notices that I wear the same dress every year needs to get a life. I am not buying a dress to wear once a year. Besides, that dress is my gauge of whether I've gained weight since the year before. I've given up hope that it will show that I lost some."

Laughter rippled around the table.

"I got a short red number that I hope will attract as much attention as the fire engine that the color is named after," Roz said. "If you're going to do something, might as well do it up right."

"I bought a royal blue two-piece dress. It might cover up everything, but it lets you know where everything is." A gleam appeared in Cathy's eye. "It's not red, but if I'm lucky it will build a fire under Stan that will last into tomorrow morning."

"Oh my." Cheryl fanned her face with her empty hand. "Such hot talk from a senior citizen."

"Child, I keep telling you young folks that you didn't invent anything. How do you think you got here in the first place?"

If kids had been in the building they would have come to the lounge to see what all the hooting and laughter was about.

"What about you, Linda? You all set for tomorrow night?" Roz asked.

"I guess so."

"So? What are you wearing?"

Before Linda could answer, Wanda spoke. "Yeah. What designer created your gown?"

Linda ignored Wanda's tone. "I borrowed a dress from my sister."

"What's it like?"

"Pink."

"Long, short, or in between?"

"It's long. You'll see it tomorrow. It's nothing fancy.

Just a dress." She turned to Wanda. "As for the designer, I don't know who designed it. I don't get hung up on looking at labels. I choose what I like. My sister does the same. If you're interested, though, you can check the label tomorrow night."

Bea almost choked on a sip of water. She sputtered as she tried to gain control.

Craig cleared his throat.

Cheryl released a quick giggle.

Everybody looked at Wanda, but she didn't have anything else to say. She got up and stamped from the room, sloshing coffee from her cup.

"Aha. The kitten does have claws. It just took a while for them to show. I was wondering," Bea said. "I don't know how you put up with her sniping at you for this long. Much longer and I would have given you 'How to deal with Wanda so she'll leave you alone' lessons." Bea laughed. "It's clear that you did some learning on your own."

"You did that so sweetly and with such class," Cathy said.

"Thank you." Linda nodded and loud laughter filled the room.

"I hope she has better sense than to take you up on that offer about checking out the label tomorrow night," Craig said. "We teach nonviolence to the kids here and a rumble between staff members might make patrons and potential donors think twice about opening their wallets for us." He paused. "No matter how much Wanda deserves a payback."

The laughter got even louder. They were still laughing when they went to their rooms.

Linda went back to the lab smiling.

Eleven

Linda picked up her gown and carefully slid it from the hanger. When was the last time she had worn a gown? She sighed. Her junior prom in college.

Purple and white, their school colors, were everywhere in the ballroom that night: in the balloons, the streamers, even the tablecloths and centerpieces. Linda and the others had been so proud. They were the first class not to have the prom in the school gym. It had taken a year of fund-raisers and a lot of their time, but they had done it.

Everyone had floated into the dance dressed in their finery. For some it had been the first time they had worn formal clothes. Linda had been to several formal affairs with her parents, so she should have been used to gowns, but when the girls in long flowing dresses had twirled around every chance they got, she had, too. The girls who wore fitted dresses glided like models on a runway.

They had filled the room with giggles and happiness. Linda had felt as light as one of the balloons floating over the table centerpieces.

Jamal went with her. She hadn't had to do much persuading to get him to go. He liked dressing up, and no wonder. He looked like he was born to wear a tux. She shook her head. Jamal looked good in everything. She sighed. *Just goes to show you how much looks mean.*

She didn't let her mind go to what had happened two weeks later.

She slipped on the dress she had borrowed from her sister, smoothed it over her hips, and stood in front of the mirror fastened to the closet door. She frowned at the image staring back at her.

"I can't wear this." Linda pulled the scoop-necked gown hugging her breasts and midriff away from her body. She let go and it molded back to her. The tiny straps looked as if they were ready to snap. "Why didn't I try this on before now?"

She stood sideways, looked in the mirror at the fitted dress contoured to her hips, and frowned. The slit up the side of the straight skirt looked higher than it had before she put it on. "I can't wear this," she repeated.

She ran to the phone and called her house. Maybe she could catch Sheila before she left. She trudged back to her room when her mother told her that Sheila was already on her way.

She looked in the mirror again, hoping she had been wrong. She wasn't. She and Sheila weighed about the same. They wore the same size. Why didn't it look like it?

Deep pink. So what if it did make her skin "glow" like Sheila had said when Linda had held it against her own body. Why hadn't she borrowed the black, sequined gown Sheila had first suggested? Linda let out a hard laugh.

Because the black fabric was stretchy and Linda hadn't wanted to attract attention. She stretched up as tall as she could. Her mother would be proud of her posture. Then she slumped a little. All that standing tall did was emphasize her breasts and make them look like they were coming out of the neckline. She shook her head. The top of the dress was too low to be called a neckline.

She sighed, brushed her curls one last time, and

slipped on the teardrop diamond earrings that her parents had given her for her eighteenth birthday. Maybe the earrings would draw attention to her face instead of her body. She could deal with that.

She sat down and pulled on the black dress heels that she hadn't worn in years. She fastened the straps and wished she had one of her own old gowns to pull out along with the shoes. At least her own gowns wouldn't have been so tight.

She picked up her small evening bag that barely had room for her lipstick and a tissue. *Men must design these things,* she thought. *They don't have a clue as to what we need to carry.*

She forced a comb into the bag and hung the gold chain strap over her shoulder. If she was lucky the room would be dark and nobody would notice her. She looked down at her dress. Maybe they wouldn't be able to see her well enough to notice. Maybe it would be so crowded she could melt in with the others. She went slowly downstairs as the doorbell rang.

"Oh, my, child." Auntie stood at the door with Sheila looking at Linda as she came the rest of the way down. "Aren't you beautiful. You're bound to give some man a heart attack when he sees you in that dress. I do like to see people dressed up. If it weren't for church, people would spend their lives in jeans and T-shirts. You don't watch out you're going to catch somebody tonight." She laughed. "I hope it's somebody you want."

Linda's thoughts flew to Avery and stayed there. She knew he'd look as at home in a tux as he did in the center T-shirt, and that was distracting enough. Would he bring a date? What would she look like? Maybe Wanda would go with him.

Linda sighed. It wasn't any of her business. Nothing Avery did, nor whom he did it with, was any of her business. That didn't stop her from wondering, though.

"You look great," Sheila said.

"This dress is too tight. Let's go by the house so I can pick out another one." Linda pulled at the dress.

"Stop that." Sheila swatted her hand. "The dress is not too tight. It's a perfect fit. Besides, we don't have time to go by the house."

"It won't take long."

"Linda, all of my gowns are fitted. I don't own any flour sacks. I'm not even sure they still put flour in cloth sacks. 'There's nothing wrong in showing what you have,' as Grandmom used to say."

"But you're not supposed to flaunt it."

"It's all right to show what the Lord gave you," Auntie added and smiled. "Stop worrying about the dress. Have fun. You deserve it."

Linda sighed. "I'll try." She pulled at the dress once more.

"Stop that. You'll stretch it out of shape."

"If it were possible to stretch it, I already would have." Linda turned to Auntie. "See you sometime tomorrow evening. Remember I'm spending the night at my parents' house."

"I remember. I guess it will get me in practice for when you desert me and move into your own apartment on Monday."

"I'm not deserting you." She hugged the woman. "You know I've grown close to you. You're like family. I've grown closer to you than I ever was to my own aunt." Linda touched her hand. "I can never forget how you trusted me and took me in when I needed someone. But it's time I got my own place. Besides, I'll only be a few blocks away. I'll be over here to see you so much, you'll forget that I don't still live here. You'll get sick of me."

"That will never happen. You're always welcome here. And I must admit I do think young people need a place of their own." Her smile widened. "Now go on before you have me crying. Have fun. Dance a hole in your shoes," she called after them as they left.

Linda was glad she had finally saved up enough money for the security deposit on the one-bedroom furnished apartment. It was small, but it would be hers. She'd miss the comfort of Auntie's home, but it was time to move on. Her life was finally moving forward again.

She followed Sheila out to the car, resisting the urge to tug on the dress again. It wouldn't do any good, anyway.

When they arrived, they got out of the car and Sheila gave the car keys to the valet. Linda took a deep breath, gave in and pulled at her dress, and led the way into the hotel.

The stream of people behind her made her walk into the ballroom faster than she'd planned to. It had been a long time since she had been in a place like this. She smoothed her hands down the sides of her dress and stepped to the side when they entered the room.

Royal blue, silver, and white balloons floated from the registration table at the door. The room was filled with tables covered with crisp white tablecloths draped at each corner with blue ribbon. In the center of each table was a low flower arrangement of white roses and blue carnations spilling from a silver bowel with a thick, white column candle flickering from the center of it. The center's colors were everywhere.

"Hi, Miss D."

The young woman at the table caught Linda's attention.

"Hi, Dawn." She touched her arm. "Aren't you something this evening. So glamorous. I hardly recognized you without your blue T-shirt and jeans. Stand back and let me look at you."

The color in Dawn's face deepened as she stood and

smoothed her peach-colored dress over her hips. She adjusted the wide strap that held the gown at the right shoulder and shifted the fitted top. Then she leaned closer.

"Don't tell anybody, but this is my sister's prom dress."

"It's beautiful." Linda leaned toward her. "I won't tell if you don't tell anybody that I borrowed this dress from my sister." As they laughed, Linda took Sheila's hand and introduced her.

"This is my basketball partner."

"We really showed them, didn't we?"

"Y'all were just lucky, that's all." Michael came over and put a folder on the table. He smiled at Linda.

"Don't you look handsome tonight."

"Yeah, I do, don't I?" The sparkle in his eyes and his laugh showed that he was teasing. "I'm thinking about buying one of these so I can profile." He looked at Dawn. "Maybe I better not. I wouldn't want to give Dawn a heart attack at her young age."

"Don't you just wish." She opened the folder. "I see they found the other guest lists."

"Yeah, though I don't see how they can call them 'guests' when they're paying a hundred bucks for a ticket."

Linda chuckled. "We better move on and let you do your job."

They located Sheila's table, then they both mingled with the others standing around eating appetizers from the clusters of tables off to one side.

"I'm afraid to eat anything. It might be the last straw, or rather the last ounce to burst a seam."

"The dress is fine. Stop worrying." Sheila put carrot sticks and several cheese cubes on a plate followed by a giant strawberry. Linda just watched her.

They only had a few minutes before the people drifted to their tables. Linda made her way to the staff table.

"Wow. Just goes to show you that there's pink and then there's pink with a capital 'P.' " Bea stared at Linda.

"Shows you what a statement 'understated' can make." Cathy smiled. She introduced Linda to her husband.

Linda smiled as she remembered Cathy's comment about building a fire. The way Stan was looking at his wife, it was obvious the dress had done its job.

"I like the way you make a statement." Les's wide grin covered his face. "You will have my full attention any time you make a statement like that."

"Pink is now my favorite color." Craig nodded slowly.

"Stop." Linda pulled at her dress. "I feel self-conscious enough already."

"Leave it to you to wear something to attract attention." Wanda, dressed in a fitted red dress, glared at Linda from across the table. Linda glared back.

"To some of us it just comes naturally. Others have to work at it but still never quite achieve it." Linda's stare stayed on Wanda until Wanda blinked loose. *So. You aren't Avery's date.*

Laughter ringed the table at Linda's response.

She admired the dresses of the other women, and was introduced to Roz's husband and Cheryl's date. She commented on how handsome Craig and Les looked. What she didn't do was let her gaze stray to the platform where Avery sat with the board members. She was glad he wasn't at their table.

The dinners were served and light conversation flowed around. After the dessert of ice cream with chocolate sauce and a huge strawberry on top, Linda's attention was drawn to the platform. The charity board president spoke.

"Thank you for taking time out of your busy schedules

to support such a worthy cause. You have done yourselves proud again this year. Here's Avery to say a few
words."

Clapping lasted long enough for Avery to get to the
podium. Linda could no longer try to ignore him.

"I want to thank all of you for coming. Your support
is greatly appreciated."

Avery told about the current programs and plans for
future ones. He introduced the staff one by one and
they stood as the other people applauded them. Linda
stood when her name was called. So much for blending
in with the crowd and remaining unnoticed.

"Miss Durard is our most recent staff member. She
started a computer program that was really needed. It
hasn't been in place long, but the kids have made great
strides. They even published a journal of their writings
thanks to the funding of the Johnson Corporation."

Linda sat back down as Mr. Johnson waved from his
place at the end of the board table.

Avery touched on a few projects still in the planning
stage. "No more commercials. I know you didn't dress
up to hear me, so I'll end there. I hope you'll enjoy the
music of Dave's Combo. Thanks again, folks, for your
support."

Taking their cue from that, the musicians started with
a soft number. A young woman came over and asked
Les to dance. The other staff members found their way
to the floor. Linda, sitting by herself now, watched cou-
ples from around the room drift to the dance floor.

Avery walked near the staff table with Veronica, a
board member with whom he had been seated. They
were on their way to the dance floor, too. He wasn't close
enough to speak to, but he was close enough for Linda
to get a good look at him. He was every bit as handsome
in his evening clothes tonight as she had imagined. So.
He was dating a board member. Linda swallowed hard.

She tried to convince herself that she didn't care, that she didn't feel like she had lost something valuable. There had never been anything between her and Avery for her to lose. There could never be. *Then why do I feel loss cutting me so deeply?* She stared at him. None of her rationalizations were working. Maybe it was the setting away from the center. Maybe it was seeing him in evening clothes. Maybe it was just time for her imagination to grow.

Why wasn't she the one with him, the one soon to be in his arms? If aching for someone could make that person come and get her, Avery would be in front of her right now. He'd walk her onto the floor and the music would be just an excuse for him to hold her close in his arms. It would give her a reason to hold him just as tightly. If imaginations could turn wantings into reality, she'd be with Avery right now.

She watched as he walked onto the dance floor with Veronica. Linda was glad he didn't notice her, didn't even look her way. She didn't want to be introduced to his date. She was already wondering too much about him. Les had said Avery wasn't involved with anyone. Evidently he didn't know everything going on in Avery's life. Linda stared at the couple.

Why wouldn't he have a date? Why wouldn't he be involved with someone? How close were he and this woman? How did she get to be so lucky? *How much longer do I have to stay here?*

She tore her gaze from Avery and found Sheila, who had just walked to the dance floor with Tony, a young man also attending. They had known Tony and his family for years. They were smiling like the old friends that they were. Her date, Jack, was dancing with someone else.

Linda went to the ladies' room. Maybe she could hang out there until the number was over. Too bad she had cut her hair so short. Now she couldn't use it as an excuse to spend more time hiding out.

She almost bumped into a woman who was coming out as Linda was going in.

"Oh. Hi, Pat." Linda smiled at her old friend. "What a surprise. I didn't know you were here. How have you been?"

"I always attend fund-raisers for the center." The woman's face didn't offer a smile. "I heard you were working for Avery. Is this some kind of work release? I didn't know convicts were allowed to work with children. I certainly didn't expect Avery to hire someone with your background."

Linda stared at the woman who had been her best friend all through grade school. They had had more sleepovers than she could remember. Their friendship had continued through high school.

They had hung out together at lunchtime and talked for hours on the phone about their latest crushes. They had double-dated for the senior prom, had almost gone to the same college so they could be together. But none of that mattered. It wasn't worth a thing. They could have been strangers, except it didn't hurt as much when strangers threw mean words at you.

Linda stood straighter and stayed in place instead of taking a step back like she wanted to. She stared at the woman she thought she knew so well, and didn't let herself flinch even though Pat's harsh words were still snipping at her.

"I'm on parole. Some people think others deserve a second chance."

She wasn't going to try to convince Pat that she was innocent. It wouldn't matter now, even if she could. It was too late. Friends accept friends and at least give them a chance.

"Yes, well. I have to go."

"Yes, you do."

Linda blinked several times and swallowed hard. She watched her former friend walk away from years of friendship as if they had meant nothing to her. Linda would not let one tear escape, even though Pat wasn't there to see it.

Linda went into the ladies' room and hoped she'd have it to herself long enough to recover.

Avery almost lost his way to the dance floor after he had seen Linda standing and talking with Cheryl. He had thought that she was too much in T-shirts and jeans. Why couldn't she have worn a black dress that didn't give a clue as to what her body looked like? That way he'd only have his fantasies about her to fill his mind. His fantasies came out at odd moments: when he saw an ad for computers. Computers of all things. An ad for machinery made his imagination about her run loose.

Whenever he saw a woman with Linda's short curly hairdo, he imagined stroking the curls while Linda was in his arms. When he dreamed, at night or during the day, of the woman meant for him, Linda's face appeared. When he imagined the woman with whom he wanted to spend the rest of his life, it was Linda.

Why didn't she wear a shapeless dress like those he saw every once in a while? Why did she wear *that* dress? He let out a deep breath. He had to be honest, at least with himself. It wasn't that it was a tighter-fitting gown than the gowns worn by most of the other women. He sighed. It wasn't the dress. It was the woman wearing it that had him wanting to sweep her up into his arms and carry her away. Linda made him want to make love to her until she and he were past wanting, if there was such a time. Then he wanted to start all over again.

If Veronica hadn't asked him what was the matter,

he'd still be staring at Linda, imagining, wishing. Of course, he couldn't tell Veronica that what was wrong was that his feelings for Linda seemed so right.

He was glad the way to the floor didn't take them close enough to speak to her. If there was anything for him to be grateful for, it was that he was with Veronica and not alone. He didn't know what stupid thing he would have done if Veronica wasn't going to the dance floor with him. He had to find his common sense that wasn't so common anymore. He had to remember Linda's background. He had to be realistic.

He shook away the idea of something developing between them. She had too much history. He knew firsthand how it was nearly impossible to break away from the drug life once you were involved in it. He had seen too many fail at it. She was strong, but not necessarily strong enough. Then, in spite of his determination, questions formed in his mind.

Did Linda come with Les tonight? Was Les holding her close somewhere on the crowded dance floor and pretending to dance? How close had they gotten? Avery imagined Les taking Linda home with him. He imagined her giving Les the right to remove that pink dress that was so perfect on her. He imagined Les's hands moving to the slit up the side of the dress. Les learning Linda's body. He frowned. *Why do I care?*

He looked around and was relieved when he saw Les dancing with Wanda. If he was still here, so was Linda.

He made it through the dance and took a path back to their seats that didn't pass the staff table, even though when he glanced over to it the last time, Linda wasn't there. Where was she?

His relief disappeared when another thought came to him. Maybe she had met an old friend. She had traveled in the same social circle as a lot of the people who were here as supporters of the center. She was bound to see someone she knew. Was it an old boyfriend? Had they decided to renew acquaintances? Had they decided to get closer than that? She couldn't have gone home. Could she? It was too early, wasn't it?

He didn't want to notice, but he saw her when she came back alone. He didn't want to admit it, but he was happy that she did. He didn't want to admit to a lot of what he was feeling tonight, feelings he had been fighting for a long time.

He sat through the next few numbers, glad that Linda wasn't sitting close to him but not at all happy when first Craig and then Les held her close in a slow dance and her teasing brown leg peeked through the slit every now and then to give just enough of a hint to almost drive him over the edge. None of what he saw made him happy. He was even less happy to admit to himself that he wasn't happy about it. He watched her go back to the table.

He sighed and stood. Without thinking, without speaking to anyone, he made his way to her as if he didn't have a choice.

He saw her smile at Les when she reached her seat. Avery looked on as Les took Cheryl's hand and led her to the dance floor. He also saw Linda's smile disappear when she saw him.

She looked as if she were steeling herself for a battle. Why not? He was always scowling at her, always putting her on the defensive. Why should she expect now to be any different?

She didn't look away from him, though, and her stare and his held just the way he would soon, finally, at long last, hold her.

"Come dance with me."

Wanda stepped into his line of vision breaking the hold of Linda's stare. Wanda smoothed her dress over her hips and left one hand in place the way some men would probably find seductive. He wished she were in front of one of those other men instead of him.

"What?"

"Avery. Come on. Dance with me. Just one dance. You always dance with staff members." She giggled and Avery found it irritating. "Female staff, that is of course." She giggled again and it was no more pleasant than the first time.

She tugged on his arm and he finally looked at her. He glanced once more at Linda before he allowed Wanda to pull him to the dance floor.

Wanda threw a final look at Linda, then smiled at Avery and moved into his arms. He took her hand in his, but she wrapped both arms around his waist. He hoped it was a short number.

Linda took a deep breath. He had been coming to her. She didn't know whether to thank Wanda or go off on her. It was only postponing the inevitable. *Too bad I didn't come here alone. If I had, I could leave now.* She sighed. *But would I?*

She waited, wanting the song to be the longest in the history of music, hoping it was the shortest.

"Girlfriend's got some nerve."

Bea came back with a soft drink at the same time Cheryl came back to the table with Les. Bea looked at Wanda wrapped close to Avery. "Look at that. He's barely touching her, but she doesn't care. When she comes back, she'll gush out a long story about how close *he* held *her.*"

"She needs to give it up. She's wasting a lot of time on a hopeless cause. She's not bad-looking. And she's not stupid. She just has a blind spot where Avery is concerned." Les looked at Linda. "She doesn't know when to quit."

Linda didn't look at Wanda and Avery. If she didn't look, then maybe she could convince herself that her imagination was as wild as Wanda's and that she hadn't seen what she thought she saw in his eyes when he came over to the table.

"Have you danced with the boss yet?" Roz asked as she sat down. "I thought I saw him coming over this way."

"You did, but he's dancing with Wanda. I haven't danced with him and probably won't. He has to spend *some* time with his date. He can only leave her for so many numbers."

"Date?" Bea said. "What date?"

"The chairlady of the dance."

"Veronica Blake? She's not his date. She's a longtime board member."

"I know that's how he introduced her, but I thought they were together."

"Only because they're seated next to each other. She chairs this function every year. It's her project. She's a happily married woman. Her husband is probably out of town on business this weekend, or he'd be here with her."

"Oh. I saw them dancing together."

"You see Wanda dancing with him, too, but I can promise you that there's nothing going on there."

Linda didn't examine the light feeling that filled her when she heard that Avery wasn't involved with the woman she had seen him with.

"Are you sure you don't want to dance this one, too?" Wanda's voice reached them before she did. She followed Avery to the table, still holding his arm.

"I'm sure."

He looked at Linda and her stare got tangled with his again. This time there was no reprieve, no Wanda to stand in the way.

Avery never glanced back at Wanda. He never released Linda from his gaze. He held out his hand to her and she placed hers in it. The others were forgotten. She and Avery could have been the only two people in the room.

Slowly he led her to the dance floor and gently drew her into his embrace. Spicy aftershave rode her next breath. It entered her, found the longing hidden deep inside her, and released it.

He didn't say anything, but words were unnecessary. His hand at her back eased her closer, and she went willingly. She sighed. She was home and it felt every bit as perfect as she had imagined.

The music could have been a jumble of unrelated notes for all the attention she gave it. Heat from his hand on her back entered her and spread itself out until it settled in a place she had almost forgotten. Words of nearness and longing and belonging came from the singer and the perfection of the words spoke to her, touched her. Her whole life until now had been leading to this.

Avery's arms tightened around her and she knew he felt the same way. She leaned her head against his chest and was glad that his heart was beating as fast as hers was; nothing like the barely moving cadence of their feet to the music that neither one of them was hearing.

His arms offered her shelter and she took it. Nothing could harm her here. Nothing from her past intruded to come between them. Her past no longer existed. There was only the present. And, if she was fortunate, the future.

She closed her eyes and, for the first time in a long time, thought about, allowed herself to hope about; the future.

Twelve

She feels every bit as good in my arms as I imagined. He breathed deeply and gardenias drifted through his body, reminding him of a tropical island, making him wish he were there with her right then. His body tightened; strangely the discomfort was a welcome anticipation. Patience. He had to use patience. He could wait patiently for what he knew would come, for what was destined to happen between them, had been destined since the beginning of time.

From the time he had seen her sitting on the steps of the center that first morning, he had known, deep down, that this time would come. He had fought against it, had tried to rationalize the attraction away. Whenever he felt drawn to her, he had told himself that it could never work. At times he had almost believed the lie that said that he didn't want this more than he had ever wanted anything before in his life.

Now, holding her close like this, he knew it was time to stop fighting that attraction, time to stop lying to himself. It was time to admit that he wanted her, that he had wanted her before he had ever met her. He had been looking for her, waiting his whole life for her to make him complete; and he hadn't even known it until now.

She fit in his arms as perfectly as if her soft body were molded to his specifications.

He eased her closer still and brushed his chin across her hair, glad she had worn those ridiculous straps that passed for shoes; that brought her up closer to his height so he could do this. Gardenias. He brushed his chin across her hair again. Soft. Her hair was soft and silky and made him want to curl his fingers in it, brush them through it. Later. He'd get his chance later. He had waited this long. He had to believe in later and be patient. He brushed his lips against the side of her face and hated to settle for only that when her mouth was so close. But it was just for now. Just for a little while longer.

He settled her head against his chest and felt her hands tighten on his shoulders after he brushed his mouth across hers. He wondered if her heart was beating as fast as his was. He hoped so, but he didn't want to check to see just yet. He didn't want to consider that he was the only one feeling this thing between them.

Their bodies would fit even more perfectly together in lovemaking than they were right now.

His body tightened at the idea and he felt hers do the same in response to his. Was she thinking the same thing? Was she anticipating being with him later? Was she imagining him inside her? *Please, let the answer be yes.*

A sigh escaped from her and he wanted to swallow it with a kiss. He had been holding back a kiss for too long. He wanted to make up for wasted time, to cover her face, her body with kisses. He wanted to set a fire burning in her like the one trying to consume him right here on the dance floor. He wanted to discover her most sensitive places and stroke them awake. He wanted to learn her body until he knew it as well as he knew his own. He wanted her to welcome his exploring, to welcome him into her body. He wanted her to want to touch him all over as much as he wanted to touch her. He wanted her to want him as much as he wanted her. He wanted her.

He breathed in gardenias again and contented himself with just holding her close, for now. There was enough time for the rest later. Later that evening, he hoped.

He remembered to move his feet. They were supposed to be dancing, not making love on the dance floor, although that wouldn't be such a bad idea if they weren't surrounded by people. Making love with her anywhere wouldn't be a bad idea; any place would be perfect as long as he was with her.

He moved another step and took her with him, just as he wanted to right now more than anything take her on a love journey with him. He hoped the music would go on forever so he could go on holding her like this. Then he wished it would stop so this part of the evening would be over and they could leave.

How could he convince her to go with him? What words could he use to tell her how much he wanted her, how much he hoped she wanted him just as much? He had taken many communications classes in college, but none of them had prepared him for a situation like this. There weren't any words that could let her know how much he wanted to make love with her; how much he wanted to bring her more pleasure than she had ever experienced before.

Don't stop the music yet, he pleaded. *I need time to find the perfect combination of words and put them together in a convincing argument so she'll change whatever plans she has and come home with me tonight.*

They could make things work between them. Her past was over. It wouldn't get in the way of what was growing between them. People weren't expected to keep paying for mistakes for the rest of their lives. Her past was before this time. Before he even knew she existed. It was just that. Her past. It had nothing to do with now, nothing to do with them. She had proven herself since she had gotten to the center. He had no reason to doubt her. And he was glad, although he wasn't sure at this point that it would have mattered if she hadn't proven herself.

The music drifted into another song and Avery was grateful that he didn't have to let her go yet. He wasn't sure he could, even if he thought he wanted to; which he didn't. What if she wasn't feeling the same need that was filling him? What if it was all one-sided? What if she wouldn't go with him tonight or ever?

His actions toward her hadn't always been friendly. What if they had been too harsh for her to move past them?

He brushed his hand slowly against her waist and her hand fluttered against his chest just enough to give him hope. He smiled. Things would be okay.

Movement around them pulled Avery from his fantasy and back to the dance floor. He looked around. He and Linda were the only ones left on the dance floor. People were leaving the ballroom. Most of the tables were empty. The keyboard player was covering his keyboard and the guitarist was leaving the stage. How long ago had the music stopped?

He eased her away from him and looked into her eyes, and almost got lost again. He smiled at her as she blinked. She had been lost in the same place as he had been. He dared to let himself hope. He eased her away, but still held her hands. Flowery, fancy phrases eluded him. He spoke from his heart.

"Come home with me."

"Yes." Her voice was low, but powerful enough for him to hear her promise.

"I have to get my folder from the table." He was glad he could think of something except what would happen later that evening. They'd never make it home if he couldn't.

He looked at the empty table on the platform. He should have thanked the board members again before they left. He should have told them good night like he did after the dinner dances in past years. He smiled at Linda again. He was glad there was nothing usual about tonight after he had seen her.

He kept his arm around her waist as he led her to her table. He had to force himself to let her go once they got there.

"I'll be right back."

"Okay."

Linda looked at Les, the only one left at the staff table. She felt color creep over her face. Then she shrugged.

He stared at her and smiled gently.

"I hoped I would be the one there when you were ready to move past friendship." He shook his head. "Just goes to show you that being there doesn't always make a difference." He stood. "Be careful. Be happy." He touched her shoulder as he went past her.

Linda went to find Sheila.

"Let me guess." Sheila was standing alone beside her table. "You're not riding home with me. You got a better offer."

"Tell Mom and Dad . . ." Linda hesitated. "Tell them I'll see them soon."

"You're not coming home at all? You're going home with Avery?" Sheila's eyes widened. "With him? After what he put you through? It wasn't that long ago that you were considering leaving the center because of him. Now you're planing to get involved with him?" She frowned. "Did you think this through? I mean, all the way through? Are you sure this is what you want, that this is what's right for you? You know how he was toward you when you first started working at the center."

"I remember his attitude and I understand it. He was just trying to protect the kids. He didn't know me. I had been convicted of a terrible crime. Why should he have taken my word for anything?" She smiled. "He knows me now. His opinion of me has changed over time. He's . . ." She sighed. "That question isn't in his eyes anymore when he looks at me. He's more trusting. I know this is right for me." She smiled. "Oh, Sheila, I've been waiting for this almost from the time I met him. I tried to deny it. I tried to fight it. Now I've decided to be honest with myself. The past isn't between us anymore. It's not important. I . . . I have to do this." Her voice lowered to a whisper. "I love him. I don't know when it happened or how it happened. I promised myself that I wasn't going to get involved with anyone else, that I'd never give anyone the chance to hurt me again." She shook her head. "I should have known that we don't have as much control over our emotions as we think we do." She released a soft laugh.

"I just don't want you to get hurt again." Sheila touched Linda's arm. "I remember the disastrous results the only other time you fell for somebody."

"I won't get hurt." Linda smiled at her. "Avery would never hurt me. He's nothing like Jamal. Really. There's nothing underhanded about him. He's straightforward. He's honest. I'll be all right. I'm a different person, now. I'm a little older and a whole lot wiser." She hugged Sheila. "Let's go get my bag from your car."

Sheila didn't try to get Linda to change her mind. She only whispered, "Be careful," to Linda as they went to the door. Linda smiled at Avery who was waiting for her there.

"I'll be right back. I have to get my things from Sheila's car." She smiled at him. She knew she wasn't making a mistake.

"I'll be right outside."

Avery was known as a self-controlled man, but for the few seconds when he didn't see her after she left him, panic had filled him. He thought she had changed her mind. Then he saw her coming toward him with her overnight bag in her hand, and his heart slowed to its normal speed. He was able to smile again. His smile got wider when she reached him, and so did hers. Everything was as it should be.

He kissed her, then put his hand around her waist and held her as they walked out. It felt right touching her, as if his hand belonged there. Both soft smiles stayed in place as she went with him.

Avery left his hand at her waist until he had to let go so they could get into the car. The only reason he was able to stop touching her was because he knew it was temporary. Soon he would touch her again. Soon he would hold her and love her and fill her until he had his fill of her and she of him. Soon. He wished he lived three minutes away instead of half an hour.

He got behind the wheel and was glad he had opted for a car without bucket seats. He started the Lincoln, then reached for her. She slid across the white leather seats and against him where she belonged.

Linda let the warmth from Avery move through her during the ride. She let the heat from his body mix with hers in a promise of what was soon to come. *How far away does he live?* She hoped it wasn't far. Now that this was going to happen between Avery and her, she was tired of waiting. She had waited too long already.

"We're here." Avery stopped the car inside his large garage and turned to Linda. "You know, it's not too late to change your mind. Are you still sure you want this?"

She smiled at him and nodded.

"It is too late. It was too late from the start. I'm sure."
She had never been more sure about anything.

"Good answer."

His smile as he helped her out of the car was wider
than ever. There was a softness she had never seen in
him before.

He brushed his lips across hers and she was positive
that she belonged here with him, for now and for always.

"I'll be back in a minute."

Avery kissed her again, this time letting his lips linger
a little longer against hers. She felt abandoned when he
pulled away. He left her in the wide hallway and walked
farther into the house.

With Avery out of sight, Linda looked around. A paint-
ing of an African family in front of a village marketplace
hung beside a portrait that Linda guessed was Avery's
mother. He had her eyes. His smile came from her, too.

Linda turned and stopped in front of a gilt-framed
mirror hanging over a small table beside the door. She
touched her mouth. How could she look the same when
inside she felt so different? She didn't try to answer. Instead she turned her attention back to the art.

Prints of African chieftains hung with European land-
scapes and still-lifes. She recognized some of the artists.
Most of the art could grace the galleries of world-class
museums. She moved farther down the hall, admiring
Avery's eclectic taste in art.

She looked closely at a group of what must have been
family pictures hanging along the opposite wall. The
same smile showed on several faces, but it didn't look
as good on any of the others as it did on him.

She moved into the softly lit living room. Pieces of
African art stood on an end table and on the black granite slab table in front of a deep blue couch. Several more
statues, carved from wood, were scattered with colorful

African baskets on a high glass-and-chrome shelf against one wall.

She knew from others at the center and from Marian that Avery had been awarded numerous trophies, but not one was in sight. How like him to keep his personal achievements out of view. She loved him more for his modesty.

This room suited him. It had everything that was needed but nothing extraneous.

"Welcome to my home," Avery's soft voice rumbled from behind her.

She turned to face him. He had taken off his jacket and tie and loosened his collar. A thick patch of hair showed above the open buttons. She tried not to imagine how that hair would feel under her fingers, but she failed. She forced her gaze back to his face.

He was more relaxed than she had ever seen him at the center. He would have looked even more so if not for the intense look in his eyes. She smiled. Her own eyes probably burned with the same intensity.

He held his outstretched arms to her and she walked into them. This was her home. This was where she belonged. He closed his arms around her and she felt as if nothing bad could reach her here. Then she just felt him against her.

He kissed her, and she leaned into him. His hard body told her that he was affected by her nearness. Her body didn't give away her reaction in the same way, but she was just as affected as he was. Her hands brushed across his chest, satisfying her curiosity about his chest hair, before they eased up and found their place around his neck. Her breasts rubbed against his chest and she knew how something could cause agony and pleasure at the same time.

He moved his head back and looked down into her eyes. Were hers as dark with desire as his were?

"Do you want a glass of wine?" His voice caressed her and she had trouble making sense of the words. "Are you hungry? It's been a while since we had dinner." His hands stroked across her back, creating a hunger that he wasn't talking about, but one that she was feeling anyway.

"I don't want anything." *Nothing but you.*

"Me neither. Just you. I'm not going to pretend otherwise."

He took her hand and led her to the back of his house. Neither spoke, but words were unnecessary.

In the light as dim as a candle's, Linda got a look at the king-sized mahogany poster bed covered with a blue, red, and black striped spread. The spread had been turned back to show royal blue sheets as if waiting for Avery to share them with her.

Then she saw only Avery, seconds before he closed her eyes with soft, gentle kisses that stoked the fires within her.

"You don't know how long I've been waiting for this." His words were as soft as his kisses. He captured her mouth in a kiss. He stroked his hands down her legs and stopped when he found the slit that ran from her ankle to above her knee. Then he did what he had wanted to do since he saw it. Slowly he brushed his fingers along the edge of the slit, skimming only the part of her leg that was easily available.

She twisted slightly to give him more access to her, but he didn't take advantage of her offer. Not yet. His hands eased up her body and lingered at her waist as he deepened the kiss. He moved his mouth to the side of her neck as his fingers brushed against the fullness of her breasts. Her gasp changed to a moan.

"I know how long you've been waiting," she whispered. "I've been waiting just as long."

He circled a swollen tip with one finger, but didn't

touch it. Still, she gasped again. Wanting, need flared within her. "They say good things come to those who wait." He eased the dress straps from her shoulder and the fabric rubbing against her sensitive breasts made her long for relief. "I think we've waited long enough." He eased the back zipper of her dress down a bit and brushed the dress down to her waist. He kissed her again. "Too long, in fact. Don't you think so?"

"What?" She frowned.

How did he expect her to carry on a conversation when he was doing such marvelous things, such magnificent things, to her?

"I asked if you think we've waited too long for this."

"Yes, I . . ."

He captured the rest of her words with a kiss, and that was all right. His kiss was worth more than any words.

She worked at the buttons of his shirt as his hands slid the zipper of her dress down the rest of the way. The dress that she thought was too tight slipped to the floor and pooled around her feet. The bedroom air tried to cool her fevered body but failed miserably.

Finally she was able to push his shirt buttons through the buttonholes so she could touch his chest. She had waited so long for this. She pushed his shirt down his arms so she could touch more of him, and he released her long enough to let the shirt slide to the floor. She welcomed his hands back on her, leaned into them, missing them when they were away from her, glad they had found her again.

He moved his hands to touch her again. A few seconds without touching her was torture for him. With one finger he stroked across the top of the dainty white lace that stood between him and her. It wasn't much and he could see her honey-colored skin through it, but it was still too much. He wanted nothing between his body and hers.

He reached around her back and unhooked the clasp. Her strapless bra, no longer needed or wanted, dropped to the floor, releasing her fullness for him, to him.

He cupped that fullness in his hands. Her moan made his body feel as if it would burst. He pressed his lips to hers and she opened to him. He tasted her sweetness that was better than any dessert in the world. He tasted her jaw, her neck before he sampled the honey breasts waiting for him. He brushed his tongue across one tip and she moaned. He replaced his mouth with his fingers and moved his mouth to her other breast. She moaned again and curled her fingers into his hair as if that was the only way she could keep from falling. If he could talk, he'd tell her that he couldn't help her. He was having trouble standing, too. If he could manage the strength needed to push a word out, that's what he would tell her.

He brushed his hands down her hips taking the wisp of lace covering her lower body with them. Then he picked her up and placed her gently on the edge of the bed and looked at her. Her breasts, her sweet breasts, stood swollen and ready. A thick thatch of curls hid her secret place. His body tightened and swelled more than he thought possible. He took a deep breath. Then another.

She'd share her secret with him soon. There was no need to hurry. She was here with him. This is what he'd been searching for. She was the one he had spent his life seeking. Now that he had found her he wouldn't rush things. They had time. He would savor every second and see that she did, too.

He kicked off his shoes. Then, although it was difficult, he knelt down and lifted her foot and brushed his hand slowly back and forth over the top before he, just as slowly, slipped the straps of her shoe from her foot. He rubbed and stroked her foot as he would soon do to her body, trying to ignore the moans coming from her, but failing. If his body tightened any more he'd have to cut his pants to get them off. He took another deep breath and gave his full attention to her other foot. His kisses on her ankle released another moan from her. "Please," followed her moan.

"Soon," he whispered his promise in answer. He forced himself away from her.

He stood and looked down at her face. She licked her lips with the tip of her tongue as if getting ready for him, and he remembered how his own lips had followed that same path. His own tongue had danced with hers, had been inside her mouth in a preview of what was to come. His mouth would feel hers, would taste hers again soon. The desire burning in her eyes was a mirror to the same desire he felt flaming inside him, threatening to consume him if he didn't soon satisfy his need.

He fumbled with his belt buckle, sorry he hadn't opted for suspenders instead. He managed to force the zipper down and shoved his pants and underwear from his body at the same time. Nothing would keep him from feeling her satin skin against all of him.

Linda stared at the perfect brown god standing in front of her, ready for her, ready to share paradise with her. Thick curls covered his chest muscles and tapered to his waist and below to the part of him that promised her relief.

She swallowed hard and breathed deeply, trying to slow the throbbing of her heart, of her body; trying to ease the ache that was filling her; trying to appease her hunger that was swelling and growing and wanting. Wanting him. Only him. Him. Now.

She watched as he took the few steps that would bring him to her so he could finally satisfy her and bring an end to her agony.

She reached out to him and at last he touched her again. He took her hand in his and drew her from the bed. He pulled her against him and she closed her eyes so she could savor his strength and power against her. He moved his chest against her breasts and she almost flew over the edge.

Then he lifted her again and laid her gently in the center of the bed. Before she could protest, he lay beside her and pulled her close again. He feathered kisses over her face while his hands worked more magic on her body.

Her hands were restless against his chest, seeking the secret to release. She kissed his chin, his jaw as she made her way to his mouth. *Sweet milk chocolate,* she thought as she placed her lips against his. He opened his mouth and she entered it the way his fingers were entering her now, the way he would soon be entering her. Her moan met his.

He pulled away.

"No," she protested.

"I know." He pulled a packet from the nightstand drawer and opened it without letting his gaze leave hers.

She watched as he rolled the thin covering over that part of him that would soon give her so much release, so much pleasure.

Then he came back to her and gathered her close again.

He covered her mouth with his, and still lost in their kiss, he shifted and was above her, against her, then in her. She welcomed him and closed around him as he completed her the way it was destined.

She followed where he led her, trusting him with her body and her heart and her soul.

They moved in the joining that was as old as time but new and different and perfect between them.

She thought about how right this was. Then she didn't think, couldn't think at all, as she rode to the crest with him, and tumbled over the edge still coupled in his arms.

Thirteen

With her eyes still closed, Linda smiled, stretched, and nestled deeper under the covers. The warmth of the sun shone through the curtains, but she wasn't ready to open her eyes yet; she was too contented the way she was.

"Good morning, beautiful. I hope you slept well."

The whisper in her ear was just as arousing as the words Avery had spoken to her last night. And again several times during the night.

"I slept well, but not much." She looked at him. His gaze on her was warm.

"Is that a complaint?" Leaning on one elbow he moved his other hand in slow circles over her stomach, inching higher, slowing when he reached the fullness of the base of her breasts. She arched toward his hand, but he moved it out of reach. His gaze never left hers.

"No." She placed her hand on his chest and her smile widened. She didn't have to wonder anymore about how his chest would feel under her hands. Last night he had given her the right to find out. She stroked her fingers through the mat of chest hair and was rewarded when his muscles tightened in response. She continued to stroke.

"Good answer." His husky words caressed her as his hand did the same beneath her breasts, still avoiding the tips. "I wouldn't want you to be dissatisfied." He kissed the side of her face.

"Good answer, yourself. I would never be dissatisfied with you."

He chuckled and moved his hand to her thigh. He held it still for a few seconds before he began to trace slow circles there. "I hope you're not in a hurry to leave."

"No. I"—His hand moved higher to the sensitive skin of her inner thigh and the rest of her sentence got lost in what he was doing. And in anticipation of what he was going to do. Again.

"Another good answer." He captured her mouth with his. Then he stared into her eyes. "Quiz shows are lucky you haven't appeared on them. You'd win every prize that they had available."

"I don't need a quiz show to win a prize." She smiled at him. "I have you."

"Yet another good answer. The lady has an endless supply." He cupped her breast in his hand and stroked across the hard tip. Then he removed his hand and captured the same tip with his mouth.

Linda gasped. His hands, his mouth, on her felt as agonizing, as wonderful as they had last night. She thought of how perfect Avery was, how perfect her life was now that they had found each other. He completed her. His hand caressed the sensitive nub hidden in her soft mound, just waiting for his touch. She tightened her hold on him lest she break into little pieces.

Finally he sheathed himself and entered her place that was moist and waiting for him; just for him; and she didn't think; couldn't think anymore; could just feel; him; them as one.

* * *

Perfect. She is perfect. Last night was perfect. So was this morning. The world is perfect.

Later—he had no idea how much later—Avery looked down at the woman still sleeping beside him. The covers were draped at her hips, allowing him to see her full breasts that had filled his hands so perfectly, that had tasted so perfect. He had to find another word for *perfect*. A stronger word. Perfect didn't begin to describe how he felt about her and what had happened between them. If a genie were to appear to him right now, there wasn't anything more he would wish for. He had everything he had ever wanted. He had found it in her.

He wanted to let his hand brush down her invitingly smooth middle and claim it. Her hips flared from her waist and he thought of how he had envied that pink dress that had clung to them, the dress that had been allowed where his hands weren't welcome. Not then, at least. Later . . . He smiled. Later he had eased that dress from her and replaced it with his hands, and it had been worth the wait. He was glad she hadn't made him wait any longer, though. He was glad that she had wanted this as much as he had. Making love with her was more wonderful than he had ever imagined possible. His body tightened at the memory, but he didn't seek relief. Not now. For now, he'd let her sleep.

He brushed a hand across her cap of curls and eased her close to him. He pulled the covers over them and wrapped his arms around her. She turned toward him and nestled against him. Her eyes never opened, but she brushed her lips across his chest before she settled back to sleep. Perfect. There was no other word to describe her and this feeling she created in him. He joined her in sleep.

* * *

"What time is it?" Linda stirred in Avery's arms.

"Why? Do you have somewhere to go?"

"No." She brushed a finger along his jaw.

"The good answers still keep coming even after the time that just passed." He kissed her. Then he sat up and took her with him as he leaned against the back of the headboard. "Nothing can compare with being in bed with you, but how about some breakfast?" He glanced at the clock on the dresser. "We'll call it brunch, although even that will be a stretch in a little while."

"Good idea to go with my good answers."

Linda watched Avery walk to the closet. He must work out. Nobody could have a body like that without working at it. She felt her body tingle at the memory of the pleasure Avery had given her. She had never felt like that before, had never dreamed such deep feelings were possible. What had she done to deserve this?

She smiled as Avery came back to her. He laid one robe on the bed and left the other across his arm.

"Here's one of my robes. I hate for you to cover up such a delectable sight, but if you don't, we'll still be in bed tomorrow this time." He took her hand and eased her from the bed. "Or next week." He pulled her into his arms. "Or next month." He kissed her, then pulled back, but still held her in the circle of his arms. "Or next year." He brushed a finger down her neck. "One day, the mail carrier won't be able to fit another piece of mail through the slot and realize that the mail is piled up on the floor inside the hallway and call the police. They'll find us still in each other's arms, here in bed, having starved to death."

He smiled, and the heat in his eyes reached her and kindled a similar heat within her.

He opened the robe and held it behind her, but still held her stare with his. She struggled to find the armholes without looking. She didn't want to take her gaze from him for a second.

"Here. Allow me." He touched her shoulder and slowly moved his hand down her arm and guided it into place. Then he kissed her other shoulder and did the same with her other arm.

"What a shame to cover up such a view." Slowly he turned her and pulled her robe together, brushing his fingers across her middle as he did. His hands stayed still and Linda had a hard time remembering whether she was taking the robe off or putting it on, until he looped the belt, then took a step back and reached for the other robe.

"Oh, no. Allow me." Linda stretched the robe behind him, rubbing against his chest as she did so, loving the feel of the rough hair against her sensitive breasts.

"You're killing me."

"I didn't ask a question, but you have good answers of your own this morning." She stroked her fingers across his chest. "I'm only returning the favor."

Avery chuckled and slipped his hands into the sleeves. He started to tie the belt.

"No, no, no." Linda brushed his hands aside. "That's my job." She pressed her lips to his chest once, then again, before she slowly drew the robe together and tied the belt. She brushed her hand across his covered body and felt his middle tighten. Hers did the same. "My view is different, but I agree with your opinion." She laughed and he joined his laughter with hers.

"I would suggest a shower, but we'd end up in bed instead of in the kitchen. We'll save that bit of togetherness until later. You can use the bathroom in here. I'll use one of the others."

A wide, soft smile spread across Linda's face as she watched him go. Then she placed her overnight bag on the bed and took out clean underwear. Her smile softened even more. When she had packed this bag she had expected to use it at her parents' house. She had never imagined that she would spend the weekend with Avery. What a development. What a glorious, marvelous, fantastic development. She twirled in a little circle. If someone had told her at the time she met Avery that he would want her, she would have accused them of being out of touch with reality. This was reality and it was better than she ever dreamed it could be. She went to the master bathroom and just looked at it. This was dreamlike, too.

Polished black marble covered the floor of the room as large as an average-size bedroom. More marble covered the lower part of the wall before giving way to a bold wallpaper striped in green, blue, purple, and white.

Linda stepped inside, expecting the floor to be cold, but the comfortable temperature under her bare feet told her that it was heated from underneath. Thick, rich mats the same colors as the stripes in the wallpaper led to the large clawfoot tub under a wide window showing a view of the large backyard. A marble ledge under the window held a large brass pot filled with ferns and two smaller ones of ivy. Baskets placed between the pots spilled washcloths of every bright color imaginable.

The tub looked old, but Linda knew it wasn't because of the whirlpool jets scattered around the inside. A huge brass pot on the floor held fluffy bath towels that matched the washcloths. An array of bath salts, soaps, and fancy bottles of bubble bath were tucked into the wide ledge over the corner of the tub. She could imagine herself soaking in the tub while thick creamy candles flickered around. It was tempting. She smiled. Maybe later. With Avery. She looked beyond the tub.

Placed in a nook just made for it, a large granite shower stall dominated one corner of the room. Shiny brass shower heads were positioned on three sides near the middle as well as near the top. She'd use the shower. This time.

She turned on the water, tested the temperature, and stepped inside. Since she was alone, she didn't linger.

She dried off with one of the towels hanging on the heated rack beside the shower. With the towel wrapped around her, she went to the vanity taking up one whole wall. Two sinks with brass fixtures where placed close to each other. A gilt-framed mirror spanned the wall above the counter.

Linda didn't spend much time admiring it. She used Avery's comb and brush and hurried to get dressed. She missed him. She pulled on a pink T-shirt and a fitted denim skirt and went to find Avery.

Avery showered quickly and pulled on jeans and a T-shirt. He never lingered in the shower, but this morning especially . . . He grinned. It wasn't morning anymore. His body tightened as he remembered why he was so late taking his shower. He set a new speed record for showering and hurried toward the kitchen. Maybe she was already there waiting for him.

Avery hummed. He stopped beating the eggs for the omelet, grinned wider, and sang a few words of a current love song. *Eat your heart out, Luther,* he thought.

He put four slices of oat bran bread in the toaster and turned the sausages. *When was the last time I felt like singing?* He couldn't remember.

The faint sound of the shower drifted to the kitchen and his body tightened again at the memory of the night he had just spent with her. With Linda. There should be a song about luscious Linda. Beautiful Linda. Sexy Linda. Linda who had spent the night—his smile widened—and this morning in his bed with him. He couldn't say sleeping with him. They hadn't done much sleeping.

He shifted from one foot to the other and was glad the shower had stopped. A few more minutes and he would have been up there with her, and again they would be not sleeping.

He placed the sausage onto paper towels to drain. He poured the egg mixture into the skillet and pushed the toaster lever down then he heard her coming down the hall.

How could he have thought anything was important enough to stand between them? He and Linda were meant to be together. What had happened before had nothing to do with them now.

"Morning, Avery." Linda's smile was soft as she went to him.

"Hi, Honey."

Avery turned off the stove and turned to face her. He drew her close. He didn't think it was possible, but she felt better in his arms than he remembered. "There's no way, not by anybody's clock, that this could be considered morning." He kissed the side of her face and caressed her back through her deep-pink blouse. "Pink. I like you in pink. After seeing you in that dress, pink is my second favorite color. Right after honey tan." He kissed her lips again as he brushed his hands slowly up and down her hips.

"Stop that, or I'll never get brunch." She glanced at the large clock on the wall. "Or whatever you call the meal between lunch and dinner." She giggled, patted his chest, and eased away from him.

She poured Avery's coffee and her tea and set them on the table in the breakfast nook under a large window that gave them another view of the backyard. Then she went back to be near him.

"I call it 'after a fantastic night and unbelievable

morning of perfect lovemaking.' If anybody else discovers it, it's sure to catch on."

He turned the perfect omelettes onto plates. Linda put the toast onto another plate and followed him to the table. There was plenty of other seating, but he led her to a bench and slid in beside her.

"To think I gave the decorator a hard time about benches instead of chairs all around." He moved closer so that his thigh was brushing against hers.

"You'll have to call and apologize." Linda tasted the omelette. "This is delicious. You can cook for me anytime."

"It's a deal as long as I can have what came before." He grinned at her. "Deal?" Avery ate a forkful of eggs.

"Deal."

"I don't like to rehash things, but this time I'll make an exception." He looked at her and his gaze softened. "I never dreamed it would be like that. It was worth waiting until our differences worked themselves out."

"It was great for me, too. I never imagined . . ." She stared at him. Finally she blinked free. "I always get lost when I look at you."

"Don't worry." Avery cupped her chin in his hand and kissed her quickly. "The same thing happens to me when I look at you, but together we'll always find our way."

They finished the meal in silence, but every few bites they stared at each other. They cleared the table and loaded the dishwasher.

"I guess I'd better go home."

"What's your hurry?"

"I know you have work to do. I figured I'd just be in your way."

"You're still trying to give me a reason to get rid of you."

Linda didn't answer. She just shrugged.

"You couldn't be in my way." He frowned. "Maybe you're ready to leave?"

"Not unless you want me to."

"What I want concerning you has nothing to do with you leaving me. Okay?"

"Okay." She smiled.

"Good. Now that we have that out of the way, would you like to see what the yard looks like? If we stay inside, I'm going to take you back to bed and then getting dressed will have been a waste of time."

Avery took her hand and led her through the back door and into the yard.

They followed a brick path winding through the huge yard.

"Oh." Linda stopped in front of a stone fountain set back from the path, spilling water from a large bowl on a pedestal into a long, wide pond. Koi goldfish flashed as they swam among the water plants anchored on the bottom. A wooden bench invitingly faced the pond. Tall hedges almost completely hid the stone wall behind them.

"Come on." Avery tugged her farther along the path. The next niche held another fountain. This one was a statue of a girl pouring water from a pot.

Other surprises were tucked on both sides of the walkway. It was hard for Linda to believe that they weren't in some European countryside miles away from any other houses.

Avery stopped when they reached a rose garden. Blossoms ranging in color from white through all shades of pink and red covered dozens of bushes.

"Beautiful."

"Yeah." Avery pulled her against him. "Until yesterday, I couldn't decide which shade was my favorite. Now I know it's pink." He nuzzled her ear. "And not just any pink. A certain shade of deep pink, like the dress you wore."

Linda leaned against him and let the perfume from the roses surround her.

After a while they moved on. Avery explained how he'd decided on the landscape plan.

"Roses were my mother's favorite flower. She was gone before the garden was completed, but I planted them in her memory."

They strolled slowly back to the house, stopping to watch birds at several of the feeders and baths scattered throughout the yard.

They both knew what would happen when they got back to the house, but they didn't rush. They had plenty of time.

Avery drew her close when they got back inside the house. He claimed her lips in the kiss she had been waiting for. Then, wrapped in each other's arms, they went to the bedroom to prove their love yet again.

Later that evening they had a light meal. It was still early, but they went back to bed.

It was barely morning when Linda opened her eyes again.

"Morning, Love." Avery grinned down at her. "Yes, it really is morning."

"Ummm." Linda stretched. "I feel like a cat looks when it stretches."

"I hope it's a good feeling, although I don't believe it could feel as good as it looks." He kissed the side of her face. "I have an idea."

"Will I like it?"

"I hope so, since you're the most important part of it."

Linda sat up and tucked the sheet under her arms.

"Now I'm intrigued." She brushed her hand across his bare chest. "What is it?"

"When I selected the fixtures for my bathroom, I was told that the shower is big enough to fit two people comfortably. I never tested it." He wrapped his arms around her. "Would you be willing to help me find out?"

Linda stroked her fingers through the hair on his chest.

"I guess I could manage to help you with your little experiment." She pulled gently. "Never let it be said that I stood in the way of science."

"Good." Avery stood. He tugged her up with him.

"Anxious, aren't we?"

"I don't know about the 'we' part, but I certainly am. You know, scientific discovery and all that." He took her hand and led her to the bathroom.

"This is strictly in the interest of science, right?"

"Of course. What other motive would I have?"

They both laughed as they went to the shower. Soon their laughter faded and they were making other discoveries about the shower and learning how it wasn't just for getting clean.

They also tested the softness of the bathroom floor mats. Linda was grateful for the heated floor. When they switched positions, she knew Avery was grateful, too. Now they were back in the bedroom.

"I really have to go." Linda pulled on her top and reached for her skirt as Avery watched her.

"Don't you want to stay tonight, too?" Avery tightened the forest green towel that was wrapped around his middle and moved to stand close to her. He nuzzled her neck.

"As tempting as that sounds, I can't. I promised my parents I'd have dinner at their house today." She looked down at her clothes. "We don't exactly dress up for Sunday dinner, but we don't wear 'bum around' clothes, either, so I have to go home to change first."

"I guess it's just as well." He caressed her shoulder. "I'll miss you no matter when you leave."

"I'll miss you, too." Linda brushed her fingers down the side of his face. She smiled when his muscles tightened and desire flared in his eyes. "Tell you what. I'll go straighten the bathroom. You get dressed."

"You don't think this is appropriate attire?" He touched the towel.

"Not for driving me home." She eased his face down to hers and slowly kissed him. "It is, however, the perfect preliminary for another activity."

"Yes." He held her close. "But you're overdressed for that." He brushed his fingers slowly from the side of her head to the side of her hips before his hands settled there. "We can take care of that, you know. We still have time." He slipped his hands under her top. "I can't get enough of you."

She took in a deep breath that swelled her breasts as Avery's fingers grazed against them.

"I just got dressed." She placed her hands on his towel and wrapped her fingers around the knot.

"I'll help you undress." He placed a kiss at the top of her breasts through her T-shirt. "Didn't I do a good job last night?"

Linda felt heat flood her face. She groaned as Avery moved his hands up and cupped her breasts. She groaned again when he brushed his thumbs across the hard tips.

"Avery." She could barely get the word out.

He lifted her shirt over her head. He dropped it and ran his fingers along the lace edge of her bra.

"Avery." His name was a plea for relief.

"Blue lace this time. I'm going to enjoy discovering the other colors of your lingerie, but right now, this is in our way." He unhooked her bra and gazed when her breasts stood free and waiting for him. He found one tip and Linda moaned when he drew it gently into his mouth.

She fumbled with his towel until it fell away, then she settled her hands at his waist. Avery covered her lips with his. She slid her hands up around his back, pulling his hips closer. Home and leaving Avery were forgotten as he took her back to bed.

"I really have to go this time." Linda eased away from Avery and stood. She gathered her clothes for the second time. "You stay there until I leave the room."

"Yes, Ma'am." Avery grinned at her.

"I'll get dressed in one of the other bathrooms this time."

"I don't know why." His innocent look was destroyed by the twinkle in his eye.

"You get dressed in here. Or in the bathroom. It doesn't matter as long as it's not in the same room that I'm in."

"So you're one of those, huh?"

"One of those what?" Linda paused in the doorway and frowned at him.

"One of those 'use them and throw them away when you're finished with them' people."

"Throwing you away is not an option. Besides, I'm not finished with you yet."

Avery swung his feet onto the floor, and Linda held up a hand as if to stop him from coming close.

"Don't come over here." She backed out into the hall. "If you touch me now, I'll never get to my parents' house." She looked at the clock on his nightstand. "As it is, I'll have to wear what I have on."

"Yes, I know." Avery stood. "I mean what I have here."

Linda's gaze followed him as he got out fresh clothes. Gorgeous. He probably wouldn't appreciate the use of that word to describe him, but it suited him.

"Don't look at me like that, or I'll feel obligated to satisfy the hunger I see in your eyes."

"Much as I'd enjoy that, don't come near me. Get dressed while I go do the same."

"Yes, Ma'am." He turned toward the bathroom, but turned back to face her. "I'm giving you fair warning. If you're still there when I come out, I'll take it as an invitation."

"Go. If you don't, I'll never get out of here."

"But isn't that a great way to spend the rest of your life?"

"Most definitely."

They both laughed. Avery went into the bathroom and Linda went to a guest bathroom. *I can think of worse ways to spend my life,* she thought as she got dressed.

Fourteen

Linda waited in the living room for Avery to finish getting dressed. Even after the past two glorious nights and the one fabulous day, she was still having a hard time believing that she and Avery had finally gotten together. She smiled. "Gotten together" did not come close to describing what had happened between them. Neither did "what happened." Her smile widened. Wow. She had thought, no, hoped, wished, that he felt about her the way she felt about him, but she had decided that it was all wishful thinking on her part. Now, here he was. She sighed. No. Here *they* were, tangled up in each other just like they had been when they made love. As they would be the next time they made love. She had never dreamed it could be like that, so intense, so deep, so fulfilling. Her smile disappeared. Too bad they couldn't stay locked up in their own little world for the rest of their lives. Reality did have a way of inserting itself on you, whether you were ready or not. She shifted her bag from one hand to the other. What would Avery say about her suggestion? He had never mentioned commitment. Maybe he just looked on her as an itch that he had to scratch.

"What's that look on your face?" Avery pulled his sport shirt down as he walked into the living room and stood in front of her.

"I don't supposed you'd like to go to dinner with me and meet my parents? I know you have a lot of work to do tonight and the next few days. You have to get ready for that meeting in Atlanta on Wednesday. And you always have a desk full of paperwork to wade through. This is probably not a good time for you." She shrugged. Maybe that was a commitment that he wasn't ready to make yet. Maybe not ever. "Never mind. It's a bad idea. Maybe some other time." She stood.

"You don't want me to meet your parents?"

"Of course I do."

"Then why did you change your mind?"

"I didn't. I . . ."

"You just thought you'd make it easy for me to refuse." He wrapped his arms around her loosely and stared down at her. He gave her a quick kiss. "I'd love to go with you if you're sure it's all right with them. If I thought it would be appropriate, I'd even thank them for you."

Linda smiled and relaxed. "I'll call Mom and let her know that I'm on the way and that I'm bringing you with me."

"Will she have enough to squeeze another person in for dinner? This is awfully short notice."

"She always cooks more than enough; you know how our folks go all out for Sunday dinner." Her smile widened. "Be right back."

Linda finished with the short call and they walked to the garage with their arms around each other. They only let go long enough to get into the car.

"What's the going rate?" Avery pulled out of his driveway and onto the street.

"For what?"

"For thoughts. It used to be a penny, but that was years ago. I know the price must have gone up."

"For you, there is no charge. I was thinking about my

parents." She shrugged. "I know I'm grown, but I'm still uneasy. They'll take one look at me and know that I spent the weekend with you."

"Let me see." Avery eased her face toward him. "Nope. I can't see it."

"What?"

"The scarlet letter. All I see is the beautiful face of a woman who is beautiful inside as well as outside. I don't even see a hint of sensuality, and I know that's a big part of you."

Linda laughed. "Okay. Tell me about the Atlanta meeting. How do you think it will go?"

The rest of the ride was spent talking about Avery's meeting with the board of a national trust foundation. The proposal he would present involved plans to expand the center's program to include adult activities such as a literacy program as well as computer training. Linda was more relaxed when Avery pulled into her parents' long, wide driveway

When they got out of the car, she put a hand on Avery's arm.

"I'd better warn you about Daddy."

"What about him?"

"He can be . . ." She shrugged. "Believe it or not, in spite of all that happened to me, he's still very protective. He was always intimidating to anyone I brought home. That was a long time ago, but he probably hasn't changed. I don't know if it's fair to subject you to his scrutiny."

"I can understand why he'd be protective. If you were my daughter, I'd want to keep you in my sight at all times." Avery's stare grew more intense. "Did he have many chances to do that?"

"What?"

"Intimidate the guys you brought home?"

"A few." She looked at him. "Not too many. None of the guys were as important to me as you are."

"The good answers still just keep on coming. You must have been an A-plus student."

Linda laughed and he laughed with her. She laced her fingers through Avery's as they walked to the house.

Sheila opened the door as soon as they rang the bell.

"Hi, Sis." They hugged. Then Linda pulled away and took Avery's hand. "You remember Avery."

Sheila stared at him for a few seconds, then she smiled.

"Hi, Avery. Come on in."

"Hi. We didn't get a chance to meet at the dance, but Linda told me about you."

"Please don't tell me that she told you all about me."

"No, she didn't." He followed her into the house. Talking hadn't been high on their 'Things to Do' list this past weekend. He squeezed Linda's hand.

"Is Dad watching the game?" Linda squeezed his hand back, but she didn't look at him.

"If there's a game on, what else would he be doing?"

"That's true."

Avery laughed with them and it seemed as if he belonged with the family.

"I'll go back to Mom," Sheila said before she left them.

"Tell her I'll be there in a minute."

She slid her hand into Avery's and led him into the family room. Some things never change, she thought as she saw her father sitting in his favorite chair. She squeezed Avery's hand. And some things do.

She introduced Avery to her father who stood and looked from her to Avery. Linda felt as if he knew that she had spent the past day and a half with Avery at his house. She held her breath as her father stared at Avery for a few seconds more. Something during the game made the crowd go wild, but none of them looked to find out what it was.

Her father's gaze slid to her again. She shook her head and hoped he would heed her plea. He held her gaze for a few seconds longer before he held out his hand to Avery.

"Football player, huh?"

"I used to be."

"We were happy for Linda when she started working for you at your center. She needed for someone to give her a chance to overcome that terrible time in her life."

"I'm glad she came to the center, too. She's been a valuable asset to our program. The kids are crazy about her." He took the hand Linda had freed from his. "I've grown to care a lot for her, too."

"She's been through a lot, which she didn't deserve. I don't want her to get hurt again."

"I don't intend to hurt her, Dr. Durard."

"You're here." Linda's mother came from the dining room. "I was about ready to give up on you."

Linda was glad her mother hugged her before she had a chance to see the color flood her face as she thought of why she was late. She hoped her color was back to normal when her mother pulled away.

"This is Avery." Linda hoped her voice didn't sound as husky to her mother as it did to her.

"Welcome to our home." Mrs. Durard looked at him for a few seconds before she smiled and held out her hand. "Come on. Let's go sit down. Dinner's ready, Charles." She called to her husband.

"I'm coming. Your timing is good today. It's half time."

"Well, come on before—"

"Everything gets cold," Linda and her father finished for her.

She laughed with them.

"At least I know my message got through."

During the meal of candied yams, ham, and peas, Avery answered questions about the center. Linda didn't allow herself to relax until her father brought the conversation to football. A good-natured discussion began about the current Eagles team, the players let go after the last season, and the new draft picks.

Linda and Sheila were as interested in the conversation as their father and Avery. They had spent many Sundays watching games with their father and had attended many home games. Then the subject centered on quarterbacks.

"It doesn't matter who throws the ball if he doesn't have anybody to catch it." Linda launched into her opinion about the draft. "They should have taken a receiver. There was nothing wrong with their quarterback."

"You're really into football, aren't you?" Avery smiled at her. "I'm impressed."

"I can't help it." Linda smiled back at him. For a few seconds they were alone. Then she blinked and looked at her father. "Daddy dragged me to games as soon as I could walk." She grinned at her father. "I think he considered it parent bonding. When Sheila was four, she came with us. My collection of Eagle T-shirts gives a history of the team logos and the players."

"So." Avery looked around the table. "Did you paint your faces green and white for the games?"

"Never. Mom wouldn't let us."

Linda and Sheila giggled. Then they and their father all began talking at the same time, giving the merits of their favorite players. Soon the conversation centered on quarterbacks.

"Stop. Enough." Her mother looked at Linda. "You had to bring home a football guy, huh?" She put slices of coconut cake onto dessert plates and passed them around. "Now. What do you think of Denzel's latest movie?"

"Don't let Mom fool you." Linda looked at Avery. "She watches football, too. She gets as caught up in it as we do. That's why she does a lot of the cooking for Sunday dinner on Saturday."

"Don't you tell Avery about the time I burned the pot of greens." She shook her head. "I still don't know how it happened. One minute they were full of water and the next thing I knew they were as dry as when they were picked." She pretended to glare at her family. "How can I help looking at a game every now and then. It's the only way I get to spend time with my family during football season." She glanced around the table. "Now I hope all of you do justice to my cake. It's Linda's favorite." She smiled. "No more discussions of quarterbacks." She picked up her fork and looked at the others again. "Everybody knows Randall was the best, hands down." Her grin widened. They all laughed, including Avery. Linda relaxed. Avery belonged here with her family. They had accepted him.

Linda turned to Sheila. "How's school? Did you get into the five-year med school program you used to talk about?"

"Yes, though sometimes I question the state of my sanity when I made the choice. I understand the usual premed/med school program is rough enough in itself. The five-year program is almost impossible."

"Don't you believe it, Avery. She's leading every class except physiology, and there she has a high 'B.' "

"But it's kicking me, though."

"You always did complain in school all the while you were leaving everybody in the dust," Linda said.

"It's hard work."

"Of course it is. But somebody has to do it. It may as well be you."

Sheila swatted Linda's arm.

"Same old Linda."

"You're going to get your doctor after all, Daddy. I know you're proud of her."

"I'm proud of both of my daughters. I just want you both to be happy. That's all I ever wanted." He smiled at them. "Now why don't you tell us about this computer program of yours? Your mother is taking a computer class and she loves it, but I'm still not sure whether I like them."

The conversation switched to computers and programs and for once the second half of the game was forgotten.

They were finished with dessert when Sheila turned to Linda.

"I've been thinking about tomorrow and I have things worked out better than what you have planned. You take my car with you tonight. That way you can get started as early as you want to in the morning. Daddy can give me a ride into school, and Mom can pick me up after classes. I'm sorry I can't help you move, but I have a full schedule tomorrow. I can help tomorrow night if you want to wait or if you're not finished by then." She looked at her parents. "Is that schedule okay with both of you?"

"You need a car tomorrow morning?" Avery asked.

"Yes. I'm moving to an apartment. It's only a few blocks from Auntie's house." She had forgotten that Avery didn't know anything about that. She felt as if he knew everything concerning her. Things had happened so fast between them. "I felt like it was time for me to get my own place."

"How can you move by yourself? Why didn't you say something to me about it?"

She stared at him and lifted her eyebrows, but didn't say anything. *Because we were busy with other things.*

Avery nodded slightly.

"It's a furnished apartment. I just have my personal things to move and a few things I borrowed from the Durard attic. I can do it before I come to work tomorrow afternoon. Having Sheila's car will give me more time to work since I won't have to take the bus. I'll return it after I leave the center."

"I offered you a car of your own. If you weren't so stubborn, you wouldn't have to borrow your sister's car."

"I know, Daddy, and I appreciate your offer, but I want to earn my own."

"I know you said not to bother, but I have a suggestion," her father said. "If you start early enough, I can help before I go into work. I'll rearrange my schedule. I have hospital visits first. I can push them back. My patients aren't going anywhere that early, anyway."

"We've been over this. I can do it by myself. It's not like Auntie gave me a deadline." She looked at Avery. "As long as I get to work on time, things will be all right. What I don't finish before work I can finish when I get off from work. Or I can do it Tuesday. Or Wednesday. The apartment is mine. It's not going anywhere."

"I'll help."

Everybody looked at Avery.

"What about the report you have to take with you to Atlanta? You have to finish that."

"It's not like it's due tomorrow. I'll have it ready in plenty of time for Tuesday's meeting. It doesn't make sense for everybody in your family to rearrange their schedules when this is a perfect solution."

"You're sure?" Dr. Durard asked Avery. "It's no problem for me to go to the hospital later." He looked at Linda. "If Miss Independent had let me know earlier, it would all have been worked out ahead of time."

"I didn't tell you because I didn't want you to change your schedule. I repeat. I only have my personal things to move. It won't take me long. I can do it myself." She leaned toward Sheila. "I thought we had things worked out until little Miss Helpful decided to make things better."

"Sorry." Sheila grimaced. "I thought I had a great idea."

"If you can help her move, Avery, then I'll leave my schedule as is."

"No problem."

"Excuse me?" Linda looked at the two men who were talking as if she weren't there. "Who's making this move, anyway?"

"You are, Baby," her father said, "but I know exactly how stubborn you can be sometimes."

"I wonder where she got that from," her mother murmured.

Sheila giggled. Linda and her father shrugged at the same time.

"I give up." Linda turned to Avery. "Okay. I appreciate your offer of help."

"Don't let her change her mind when she gets away from me." Her father took a sip of coffee.

"Would I do that?"

"Absolutely, if you thought you could get away with it."

They all laughed. Linda stood.

"We'd better be going if we want to get an early start in the morning." Linda smiled. "It won't take as long, though, with the help I'll have."

Linda hugged everybody good-bye and she and Avery left.

"Are you sure you have time to help me? I really can do it by myself."

"I'll tell your daddy if you don't let me help."

He pulled her close and she snuggled against him. "It's been a long time since I've touched you." He kissed her before he started the car. "I missed you."

"I missed you, too." Linda patted his chest. They finished the ride to Auntie's house touching from their shoulders to their thighs. Linda smiled the whole way. It had been a good visit. It was as if her family had known Avery for years.

Avery parked in front of Auntie's house.

"I'll walk you to the house. It's been a long time since I've seen Auntie."

He helped her out. Then, with one arm around her waist and the bag in his other hand, he walked with her to the house.

Linda called out to Auntie, but there was no answer. The note propped on the mantel told her that Auntie had gone with the choir and the pastor to help an out-of-town church celebrate its anniversary. Linda couldn't help the feeling of relief flooding through her at not having to face Auntie with Avery.

"I saw that."

"What?"

"How you relaxed when you found out that Auntie isn't here."

"I can't help it. I know she'd be able to look at me and tell I spent two nights with you." She shook her head. "I know I'm grown." She shrugged. "But I can't help it."

"That's okay. That's just another thing about you for me to love." He kissed her. "What time should I pick you up tomorrow morning?"

"What do you think would be a good time? I don't want you to have to wake up too early."

"What makes you think that I'll be able to sleep?" He nuzzled her neck.

"I know what you mean." She wrapped her arms

around him. "I'd suggest we start tonight, but I don't want to start off wrong with the neighbors by disturbing them."

He brushed his lips across hers.

"Is eight o'clock too early or is nine better?"

"Eight is fine. I won't be able to sleep much, either."

"Okay." He kissed her deeper then pulled away, still holding her in the circle of his arms. "I'll see you tomorrow morning."

"Yes, tomorrow morning." Her voice was husky. Avery brushed his hands along the sides of her breasts and Linda moaned.

"I'd better leave while I can."

"Yes." Her voice was lower and weaker.

Neither one moved for a while. Then he stepped away from her and sighed.

"My bed will be too big and impossibly empty without you to share it with me tonight." He smiled. "How did you get to be a habit so quickly?"

"I don't know." She shook her head. "If you find out, tell me so that I'll know how you did the same thing to me." She widened the space between them.

"Good night, Love." Avery kissed two fingers and touched them to her lips.

"Good night, Avery. I'll see you in the morning."

Linda locked the door behind him and leaned against it until she heard him drive away.

She took a deep breath. Her body tingled with remembering. Something long dead had awakened under Avery's touch. Avery. She smiled. She had never met anyone like him before. No one had ever made her feel as deeply as he did. He completed her. When he held her, nothing existed except the two of them. She pushed off from the door. She could hardly wait for tomorrow to come.

She picked up her bag and floated up the stairs.

***

Linda. From the start Avery had known there had been an attraction. It had pulled at him in spite of the anger he had felt at what she had done. He had wanted her almost from the beginning. He didn't know exactly when. One time anger swelled in him whenever he saw her, and the next time his anger had been replaced by desire, and soon after that need had replaced his desire. He had needed to feel how her soft body felt against his, needed to taste her sweetness. He smiled. It had finally happened. She had spent the weekend with him in pleasure more sensual than he had thought possible. And it would happen again. He'd see her tomorrow. He shifted as his body tightened in anticipation. If they worked really fast at moving, maybe, just maybe, they'd have time to see if there was anything new for them to learn about the other's body.

He glanced at the dashboard clock. A lot of hours lay between then and now.

Avery drove past his street, turned around, and pulled into his garage. He sat there lost in the possibilities that the next day held until the automatic light in the garage went out, leaving him in darkness and reminding him that he was still in the car.

He grinned as he went into the house. Tomorrow. He would see her tomorrow. His body tightened in anticipation at the promise that tomorrow held.

Fifteen

At six o'clock in the morning Linda stopped pretending she expected to go back to sleep. She looked at the jeans and T-shirt she had left out to put on. She knew that she was going to get dirty, but she stared at the blue slacks set on top of the pile of clothes on hangers on the chair. She smiled. She had tried on everything she owned trying to find the perfect outfit to wear for Avery. Then common sense took over and she decided on a royal blue T-shirt. And blue socks. Even her sneakers had blue stripes. Her smile softened. Avery had a lot of blue in his house. That must be his favorite color. His bedroom drapes and bedspread had a lot of blue in them. She sighed. His sheets were blue, too. Warmth spread through her body. She took a deep breath and closed her eyes.

When he took her in his arms and made love with her, she forgot all about the color of the sheets. She forgot everything except Avery fulfilling the promises his hands and his kisses had made.

She ran a brush through her hair. Then she slipped it into her purse, folded the rest of her clothes over her arm, and went downstairs to wait for Avery.

By seven o'clock she was sitting on the couch peeping out the window, watching for Avery. Bags and boxes filled the hall. She had moved them downstairs the night before so that she and Avery wouldn't disturb Auntie, who had gotten in late, in the morning. Despite Auntie's vow to get up early to see Linda off, Linda had insisted they say good-bye the night before just in case.

She sighed. She'd miss this woman who had become like a grandmother to her. Linda was glad she wasn't moving far away. She'd see Auntie at least once a week.

She looked at her watch. 7:15. Still a long time before she could see him. She had started to call him when she woke up, but she didn't. Maybe he had spent a better night than she had. She could have blamed her restlessness on the excitement of moving, if memories of Avery hadn't kept springing up. How had so many strong memories about him formed so quickly?

She glanced at her watch again. 7:25. A snail moved faster than time's pace this morning. *Maybe he will come early.*

This is ridiculous, Avery thought. He glanced at his watch. 7:06. Almost an hour early. He parked around the corner from Auntie's, the only spot he could find. He sighed. He hadn't been this early for his first date. He smiled. Of course, Linda hadn't been the one waiting for him back then.

Linda. In a few minutes he'd see her, touch her. He wouldn't be able to hold her the way he wanted to, but he could hug her, kiss her, and remember and hope they'd finish early enough. His body tightened at the idea. His hormones were raging worse than ever. He hoped she would wear that gardenia perfume. Of course he didn't need her near in order for him to hope.

Finally, at twenty minutes before eight o'clock, he pulled up in front of Auntie's house. He double-parked and put on his blinkers. *There isn't anything wrong with being early.* It was better than being late.

He smiled as he walked up the steps. If she didn't want to go to the apartment early, they'd find some way to spend the twenty minutes that they both would enjoy. He grinned as some of the possibilities trotted through his mind.

Linda opened the door before he had a chance to ring the bell.

"Hi, Avery."

His grin widened. She had been waiting for him, watching for him. She had been as impatient to see him as he had been to see her.

He let his gaze travel over her body before it settled on her face. She was every bit as beautiful as he remembered. His memory hadn't been playing tricks on him when it disturbed him throughout the night. His body tightened at the eagerness in her eyes.

"Hi, Love."

He stepped inside and gathered her into his arms. "I missed you," he whispered before he kissed her. She tasted better than he remembered. He didn't think that was possible.

He let his lips sample her jaw and the side of her neck before they moved back to claim her mouth again.

When he forced himself away from her, she had as much trouble breathing as he did. Good.

"Did you sleep well?" The twinkle in Linda's eye told Avery that she already knew the answer to her question.

"As well as you probably did."

He skimmed his hands down the side of her breasts before they settled at her waist.

"That well, huh?" Linda kissed his jaw and stared at him.

"Yeah. You worked magic on my bed. I don't know how you did it, but it's too big for me, now."

"I know what you mean." She grinned. "You haven't even been in my bed, and it was too large last night."

"Of course, along with that magic thing you did with the bed"—Avery slid his hands to her hips and eased her against him—"there's the spell you cast on my body." He kissed her.

"I know that feeling, too." She gasped as his hands cupped her bottom and pulled her even closer against his hardness. "You've perfected some magic skills of your own."

Avery sighed and moved his hands to her shoulders. He took a step back.

"We'd better go while we can or we'll still be here when it's time to go to the center."

Linda stepped aside so he could come into the house.

Avery stood with his mouth open. "You were going to move all of this by yourself?" He stared at the boxes and bags and suitcases taking up so much space there was barely room to stand.

"I didn't want to inconvenience anybody. As I said last night, I'm not on any timetable."

"But you do want to finish sometime this year, right?" He stared at her. "You know, there's nothing wrong with accepting help from somebody who cares about you." He brushed his lips across hers.

"I know." She stayed within his arms.

"Much as I love holding you"—he kissed her cheek—"and want to take it further . . ." He brushed his lips along her neck. "We'd better get started."

They sighed at the same time. Then they grabbed some of the things and began carrying them to the car.

Hours later the last of the things had been carried into the apartment and placed in the living room.

"What do you want to unpack first?"

Linda looked at her watch.

"Nothing. We'd better go."

Avery glanced at his watch and shook his head. "I'm afraid you're right. We can stop for lunch on the way."

"We'd better make it fast-food to go." Linda smiled. "I don't want to be late. My boss had a fit the first day because I showed up early. I don't know how he'd react if I was late."

"I think he's changed into a more reasonable man. He realizes how dumb that approach was." He kissed her before he let her go. "I didn't think it would take this long to move your things. The only reason I can take you out of here now without christening your new home is because I expect to be invited in when I bring you home tonight." He leaned forward and kissed her again. "I want to make sure you understand that while I'm willing to help you finish unpacking, that's not what I'm looking forward to." He brushed his lips along the side of her face. "Even if it is too many hours from now." He kissed her forehead. "Way too many hours."

"Consider yourself invited in if you have time." She brushed a finger down his jaw, kissed his chin, and eased away from him.

"I always have time for you."

They held hands as they left and only let go when they got to the car.

They were holding hands again as Avery carried their lunches into the center.

"You're later than usual." Bill smiled at them.

Linda realized she was still holding Avery's hand and pulled away. Bill's smile widened.

"I moved into my own place this morning. Avery was kind enough to help me."

"Congratulations. That's an important step. Everybody needs their privacy no matter how pleasant a situation they're leaving."

Linda agreed. "I'll go put the water on."

"I'll be there by the time it's hot. I want to check my messages first."

The day dragged for Linda. She didn't see Avery at all. She knew it would have been painful to see him and not touch him, but that didn't ease her disappointment. She had steeled herself for the confrontation with Wanda and was relieved to hear the woman wasn't in.

"I don't need to ask if you had a good time at the dance," Bea said to Linda.

"Neither do I," added Cheryl.

"Me, neither," said Craig.

"Man, don't even try that. You were so wrapped up in your date, you didn't even know where you were," Roz said to him.

Everybody laughed.

"She is fine enough to make a man forget his own name." He looked around the table. "I think I found what I've been looking for for so long."

"I'm glad I'm sitting down." Bea laughed. She looked at Craig. "If it's true, I'm happy for you."

"I think you did some finding of your own, didn't you?" Roz looked at Linda.

"I hope so." Linda felt her color deepen.

"You deserve it," Les said.

Bea looked at Cathy. "Now, Miss Sexy Senior, did that blue dress live up to your expectations?"

"I'm here to tell you that there is more than one kind of lost weekend," Cathy said. "I had to come to work this morning to get some rest from Stan." She sighed heavily. Then she smiled as she looked around the table. "You don't know how tempted I was to take a sick day, although I was as far from sick as I could get."

They all laughed.

She leaned closer to the table. "Do you think we can have another dance real soon?"

The laughter grew louder.

Linda was still smiling when she went back to the lab. She hoped she would be as lucky as Cathy. Her smile faded. She shouldn't get her hopes up. Things had flared between her and Avery so fast. She'd have to take things one step at a time. Her smile returned. That certainly wasn't how they took this past weekend. She was looking forward to this evening's "flare up."

At the end of the evening she tried to slow her steps as she left the lab. She gave up by the time she got to the door to the upstairs hall. She ran down the stairs forgetting all the time she had admonished the kids to take it slow.

"Do you want me to catch the bus?" Linda looked at Avery still sitting at his desk.

"You're kidding, right?"

"Don't you have work to do?"

"Absolutely." He closed the folder and walked toward her. "But I'm not sure work is the correct way to describe it, and what I have in mind has nothing to do with the center." He tucked her arm through his. "Let's go. I don't mix business with pleasure in here, but it is after hours, and if I have to be this close to you and not kiss you, I'll break my rule with a vengeance."

Linda laughed as they left the center.

"Finally." Avery reached for Linda as soon as they were out of the car at her apartment building. He wrapped his arms around her and kissed her. She clung to him as if they had been away from each other's arms for weeks instead of a few hours.

The kiss ended, but they still held each other close as they went up to the apartment.

Unpacking was forgotten as they picked up where they had left off. Was it only two nights ago that they had discovered each other? Linda moved even closer at Avery's urging. He picked her up. She was glad she had made the bed this morning. Then, after Avery carried her to her bedroom, she had other things to be glad about.

"I have to go home."

"I know." Linda cleared away the rest of the take-out that they had ordered after a different hunger drove them from the bed.

"If I had been smart, I would have packed a change of clothes this morning."

"It's probably just as well. Go wrap up your presentation."

"Use me and throw me out when you're finished with me, huh?" Avery grinned at her.

"I am most definitely not finished with you." She kissed him. "I never will be."

He deepened his kiss before he slowly pulled away.

Linda wrapped her arm around his waist and walked him to the door.

"See you tomorrow at the center." She brushed a finger over his lips. He drew it into his mouth before he let it go.

"I really have to go." His words were rough.

"Yes." Linda stepped away. "I'd give you a little shove out the door, but if I touch you again we both know what would happen, don't we?"

Avery's laugh rumbled as he stepped into the hall. His stare caused heat to flow through her.

"I'd better take the stairs. I have to find some way to get rid of this excess energy."

Linda laughed. She didn't close the door until she

heard him on the stairs. Then she ran to the window, glad he had parked close enough for her to watch him drive off.

She remade the bed and got into it, wondering how she was going to sleep without having Avery beside her, touching her.

The next morning Linda was up early. She opened the door as soon as she heard the elevator stop.

Avery walked toward her looking as fine as ever.

"Miss me?" He drew her into his arms and kissed her. Then he gazed at her face. "Are you ready?"

"I'm definitely ready." She grinned. "I'm even set to go, but don't you want to come in for a cup of coffee?" Linda had trouble breathing. She liked the feeling. "We have time."

"If I come in, it won't be for coffee, and we don't have time for what I want." He leaned forward and kissed her. "What *we* want, I mean."

"That's true." She grabbed her purse, pulling the door closed and locking it.

"Are you all set for the presentation in the morning?"

"I will be by the end of the day. It's just about there."

"You didn't get much sleep."

"I wouldn't have gotten much even if I didn't have to work on the plan."

"I know what you mean." They walked to the car.

"I hope it's so perfect that they say yes, open their corporate pockets immediately, and let me come back to you."

"I hope so, too." Linda sighed. "I miss you already."

The ride to the center was spent discussing the presentation that Avery had spent hours working on the previous night.

"I don't know how I'll survive without you for a week."

"I don't want to think about it. I was tempted to ask them to reschedule the national conference, but almost a week away from you at anytime would be nearly impossible."

He held her hand for the rest of the ride. Neither one dared to anticipate their reunion when he returned.

"Hi, Linda, Avery." Bill's usual smile wasn't in place. He looked at Avery. "A buddy of mine on the police force was waiting outside when I got here this morning." He glanced at Linda then back at Avery. He hesitated before he went on. "He said there's been an increase in drug activity in the neighborhood and he thought we should know about it. He suggested that we keep a close watch on every new kid, just in case."

"Thanks, Bill. Let me know if you see anything out of the ordinary or if you hear anything more about it." Avery turned to Linda. His stare seemed to enter her and search for something. Then he blinked.

Had she imagined that look? For a second Linda caught a glimpse of the Avery from weeks earlier. She shook her head. No. It couldn't be.

"I'll be in for coffee in a little while." Avery left Linda in the hall. He didn't touch her, didn't even look at her face.

Linda walked slowly to the lounge. She didn't feel as carefree as she had earlier. Bill hadn't meant anything when he had glanced at her, had he? She swallowed hard. Avery hadn't looked at her differently after he had listened to what Bill had to say, had he? She shook her head. *Please, no.*

She put the water on to heat, all the while trying to deny the accusation she had seen in Avery's face. It was gone almost as quickly as it came, but it had been there. She shook her head. She hadn't seen what she thought she saw. She and Avery were past that. If they weren't, the past weekend wouldn't have happened, would it?

She blinked hard. She was just imagining things, seeing ghosts where there weren't any.

She was glad when the kettle whistled. It gave her something to do.

She turned quickly toward the door when Avery came in. She searched his face for some hint of the Avery of just this morning. She was still looking when he turned his back on her and poured his coffee.

"I'm going to take this back to my office." Avery stirred sugar into his coffee. He was still stirring long after it had dissolved. "I'll see you after we close."

"Do you think there's anything to the police suspicions?"

"I don't know. There's always a possibility."

"But none of our kids would be involved in something like that."

"Some of them could. Remember, we have new kids in here all the time. That's one reason why we're here. There's no way we can keep a close watch on all of them." He stared at her. "Besides, even good kids sometimes get mixed up in bad stuff."

His look grew more intense. Linda knew he was remembering her involvement. She stared back at him. Then she let her gaze slide away. She'd probably do the same if she were in his place. More sadness than she had known existed filled her.

Avery leaned forward and kissed her forehead, but there was no warmth in it. That was his only touch. Then he was gone.

Linda stared after him. Why did his kiss feel like the end?

She went to the lab. She glanced at her watch. Too much time before the kids came in.

She let her mind focus on where she would place every knickknack, every personal item, in her new home. Anything to keep her thoughts away from Avery. How could the death of something that never developed fully hurt so much?

Avery went to his office. An open file lay on his desk, but he didn't even pretend to read it. *She's not involved. She can't be.* Centers all over the area have drug problems flare up from time to time. One or two of his kids got in trouble a few times. The fact that the problem surfaced after Linda got there was just a coincidence.

He stared at the papers and tried to make sense of them.

Fifteen minutes later he was still on the same page. He stood and stared out the window.

Linda and this past weekend drifted through his mind. The image of her in his bed on Saturday morning was as sharp as if it were happening right then. His body tightened, but desire wasn't the only reason this time. Uncertainty and an aching clamped together with his desire.

She couldn't be involved. He couldn't want a woman tied to the drug trade. He frowned. He knew she would never put the kids in jeopardy. He hadn't known her long, but he knew her well enough to swear to that.

He sat back down and shifted a pen through his fingers. He didn't even pretend to write.

When the bell rang to signal the closing for dinner, he forced himself to leave his office. He walked to the lounge, dreading every step.

"I'm sorry to interrupt your meal. I know that you need the time to unwind and then gear up for the rest of the night, but there's something you need to know."

If someone had been in the hall they would have thought the room was empty.

Avery took a deep breath. He looked around the table at the others, but he would not look at Linda. "The police have noticed increased drug activity in the neighborhood. They warned us to be aware of anything unusual."

"They don't think some of our kids are pushing, do they?" Bea asked.

"It wouldn't be the first time that some of them are involved with drugs. This neighborhood is typical. No matter how hard the decent people fight against it, you get a neighborhood full of need and somebody looks for a quick way to make money," Craig said.

"Yeah, and they find it by supplying people who think they can escape by using," Roz added.

"What are the folks from the suburbs who find their way down here for their supply trying to escape?" Les asked.

"Maybe it's not kids who the police should be looking for." Wanda glared at Linda.

The room filled with silence. Was Linda just imagining that everyone had glanced at her?

"I didn't bring it up so we could guess who's involved. I just want everybody to be on the lookout for trouble."

Avery looked like he was working hard not to look at Linda. She shook her head slightly.

She wasn't surprised at hearing something like that from Wanda. Wanda had never tried to hide her feelings. She had been open from the start.

Linda blinked hard and stared at the table in front of her. She had been here so long and eaten with them so many times. They had shared their problems and helped each other with solutions. They had teased and empathized with each other. She thought she had formed solid friendships. She glanced at Bea and then at Les. Then she stared back at Avery and tried not to let her hurt show. There wasn't any use. If they didn't know and trust her by now it would never happen.

Avery left, but no conversations started. Linda dared

to glance around the table. Everyone was lost in their own private world. Their food remained untouched.

Bea didn't have a playground story to tell. Craig didn't tell them about his newest lady friend. Cathy didn't mention Stan. Nobody rehashed the dinner dance, even though they had barely touched on it the day before. It was as if it had never happened.

Linda wished it hadn't. She wished Avery hadn't asked for that first dance. She wished he had never held her close, never let her body learn his. Did she wish she had never gone home with him? Never made love with him? Never let him teach her, never let him awaken her soul?

If it had never happened, if I had never lain in his arms this past weekend, I wouldn't be hurting as much now, would I?

She had been drawn to him from that first day. He had stood in front of her, intense and strong with fire in his gaze, and it had grown ever since.

If last weekend and last night hadn't happened, would she be hurting any less now that she knew that it would end so soon? Could she wish it all away? Would it hurt more to imagine them never making love and to be consumed by longing for Avery to fulfill her need, or for her to never have felt him inside her, filling her body and her heart and to know it would never happen again?

She could never have known how much just imagining could hurt. She only knew that knowing him and making love with him and knowing she'd never hold him close again was ripping her heart apart.

The bell rang and everybody was as relieved as she was to leave the lounge.

The hours back in the lab were torture. Linda had done her job well. Except for a few questions now and again the kids worked on their own. Her lab was so different from what it had been when she had come.

She shook her head. She had to change her thinking. It wouldn't be her lab much longer. She knew what she had to do.

She took out her long-range plans and read through them, adding suggestions and making changes as she went along. In some places her enthusiasm had made her writing almost illegible, even to herself. She carefully rewrote those sections. It was a good plan and wouldn't be too difficult for someone else to either follow it or make adjustments to suit himself or herself and Avery.

She shook her head. No. She wouldn't think of Avery. Not thinking of him was the only chance she had of keeping herself together. She made her mind go back to the plan.

If the plan was followed, literacy and job training programs for adults would be added in the fall after the schools opened again. She closed her eyes.

Two weeks until Labor Day and then the following day the schools reopened. She swallowed hard. How ironic. Two weeks.

She opened a new file on the computer and began writing, surprised at how few mistakes she made as she typed the words that would change what she had been foolish enough to think would be her future.

Sixteen

An hour before the center closed and Avery should have been impatient with time for moving too slowly. He was going to be with Linda, and that thought should have him filled with anticipation. This morning, before the world closed in on them, he could hardly wait for this day to end. How had things fallen apart so quickly? How could he still suspect her after she had done nothing to make him doubt her motives?

She had opened herself to him; she had let him see her vulnerability. She had given all she had to him and this was how he repaid her. The first mention of trouble and his thoughts automatically went to her. It wasn't for long, but it was for too long. He stared at the wall.

She had done nothing to deserve his suspicion. Her program was exactly what the kids needed. They loved her. They trusted her. Why couldn't he? He shook his head. He thought he had severed his ties with his past. He thought he had dealt with the problems with his brother and moved on with his life. He let out a deep breath. Now he realized he was still back there, held prisoner by it. And he had made her suffer for his memories.

He stood and looked out the window. He had to talk to her. He glanced at his watch. Still fifty-five minutes to go before he could take her home. He frowned. Was that enough time to figure out what to say to try to put things back the way they were?

He rearranged the papers on his desk, not even pretending to read them or do any work. Anything he did would have to be done over once he had made things right.

The bell rang and kids started passing by Avery's office. He hoped he had found the right words between him and Linda.

Just as he got to the door, the phone rang. It was on its twelfth ring when he decided to answer it.

"Hi." Linda stood in the doorway to Avery's office.

"Be with you in a minute." Avery frowned and continued to talk on the phone.

Linda resisted the urge to leave. She crinkled the envelope in her hands and smoothed it out. She looked back at Avery, and, without being aware of it, clutched the envelope again, undoing her smoothing effort. This paper was the last thing on her mind.

She let her gaze wander over Avery before settling on his face, as if trying to memorize it for when she could no longer see him.

She took a deep breath, brushed her hand over the envelope once more, and took a step forward.

"I . . . I decided to take the bus home."

"No." Avery looked at her. He frowned. "I'm not talking to you," he growled into the phone. "Let me call you back as soon as I get a chance, Tim."

"Don't hang up because of me," Linda said. "I'm leaving."

"It will wait." He hung up and walked to her, but he stopped too far away to touch her. Did he do that on purpose?

"I'm supposed to take you home."

"A lot has happened since we got here this morning." Was it just this morning that her future fell apart? A lifetime of life-changing events had happened. She blinked, but she managed to keep her gaze on him. "I think it's better if I take the bus."

He stared at her. She hoped he wasn't going to pretend that things hadn't changed between them. He had always been honest with her. She hoped he didn't destroy that illusion, too.

Linda . . ."

"Here." She held out the envelope and waited, when what she wanted to do was drop it on his desk and get out of there.

"What's this?" He frowned as he took it. He turned it over and over in his hands as if expecting to read it without opening it.

Didn't he know nothing came as easy as you wanted it to?

"It's all there." She swallowed hard. "I'll see you tomorrow."

"Don't go. We have to talk."

"There isn't anything left to talk about. I have to go before I miss my bus."

"You don't have to take the bus. This is crazy."

"Yes, I do and yes, it is."

She turned away from him. It was hard, but she'd get used to it. She had gotten used to things she had thought were impossible at the time, but she had managed.

The phone rang and she heard Avery snap at whoever had been unfortunate enough to call him at this time.

She blinked hard to stop her eyes from filling with tears. Somehow she'd manage this time as well.

She took a deep breath when she got outside and cut through the parking lot.

* * *

Avery slammed the phone down a few seconds after he answered it. He ripped open the envelope Linda had given him. The piece of paper inside said exactly what he was afraid it would. He tightened his hand around it, making new creases. He read it again even though he had it memorized. He shook his head. There weren't many words, but then it didn't take a lot of words to quit a job, especially when the two people involved both knew the reason for it.

He still stared at the words as if expecting them to change into something that wouldn't hurt him.

He had really thought he was over his hang-ups. He had thought his feelings for her were stronger than anything that could crop up. When *would* he be through with the past? When would it go away and let him get on with his life? He closed his eyes and leaned back. It didn't matter, now. Nothing mattered. It was too late to make a difference.

He should be with her right now. If this morning hadn't happened, he would have been. Tonight they should be sharing her new apartment, her new bed. They hadn't last night, and he had missed falling asleep with her still in his arms. Already he had gotten used to waking up with her beside him. How had she become a habit so fast? He had allowed himself to think that, just maybe, they had a future together.

He stood. He could catch her before she got the bus. If not, he would go to her apartment and wait for her. They'd talk until things were back the way they should be. The phone rang again, but this time he ignored it.

"Hey, Linda."

"Jamal." Linda whirled around as the tall, wiry man came toward her from across the street. "What are you doing here? How did you find me?" Linda backed up.

She was sorry he hadn't approached her when she was on the steps of the center instead of a few doors away. Bill was back there. He would help her. She looked around for somebody, for anybody.

"You ain't gotta be afraid of me no more. I ain't here to hurt you. I never did hurt you"—he shrugged—"not physically anyway." He didn't try to close the gap between them.

"Then why are you here? How did you find me?"

He shrugged again. "It's not like you're hiding out or something. I still know some people who know some people."

"Same old Jamal."

"Naw, I ain't the same old Jamal."

"I can't associate with you. If my parole officer finds out I even saw you, I'll be in trouble." She swallowed hard. "I can't go back in there."

"I know. You shouldn't a been there in the first place."

Linda frowned at him. His voice was different. Oh, she had heard it soft before, persuading, anything it took to get his way, but she had never heard it like this before.

"Too bad you didn't say that before it was too late."

"Yeah, it is." He held out his hand and Linda stepped back. He moved farther away from her. "Look. I been through some changes while I was in there. I'm trying to get my life together. I know you ain't gonna believe this, but folks from a church used to come visit us. At first I laughed at the dudes who went to the services. Nothing like that was for old Jamal. I was too smart. My cell mate kept after me to go with him. Finally I went just to get him to shut up." He shook his head. "I had to keep going back." He shrugged. "One day, I still don't know what happened, something pushed me to the front when the doors of the church were opened." He blinked hard and his stare intensified. "I . . . I don't remember walking up there." He sighed. "I know they say 'come as you are,' but I got to make things as right as I can before I get baptized. I got out this morning. I knew I had to try to fix things with you."

"Whatever you want from me, forget about it."

"I just want to apologize. I know it's too much to expect your forgiveness."

"Excuse me if I don't believe you."

"I don't blame you. I wouldn't believe me, either, if I was you." He stared at her. "I'm so sorry for the way I used you. I just came back from talking to the cops and trying to see what I have to do to put things right. You shouldn't have a record."

Linda stared, wondering if she could believe him. When she didn't say anything, he continued.

"I'll see you tomorrow after they let me know what I have to do next. They said something about a hearing. I'll come let you know how things went."

"You plan to come here, Jamal?"

"Why not? Be seeing you, Pretty Lady."

Linda watched him walk away. A sound behind her pulled her attention.

"Avery?"

"Yeah."

Avery stood as if he had taken root. The look in his eyes told her he had either heard too much or not enough. She shook her head and slowly turned away.

"It's not what you think. Let me explain."

"What I saw is enough of an explanation. Tell him to stay away from my center."

"You only heard part of it."

"I heard enough. I was a fool."

Linda shook her head. She didn't bother to wipe the tears staining her T-shirt. It wouldn't do any good. She ran to the bus stop and got there just before the bus pulled away.

During the ride home, Jamal's words whirled through her head. If he meant what he said, then her record could be cleared. She should have been happier than she was. She should be dancing down the bus aisle. Instead she tried to blink back fresh tears. Jamal might undo her record, but he couldn't undo what the record had caused.

Linda tried to keep her mind empty, but thoughts of Avery kept filling it and she couldn't keep them away. Tears spilled over again.

She had expected to have shared her bed with Avery tonight. Now it would never happen. How could she see him every day and know she'd never feel his arms around her again? How could she survive the next two weeks while her dream died inside her? She spent the rest of the ride trying to convince herself that this was for the best. Better for it to end now. Later would hurt even more. She sighed. *It can't hurt more than it already does.*

She closed her eyes, but tears escaped anyway and rolled down her face. She didn't bother to brush them away. What was the use? What was the use of trying to change anything anymore? Anyone who thought you could overcome your past was a fool.

Avery stood staring down the street. Then he went back to the parking lot. So. That was Jamal. He was out and Linda was hooked up with him again. Avery's jaw tightened. Maybe it wasn't again. Maybe it was still.

He had thought her feelings for him were as strong as his were for her. How could his judgment have been so wrong? Should he have let her explain? He shook his head. He knew what he saw and heard. What could she say to change that? Should he have let her try? There had to be a good reason for Jamal to be here. One that didn't have anything to do with the new drug activity at the center. Didn't there?

He walked slowly to his car and got in, but he didn't start it right away.

If he cared as much for her as he thought he did, would an explanation even be necessary? He closed his eyes and leaned his head back. *So this is what losing love feels like.* He sat up straight. His feeling couldn't have been love. He had waited so long for it to happen. It couldn't be gone so easily, so quickly. He stared out the windshield.

It hadn't gone on its own. He had chased it away before it had time to flourish. You have to take care of something that's developing. You have to nurture it, allow it to grow. He hadn't. His lack of trust had killed it. He shook his head. Even though the hurting was tearing him apart, he still wasn't sure, deep down, that he was wrong.

He thought his hatred for drugs was strong before. Now it was more intense than ever. This was the second time drugs had taken something valuable from him.

"Are you all right, Avery?" Bill was standing beside the car.

"I was just thinking." He started the car. "See you tomorrow."

As he drove away, an image of large, brown eyes filled with hurt and spilling tears stayed with him.

He went home, not because he expected to sleep or even get some rest. He went home because he had to try to get himself ready to face her tomorrow knowing he had no chance of ever holding her again.

Linda finally reached her apartment. She was relieved that she didn't have to face Auntie's concern. She didn't have to worry that Auntie would hear her crying. She took a deep breath. She could use all of her worry on wondering how she was going to get through the next two weeks knowing things were over between her and Avery. When she first knew he'd be gone for almost a week, she wondered how she'd survive without him. Now she wondered how she'd survive the days after he returned. She'd work on surviving for the rest of her life later.

She nearly fell apart when she went into the bedroom and looked at the bed. She stared for a few minutes. Then she wiped her face and stripped the sheets off, taking every trace of Avery with them.

She went back to the living room and looked at the boxes. Then she began unpacking, glad to have something to do that didn't require a lot of thinking.

It was after two o'clock when she shoved one empty box into another in the pile beside the door. She looked around. She had done more than she had planned to do. She sighed. Things didn't always go according to plans.

She showered, wishing she could wash away the misery that threatened to overwhelm her. She made the bed, crawled into it, and curled up in a ball, hoping that primitive position would help her, but knowing that nothing could. She pulled the top sheet over her trying not to remember how she had shared this bed with Avery, but her memory was functioning perfectly.

She turned out the light, but she didn't expect to sleep. She waited for morning to come so her mind could have other things to do besides dwell on the loss of Avery's love.

At seven o'clock Linda awoke. Her body was sore from unpacking and tired from not enough sleep. Her mind wasn't much better. Could a mind get tired? She felt as if her mind had been at work while she slept. She was emotionally drained. With any luck she'd stay that way all day.

Linda arrived at the center early as usual, but this time it wasn't enthusiasm for her job that had motivated her. She wanted to make sure that she arrived before anyone else did. She was not up to facing accusing stares today. She spoke quickly to Bill and went to the lab.

"Hi."

Linda turned to see Les standing in the doorway. She took a deep breath. *Please don't let him accuse me this morning.*

"Hi, Les. Can I help you?"

"I came up to ask you the same thing." His smile was gentle. "I know you aren't involved in this problem. So do the others. We don't count Wanda. She'd never accept you no matter what. You took Avery from her. She must have had a premonition about you from that first day."

"I saw the looks in everybody's eyes yesterday when Avery made the announcement." She stared at him.

"Linda, I . . ."

"It's okay, Les. I would have been suspicious, too, if the situation had been reversed."

"No, you wouldn't have. You've been there, so you know what it's like to be unable to prove your innocence. I'm sorry I thought, even for a second, that you could be involved. I know you better than that. I've seen you with the kids. There's no way you could do anything to hurt them." He looked more serious than Linda had ever seen him. "I don't believe that you were involved the time you went to jail, either. I had my doubts when Wanda first told me, but I was sure of your innocence after I got to know you."

"Thanks for that, Les." Linda swallowed hard. "It's

good to know somebody believes me." Why didn't the one who mattered the most?

"I'm not the only one." He smiled. "You coming down for dinner this evening?"

"I don't think so."

"Think about it, okay?"

He kissed her cheek and left. Before Linda could leave the door, Bea walked in.

"I tried to call you last night, but I don't have your new number."

"My phone isn't connected yet."

"I figured as much." She took a step closer. "How are you holding up?"

"I think the term is 'as well as can be expected.' "

"Don't pay Wanda any attention. You know how she is."

"I don't care about what Wanda thinks about me." She blinked hard, but it didn't stop her eyes from filling.

Bea put her arm around Linda.

"He doesn't really believe you could do something like that. He'll come to his senses."

Tears started down Linda's face.

"It's no use. He'll never trust me. I never should have come here."

"What are you doing to that child?" Cathy asked from the doorway.

Her question made the tears flow faster down Linda's face.

"Don't cry." Cathy patted Linda's shoulder. "It's going to be all right. Just give it time."

"I can't. I gave Avery my two-week notice." She sniffed. "But I won't be surprised if he comes in today and tells me I don't have to wait two weeks before I leave."

"You can't leave. If you do, Avery will make me come

up here, and I don't know what these machines will do to me," Bea said. "You know they don't like me."

Linda managed to laugh with the others, but the sadness never left her face. She took the tissue that Bea offered her.

"Avery . . ." Linda's voice broke. Would she ever be able to say his name and not feel her heart tear? She wiped her eyes again, but she continued. "He won't have trouble finding somebody else to work up here. A few graduates from the computer program at Temple already came to see about jobs. He plans to hire another person anyway, if things go well in Atlanta and he gets the funding to expand the computer program. Now he can hire two people instead of one."

"Don't rush into it. He'll realize how wrong he is and you two can work it out."

"It doesn't matter. I'm leaving anyway." She swallowed hard. "Even if things had worked out between us"—she took a deep breath—"I would still have to leave. It would be too awkward working with him and . . ." She shook her head. "I'd have to go anyway." She smiled at them. "Thanks for believing me. You don't know how much this means to me."

The two women hugged her again and left.

The other staff members, except for Wanda, came up to reassure Linda that they believed in her. Everyone came to the lab but the person who was most important to her.

Linda stayed in the lab at dinnertime and picked at her food. She was positive Avery didn't care about her not following his rule about taking a break from work during the meal. He no longer cared anything about her at all.

Seventeen

Avery had an hour and a half before he had to catch his 6:30 flight. He should have gone directly to the airport instead of coming to the center. On a smooth traffic day it would take him forty-five minutes to get to the airport. Nothing would be smooth about traffic today; he would be driving the expressway in rush-hour traffic and there was no telling how long it would take, but he had something important to do before he got on that plane.

Why did Nate have to pick last night to get into trouble? He had been doing fine before last night. He was sure to get a scholarship next year when he graduated. He had just been stopped for breaking curfew, but instead of going home when the officer told him to, he had decided to mouth off.

Nate's mother had waited until eleven o'clock this morning to call Avery. She thought she had been doing him a favor by not disturbing him the previous night or earlier this morning. She had no way of knowing that he would rather have stayed up all night working on Nate's problem than use the little time he had today before his flight. He had important plans for today.

He let out a hard breath. It didn't help that the rookie officer who had picked Nate up was determined to make an example out of him. It took all of this time to contact him and then to talk him into dropping charges back to a curfew violation. The easiest part was getting Nate to apologize. A night in the lock-up had scared him enough so that he was willing to say anything to get out. The chewing out Avery gave him would make sure that this was the last time he'd do something this stupid. Avery shook his head. But why today of all days?

He had planned to get to the center early enough to talk with Linda and try to regain her trust. He had his own stupidity to deal with and nobody but himself to undo his mistake. He knew it would take more than one conversation to set things right with her, but he had hoped to have hours to at least get her to listen to him. Now he didn't even have the minutes that he was taking.

He stood in the doorway of the lab and looked at Linda. She didn't look at him, and he was glad. He knew her eyes would be filled with the hurt that he had put there.

Since Avery had seen her with Jamal he had done nothing but think. Had she meant so little to him that he was willing to let her go without talking things through? She hadn't called Jamal. She couldn't have. If she had been involved with the drug problem in the neighborhood, the center was the last place where she would meet Jamal. All that aside, he knew she couldn't be involved. He didn't know why she hadn't been able to prove her innocence in her court case, but she hadn't been guilty then, either.

He let out a deep breath. He needed the funds he hoped to get at the conference, but the timing couldn't be worse. If he thought it would do any good, he'd cancel his trip in spite of the center's needs and worry about funds for the new programs later.

It was a good thing he had finished his presentation before this stuff came up. He hadn't gotten any work done since then. All he had been able to think about was Linda and what his life would be like without her in

. She was innocent. He knew that now. He should have realized it from the start. If his love for her had been strong enough, he would have trusted her, no matter how things looked. At the least, he would have given her chance to explain. He couldn't blame Jamal or anybody else. This was his own fault. He had been tested, and he had failed miserably.

He swallowed hard and stepped into the lab. He didn't know what he would say. He hoped the right words would come to him that would make her, if not forgive him right now, at least not shut him out forever. He couldn't stand the thought of spending the rest of his life without her.

Linda heard a sound and turned. Avery. Had he come to tell her not to be there when he returned?

She blinked hard. How could she have forgotten how fine he looked dressed up. His dark gray suit and light gray shirt gave him an air of authority, but she knew about the warm sensual man hidden underneath. She knew, and it was killing her. How could she have forgotten how fine he looked, period? Her body warmed at the memory of his pressed against hers. It made her heart hurt to know she would never know that feeling again.

She allowed her gaze to roam over him this one last time. She tried not to remember how it felt to have those strong arms around her. She didn't want to think about how she'd manage to live without ever feeling them again. She let her gaze caress his face the way her hands never would again. She sighed. It was for the best that he go while he was away. It would never work out even for the two weeks she had left at the center. She sighed again. She should have realized that any relationship between them was doomed before she allowed him to get close enough to break her heart. She took a deep breath and stood straighter.

"I didn't think you'd come in today."

"I had to see you before I go. I have to talk to you."

"Have you come to tell me not to be here when you get back?"

"Still trying to get me to fire you?"

"No. I'm just facing reality."

"Reality is that we have things to talk about."

"No." She shook her head. "Reality is that I have a new job lined up and that I start in three weeks. I found it when . . ." Her words trailed off. "When things between us fell apart. Reality is that it was a mistake for us to get involved in the first place. Too much stands in the way." She blinked hard. "There's nothing you can say to change that reality. Last night proved it."

"Last night I was stupid. Today I'm smarter."

"Until the next time something comes up that makes you suspicious. You'll always question me." She shook her head. "I can't spend the rest of my life defending myself to you."

"I need you in my life." He took a step closer. "I love you."

Linda wiped her eyes. "Sometimes love isn't enough. Even if you do love me, this is one of those times."

"Please." Avery took a step toward her and reached out.

"Don't." Linda stepped back. "Don't touch me. I don't want you to ever touch me again." She made herself look at his face as she told him the lie. No matter how much she was hurting, it was better for her this way. "You've caused me nothing but pain." She refused to remember those moments spent in his arms. "I never should have let you get close to me. That was one of the worst mistakes I ever made. I'm not the smartest woman in the world, but I never repeat my mistakes and I'm

not about to start now. I don't want you back in my life.
I won't let you hurt me again. All I want from you is for
you to leave me alone so I can move on."

Avery stood there staring back at her, silent.

If I wasn't right, he'd say something, wouldn't he? "Go
catch your plane." She turned her back on him and sat
at a computer as if she expected to do anything that
made sense. "Leave me alone from now on."

She heard the door close softly. He did what she'd
told him to. *So why did it feel all wrong?* She had told Avery
the truth. She had a new job waiting. Now all she needed
was a new heart to replace her old one, which was in
shambles.

She lowered her head to her arms and let her tears
come. Just for a little while. Just until she could find a
way to get them to stop.

Avery drove to the airport. Traffic was so heavy that
it took all of his concentration to keep his car under
control, but that was all right. It gave him less time to
think about what Linda had said.

She was through with him. She didn't believe that he
trusted her now, and why should she? He had talked a
good talk, but when it came time to prove it, look what
he had done.

He tightened his fingers on the steering wheel. How
ironic. He trusted her now, but she didn't trust him. He
let out a hard breath. He wasn't finished. He couldn't
accept that it was over between them. He'd try again as
soon as he got back. And, if he didn't succeed, then he'd
try again. He wouldn't be where he was today if he were
a quitter.

Maybe when he got back she would have cooled off
enough to hear him out; maybe she'd be willing to give
him another chance. Maybe this trip was at a good time.
Maybe time apart was just what they needed. Maybe he'd

have time enough to figure out how to persuade her to give him another chance.

He sighed. His future was riding on a lot of maybes.

He parked and ran into the airport. The last boarding call was announced as he got to the gate.

In spite of what he thought about the timing being good, he was almost sorry that he hadn't missed the flight.

Linda put cold towels over her eyes and hoped that enough of the puffiness and redness would be gone by the time the kids came back. It would help if the tears would stop flowing.

She took several deep breaths and let them out slowly. She just had to get through the rest of the night. That was all. It was too much to think about what would happen after that.

She made her thoughts go to the new job that she had gotten this morning. She would have tried to get a job with the school district, but her record would block that. If Jamal meant what he said, she might be able to get her record cleared. She'd call Marian tonight and find out. She wouldn't get her hopes up, though. Jamal seemed to have changed, but she still didn't trust him. She sighed. At least she got a new job.

Despite her lack of experience, her computer background was a big asset. The first time she'd thought the job wasn't going to work out, she had gone to an employment agency. She had forgotten all about it until Auntie told her they had called. The employment agency sent her on an interview for temporary placement in the computer department of an investment firm. The interview with the firm had gone well. She would start in three weeks and she was told that the position might become permanent. The job was nothing like what she was doing at the center. Linda was glad. Maybe that would make it easier for her to forget the center.

She shook her head. She had to be honest at least with herself. She'd never forget the center. There was no question about forgetting Avery, either. That was even more impossible. He was too deeply rooted in her heart.

She heard footsteps in the hall. She hoped the kids would be too busy with their work to notice that she had been crying. Most of all she hoped for the courage to get through the rest of the evening.

The call she made to Marian from a pay phone around the corner from her apartment building would have filled her with happiness under other circumstances. At the moment she didn't have any room inside for happiness. It was taken up by thoughts of Avery.

"I'll see what I can find out. If Jamal really did go to the police, we'll start the process to try to get your record cleared. If I find out anything tomorrow I'll give you a call. I think the term we want to use is 'cautious optimism.' "

"Thanks, Marian."

"How are things going?"

"I . . ."

Linda was surprised at the tears that streamed down her face. In between crying, she told Marian everything that had happened.

"I . . . I was supposed to check with my parole officer before I changed jobs, wasn't I?" She wiped her face. "It's all right, isn't it? I can't work at the center anymore. The new job is good. I can give her the information so she can check for herself. Do you think I'll get in trouble? I . . ."

"Don't worry about it. If things go well you won't have to get approval from anybody anymore. Don't worry," she said again. "Try to get some sleep, you hear?"

"Okay."

Linda knew she'd never be able to sleep. All she could do was wait for time to pass so she could try to escape from her memories at work tomorrow.

Linda rode to the center the next morning relieved that she didn't have to face Avery. When she'd first learned about his trip to Atlanta, she had been desolate at the thought of not seeing him for five days. Now she was relieved. Those were five days when she wouldn't have to see him and remember what she didn't have anymore. She only had to get through one more week and two days after he got back. She wondered how she would manage that. She was sure that he, too, felt relieved at not seeing her.

Linda told the first kids into the lab that she was leaving.

"Why you got to go?" Tyree asked.

"Yeah, why you dissing us?" Lamont asked.

"Did we do something to make you mad?" Helen and Kira stood in front of her. All of the kids looked at her.

Linda took a deep breath. *Please let me get through this without crying.*

"There are reasons that you can't understand." She managed to smile at them. "I don't think much will change in here after I leave. The computer program is off to a good start. Actually, you guys could handle the lab by yourselves, but I think Mr. Avery . . ." She stumbled over his name but forced herself to go on. "Mr. Avery will insist on you having a staff member here. I have two more weeks and the new person will probably be here before I go. A lot of people were interested in working in the lab with you guys. A week after I'm gone you won't even remember me."

"You know that's not true." Helen shook her head slowly.

"It's not like I'm leaving the city."

"You may as well be. We won't ever see you again."

Linda took a deep breath. "I'll make a deal with you. If you have a special program, tell Miss Bea and she'll tell me. I'll come see you, okay?"

"It's got to be okay." Tyree stared at the floor. "We don't have no, I mean any, choice."

"I'm here now. Why waste this time? Go ahead and work on your projects. See what you can finish before I go."

The next morning Linda's phone was connected. She called Marian and left her the number. Then she went to work on day two of her life without Avery.

Avery stared at Linda's door for a few seconds. Then he sat on the floor across the hall. He glanced at his watch. He wouldn't awaken her at six in the morning even if they were on good terms. Not unless she were sleeping beside him. He shook his head. He couldn't think about that. What would he do if she meant what she told him before he left? What if she really didn't want to have anything more to do with him? He couldn't deal with that now. He wasn't even sure he'd be able to deal with it later.

He hoped she had had less trouble sleeping than he had while he was away. He didn't even consider knocking on her door, even though he knew that wouldn't make a difference as to whether she listened to him.

He shrugged. Sooner or later she had to come out. This time he spent waiting would give him time to plan what to say. He frowned.

Did she go out for the *Sunday Inquirer* on Sunday, or did she get it the night before? He didn't know. There was a lot he didn't know about her, but none of it was as important as what he did know. He knew that he loved her. And he knew that she was innocent. That was all he needed to know. Those two things and one more. He needed to know that she still loved him.

He let out a hard breath. He didn't know if time would make any difference. He wasn't even sure that it wasn't already too late to undo the mess he had made, but he had to try.

He leaned his head back and closed his eyes, but in spite of getting no sleep the night before, he knew that, even if he were in his own bed, he wouldn't be able to sleep.

He would have come to her earlier, but there weren't any flights before the one he'd caught. He was supposed to meet with somebody for breakfast this morning. He glanced at his watch. In three hours.

He swallowed hard. She had to give him another chance. He didn't deserve it, but he desperately needed it. She had to trust him, had to believe that he had changed.

Linda sat at her kitchen table staring at her cup of cold tea. The second one she had let get cold. In a little while she'd go get the paper. She wouldn't be able to concentrate on what was in it, but going out would give her something to do besides think.

She sighed. That would take care of ten minutes. What about the rest of her life?

Her police record would probably disappear, but suddenly that wasn't as important as it would have been a week ago. Nothing was. Had Avery meant it when he'd said he loved her just before he left? He looked like he had. He looked like he had been hurting as much as she was. She shook her head. If he loved her, he would have trusted her instead of jumping to conclusions. He hadn't used words. His look had done a more effective job than words could.

It took a lot of energy for her to leave the table. She gave up on the tea and poured it out. If she walked really slow to the corner store for the paper, it would mean less time she would have to spend thinking. She opened the door and forgot why. Avery. He was sitting on the floor staring at her. Was she imagining this? Did she want him so much that she was hallucinating?

Her gaze followed him as he stood strong and solid in front of her. He didn't come closer. Had he changed his mind? Had he decided to fire her after all? Was that why he came back early? If so, it would be for the best. Then why didn't it feel like it?

She stared into his eyes. Was she imagining that she saw pain and regret there? She frowned.

"What are you doing here? Why aren't you still in Atlanta?"

"This is more important."

"The center needs the funding for the new programs." She took a deep breath and hoped it would help her gain control and keep her from touching him just one more time.

"This is more important."

She watched as he swallowed hard. He seemed to be having control trouble, too.

"Go away."

"I can't. I love you. I need you more than I thought I could ever need someone."

"For how long? Until the next thing comes up and makes you doubt me?"

"For forever." He took a step toward her and stopped. He looked as if he were waiting for her to step back. When she didn't, he took another step.

She closed her eyes. He was close enough for his aftershave to touch her. Memories of being even closer to him washed over her. Why couldn't he have changed his aftershave? Didn't he care that it was torturing her?

"It won't work." She looked away from him. She never could stand to look at something she wanted but couldn't have.

"It has to work. I can't live without you. These past five days have been impossible." He reached toward her but pulled his hand back. "I . . . I know I don't deserve your trust, but please give me another chance. I love you more than it's possible to say. I know you aren't involved in this latest problem. I know you were never involved in drugs or anything else illegal. I swear, I'll never mistrust you again." He took a deep breath and brushed a finger down her cheek. She barely felt it, but his touch released all of the emotion she was holding in check. Tears rolled down her face.

"Please don't cry." Through her tears Linda saw the pain in Avery's eyes. "I didn't come here to make you unhappy. Please don't. Your tears are ripping me apart."

Linda wiped at her face and stepped away from him. More pain crossed his face. Then he looked as if something had died inside him. She knew that feeling. That was the way she had felt.

"Come inside." She stepped back, but not so far that his anguish couldn't reach her. She had complained about his lack of trust in her. Now it was her turn to trust him or face the rest of her life without him. It all came down to one thing: Did she love him? She let out a deep breath.

"Do you want a cup of coffee?"

"Yes." His voice sounded as weak as she felt.

He followed her into the kitchen, trying not to hope for more. Maybe. Just maybe.

What were the words he needed? What could he say to make his time with her last longer than a cup of coffee? Like, maybe for the rest of his life?

"What do we do now? How can I fix things?" He stared at the face he had grown to love so quickly. He reached toward her.

When she didn't move away, he caressed her face.

Then he gently, giving her a chance to pull away if she wanted to, eased her into his arms. He stared into her eyes that didn't seem to hold as much hurt as they had before. Or was he just seeing what he wanted to see?

"I know I hurt you." He brushed his lips across her hair. "I know I can never undo the pain I caused you." He kissed the side of her face. "I know I love you more than I ever imagined possible. I don't just want you, although my want is killing me. I need you to make me complete. Please let me spend the rest of my life proving that to you. I know I don't deserve it, but please give me another chance."

For what seemed like hours, Linda just stared back into his eyes, and his heart felt like it was waiting for something from her so it could start beating again. Then she brushed her hands across his chest and his heart made up for the beats it had held back.

"You did hurt me more than I thought anyone ever could." She glanced away and took a step out of his arms. She stared back at him. "While you were gone I had time to think. I complained about you not trusting me, but I'm doing the same to you." She sighed. "I've thought about what my life would be like without you. I'm barely hanging on after five days. Forever without you would be impossible." She blinked. "My love for you is so deep that it scares me. I have to give you another chance."

"Oh, Linda." Avery pulled her back into his arms where she belonged. He trailed kisses down her face. "I'll never make you sorry. I'll never hurt you again. I promise. I'll trust you."

"I'll trust you, too," Linda said. "I . . ."

But the rest of her words were swallowed up by Avery's kiss, the kiss sealing their love and their trust for all time to come.

Eighteen

"You should see Daddy." Sheila smiled at Linda fussing with her veil and the tiara it was attached to. The small room at the back of the church seemed even smaller as it tried to contain the yards of wedding gown pooled around Linda's feet. "Leave that veil alone." She pulled Linda's hand away. "And don't touch the tiara again. If you mess it up Mom will be angry and so will I. I have to wear it next, you know." Her smile took the harshness from her words. She patted the folds into place. "It's perfect already."

"My daughter will probably get to wear it before you do."

"Cold words from a bride-to-be on her wedding day."

"You're the one who's married to school."

"Not married." Sheila smiled. "More like engaged." She stared at Linda and leaned forward. "It's only a temporary engagement, too." They both laughed.

"Good." Linda's smile filled her face. "I want you to find some of this happiness as I did." She swallowed hard. "Baby Sis, I never thought it was possible to be so happy." She blinked hard.

"Don't do that." Sheila pressed a tissue to Linda's eyes. "You'll mess up your makeup."

"Yes, Mother." She let out a deep breath. "Speaking of which, where is Mom?"

"Trying to calm Daddy. She said she was putting you in my hands this morning, She said she wouldn't subject you to two Durard women fussing over you."

"The way you're acting, I would rather take my chances with her."

"I'll think of a way to get even later."

"What's the matter with Daddy?" Linda adjusted the high neckline of her off-white wedding gown.

"Leave that alone, too." Sheila slapped Linda's hand away. "We'd better hurry or you will have messed everything up."

"Yes, Ma'am." Linda smiled at her sister. "What about Daddy? He's okay, isn't he? It can't be anything serious since you're smiling."

"He's as okay as any father in this situation, I guess." She laughed. "He was pacing up and down in front of the church muttering 'I never thought she'd do it. I never thought she'd do it' as if you had committed murder."

"He never acted that way when I was convicted, did he?" The light had gone out of her face.

Sheila's face lost its smile, too. She shook her head as she stared at Linda. "That time he kept saying, 'I know she didn't do anything wrong.' " She stared at Linda. "He . . . make that we, didn't need the pardon you just got to tell us that."

"A pardon is better than a parole, isn't it."

"Absolutely. It tells the world that you were never guilty in the first place."

"Marian never told me that she was working on it. I guess she didn't want me to be disappointed if it didn't happen."

"She didn't want you to have false hope."

The two stared at each other for a few seconds before Sheila broke in. "Enough of the past. The future is galloping toward you. We have to make sure you're ready."

"I'm ready. As soon as Bea gets here with the busload of kids from the center, we can start. She had better hurry or Daddy will need a casket instead of a seat in the front pew." She shook her head as she stared into the mirror. "I can't believe it." She took a deep breath. "I'm looking at me dressed in my wedding gown and I still can't believe it. I don't deserve to be as happy as I feel right now."

"Yes, you do. Don't even think that way. After all you've been through, You have earned every happiness imaginable."

"I'm marrying Avery." A dopey grin.

"Yes, you are."

"I'm going to be Mrs. Avery Washington."

"Absolutely." Sheila grinned.

A knock on the door drew their attention. Sheila opened the door.

"What are you doing here? You can't see Linda. It's bad luck."

"That's nonsense. I don't believe in luck. I want to see Linda."

"Hi, Avery." Linda peeked around Sheila.

"You may as well come in. I'll see if I can find out what's holding up Bea." Sheila smiled and shook her head. "Some people have no regard for tradition."

Her words were lost on Linda and Avery. They were lost gazing at each other. The church could have disappeared and they wouldn't have noticed.

"I missed you." Avery stood in front of Linda, but he didn't touch her.

"Don't you crush her dress," Sheila warned as she left them alone.

"I missed you, too." Linda closed the space and caressed the side of his face.

He touched her cheek and stepped back from her. "I don't want Sheila mad at me.' "

"That's okay. She's not the boss of me." Linda stood on tiptoe and brushed her lips across his.

"The bus is here." Sheila opened the door and stared at them. "And not a minute too soon, I see." She shook her head. "Leave you two alone for a minute and look what happens." She smiled. "Okay, Avery. Go stand where you belong." She held up her hand. "Don't even try to tell me that you belong with Linda. You can wait a little while longer. Go," she added when he stayed in place. "The sooner we do this the sooner you guys can get married."

That made Avery move. "We should have eloped." He kissed Linda's cheek and left the room.

"Okay. Let me touch up your lipstick since you let somebody mess it up."

"Not just somebody. Avery."

"I had heard that the reason brides need attendants is to keep them focused. Now I see why."

A tap on the door was followed by 'we're ready.' Linda quelled the flutter in her stomach and reached for the door.

"Not yet." Sheila eased Linda back in place. "Let me check you one last time." She patted the veil. Then she smoothed the sides of the pearl-encrusted skirt over Linda's hips. "Okay. I assume the borrowed and blue and penny in your shoe are still where they belong."

"Yes. Can I go now? Avery is waiting."

"Avery will wait forever if he has to. I know he doesn't have to," she added quickly when Linda started to disagree. "From now on you two will see so much of each other that you'll probably be sorry that you decided to go back to the center to work." She stared at Linda's radiant face. "Or maybe not." She sighed. "You are a beautiful bride." She cleared her throat. "Okay. I'm going to put you back in the capable hands of your wedding coordinator, Cindy Granger." She smiled. "See you in a few." She hugged Linda loosely. "The next time I hug you, you'll be Mrs. Avery Washington."

"Yes. I will." The dazed look was still on Linda's face after Sheila left.

"It won't be long," Cindy said as she came into the room to make one final check of Linda. Then she handed Linda the bouquet.

Mrs. Long played the opening song and Linda's new life moved forward.

Linda quit trying to make deep breathing calm her. It wasn't working anyway. The music changed and she knew from the rehearsals that the others in her wedding party were marching in to take their places at the front of the church. The music changed once more and Cindy touched her arm.

"It's your turn." She smiled encouragement to Linda who had suddenly forgotten how to walk. "Avery's waiting for you."

That freed her. A calmness washed over her and, clutching her bouquet in front of her, she went to meet her love.

Linda stood at the back of the church, holding her father's arm and stared. The church was packed but every face held a smile. Roberto waved from near the front and the other kids imitated him. Linda's smile widened. She was glad she had decided to go back to the center to work. She would have missed the kids. Then her gaze found Avery and everybody and everything else disappeared.

She didn't remember her feet touching the white carpet spread down the aisle, but they must have because, there she was, standing in front of everybody, ready to pledge her love for all to see.

"It's okay, Daddy," she whispered when her father still held her arm after it was time to let go. "I'll be all right."

Her father put her hand into Avery's, patted it and left her side.

Linda's gaze found Avery again and held his. Again everybody else faded.

"I understand you have your own vows." Reverend Dent's voice brought them back to the present.

"Yes." Avery found his voice first.

He clutched Linda's hands in his. His love for her shone in his eyes and filled his voice. "Linda, you are the love I have needed but thought I would never find. You have given me a reason to breath. Before you I was nothing. With you I am everything. With you there is no past only our future together. You complete me. I will spend the rest of my life trying to earn your love."

Linda forced herself to remember the words she had written and to say them when what she wanted was to say "I do" and feel Avery's arms around her.

"Avery, I love you. I thought I would spend my entire life searching for you, but not finding you. With you I am whole. You are the piece that was missing from my heart. You are my life, my only love. With you, there is no past, only our future together. I love you now and for always."

Their words hung in the air, drifted over them, seeped in and were absorbed, became a part of them. Her mother sniffed and the spell allowed time to move on; let the ceremony reach completion.

Reverend Dent announced them husband and wife and applause filled the sanctuary.

Cindy, the only one who seemed to remember protocol, prodded the members of the wedding party into place to receive the guests. Avery refused to release Linda's hand and she clung just as strongly to his. Finally Cindy gave up.

Linda's already wide grin stretched even wider as the kids from the center stood in front of her.

"Yo, Miss D. I wish you much happiness. Maybe Mr. Avery won't be so grouchy anymore. You know he's been on my case and everybody else's. Now that he knows you ain't going nowhere, maybe he'll chill."

"I'll chill when you do right." Avery shook Roberto's hand.

"I got that covered, Mr. A."

"Mr. A?"

"Yeah, you know: Miss D. and Mr. A."

"It won't be Miss D. anymore," Michael said. "It will be Mrs. W."

"Whatever goes as long as you're gonna be at the center."

"I have to be there. Somebody has to call you on the double negatives."

"I wish you a lot of happiness, Miss D." Helen's shy smile showed. "I wrote a poem to you and Mr. Avery and we plan to have a special edition of the newsletter. Kira and the others are helping. It will be ready when you come back from your honeymoon."

Linda hugged both girls and thanked them.

Marian and Auntie stood in front of her next. Tears filled Linda's eyes and spilled over.

"I . . . I can't thank you enough. Neither of you. I owe you so much." She took the tissue that Sheila handed her and wiped her eyes. "On top of everything else, if not for you I never would have met Avery."

"And I never would have met Linda." Avery hugged Marian.

"Yes, you would have," Auntie said. "When two people are meant to be together as you two are, they will find each other. Now give me my hug. I don't think I've gotten my allotment for the day yet." She folded Linda to her, patted her back and moved on.

"Girl, you know how happy I am for you, right?"

"Yes, Bea. Why does it sound like a 'but' is coming?"

"Because it is. I know you two deserve a honeymoon. After the tribulations you have been through. I'll be the first to admit that. But you know that means that I'll have to spend time with those machines. I just know they are waiting to get at me. Why can't you just take a weekend; a short weekend since this is Saturday; and come in on Monday?"

Avery and Linda laughed even though Bea wore a serious look. "Roberto promised to help out," Linda said. "All you have to do is be there. The kids know what to do. It will be all right."

"It has to be."

"Don't pay her any mind." Cheryl stood with Bea. "I think that she really has a thing for computers and just doesn't want anybody to know."

"Congratulations, Avery." Les shook Avery's hand. "I hope you realize how blessed you are."

"I do, Les, believe me, I do."

"Much happiness, Linda." Les kissed her cheek and moved on.

"I hope he finds the one meant for him soon," Linda said to Avery. Then they turned to greet the next people in line.

Finally the last people had left for the reception. Linda and Avery were all alone in the now quiet sanctuary.

Avery pulled her close. His lips brushed across hers. "Hello, Mrs. Washington, my wife." He gazed down at her. "I like the sound of that."

"I do, too, Mr. Washington, my husband." She sighed. "Oh, Avery, I'm afraid that I'm dreaming; that I'll wake up and find that this never happened."

"This is for real, love. You are stuck with me for the rest of your life." He cradled her in his arms.

"I like the sound of that, too. I'm going to hold you to it."

"I hope so." She eased his mouth to hers and got lost in his kiss.

"Save that for later," Cindy said as she came into the sanctuary. "The others have left and the limo is waiting for you. You have the rest of your lives for that."

"That won't be long enough." Avery wrapped his arms around Linda. She brushed her hands over his back.

"I agree." She leaned into him and his mouth found hers. "Not nearly long enough."

Their kiss was full of promises and trust and hope for the future as the rest of the world was forgotten and only the two of them existed.

Dear Readers:

There are times when I sit at the computer and the words hide, pull away like an elusive child playing hide and seek. For a fleeting moment, I'm tempted to quit looking for the right words or waiting for the muse; I'm tempted to go watch TV, read somebody else's hard work, go for a walk, or do anything except search and dig for words that don't want me to find them.

Then I remember the appreciation of you readers—your enthusiasm and loyalty—and I try once more to find the perfect phrase. I am still in awe of the fact that people who don't even know me buy and read my books. Thank you for your continued support. I will continue to try to give you something worth spending your time on. I can be reached at agwwriter@email.com or P.O. Box 18832, Philadelphia, PA 19119. If you wish a reply by U.S. mail, please enclose a self-addressed stamped envelope.

Alice Wootson

P.S.—Look for TO LOVE AGAIN, a New Year's love story, in October 2002.

ABOUT THE AUTHOR

Alice Wootson retired from teaching and embarked on a second career. She follows in her sister, Marilyn Tyner, into writing romance novels.

TRUST IN ME follows DREAM WEDDING and SNOWBOUND WITH LOVE into print.

She invites you to visit her website:
www.alicewootson.net